# THE SHADOW OVER DOGGERLAND

*North Sea Trilogy Parte One*

Tim Mendees/Emil Haskett/ Lily Jasmine Bergh/

Lee C. Conley/Simon Bleaken/Vincent H. O'Neil/

Robert Poyton/ E.L. Giles/ S.O. Green/ Chris McAuley &

Claudia Christian/ Gavin Chappell/ E.W. Farnsworth/Jasmine Jarvis/Carlton Herzog/ John D. Chadwick

Published by
Mythos
An Imprint of Nordic Press
Kindlyckevägen 13
Rimforsa, Sweden.
2022
This is a work of fiction.
Similarities to real people, places, or events
Are entirely coincidental
The Shadow Over Doggerland
978-91-987508-8-1
Cover Design by
C. Marry Hultman
Formatted by
C. Marry Hultman
Edited by
Tim Mendees

# TALES

# FOREWORD

That Cthulhu chap certainly gets around a bit!

As a lifelong devotee of all things Lovecraftian, one of the delights has always been finding out where that Eldritch monstrosity will poke his tentacled head out next. One of the delights of the genre is that it can be extrapolated to almost anywhere you can think of. As long as there is sentient life around to be driven to madness or existential despair, you are good to go. When H.P. Lovecraft created what he called Yog-Sothothery back in the roaring twenties he created an enduring mythos that can invade any time and place.

Even during his lifetime, his themes and creations had been taken to places as disparate as Atlantis, mediaeval France and the gulfs of space. Since then, we have seen everything from the Golden Age of Piracy to the far future play host to his themes and creations. Over the last ten or so years, interest in his work has had something of a renaissance so it is only expected that the current crop of mythos authors should be looking for new environments to corrupt. This thinking is what has led to the tome you currently have in your grubby mitts.

After completing work on an anthology pitting The King's Musketeers of Dumas against the Cthulhu mythos, I got chatting with Christopher Marry Hultman from Nordic Press about a trilogy of anthologies centred around The North Sea. One of our authors, E.L. Giles, had suggested a Vikings VS Cthulhu mash-up on some video I was hosting and it kind of went from there. We had been kicking around ideas for what will be the third book for a while so this slotted in nicely. This left us with only one problem, what to do for the first book?

Mr Marry Hultman had recently watched a documentary about the so-called Atlantis of the North Sea, Doggerland, and asked me if I was familiar with it. As it happened, I had watched a Time Team special on it some years ago and had recently read *The Dunwich Trilogy* by Robert Poyton which features Dogger Bank so I knew a little. As it turned out, that little was all there really is to know about it. Outside of the odd antler headdress and things of that nature, not much is known of its nomadic denizens. I pulled off all the archaeological studies I could find from Academia.edu and got to researching. What relatively little I uncovered turned out to be a perfect fit for the mythos.

Doggerland, that doomed patch of land between mainland Europe and The British Isles was forever submerged during a catastrophe called the Storegga Slide. This tsunami wiped it off the map in one fell swoop. It wasn't much of a stretch to imagine its cause being something other than natural. So, we had the place, we had its inevitable doom, and we had the antlers, all we had to do was figure out the style. The issue was, as the people of Doggerland would have been stone age hunters, the last thing we wanted to do was fall into caveman trappings. The thought of over a dozen stories filled with people called Ug grunting at each other as they banged rocks together to make fire filled me with a cold dread. Luckily, the answer lay in the past.

Authors such as Robert E Howard, Karl Edward Wagner, Fritz Leiber and Clark Ashton Smith had, since its inception, injected their sword and sorcery yarns with a big dollop of the Lovecraftian. Smith especially jumped out at me as his Atlantis and Hyperborea cycles had dealt with similar doomed lands that would have existed *before* Doggerland's destruction. This gave us a stylistic jumping-off point. The fact that these more advanced civilisations had given way to a more primitive time added a nice bit of continuity with Smith's themes of decay and devolution. It also gave us free rein to add some cheeky anachronisms here and there.

Once I had *finally* come up with a brief, it was a case of gathering a team together and I couldn't have hoped for a better bunch. Everyone involved embraced the idea and ran with it. I'm a firm believer in letting authors have as much freedom as possible and the result has been better than I could have hoped. The first part of this book contains all the stories that fit together, without much developmental hammering on my part, into a loose narrative covering the final days of Doggerland and the machinations of the Antlermen and their watery allies. It all flowed so nicely that all that remained was for me to tie them together, put a neat bow on it, and send the concept off towards book two. The second part of the book contains those stories that told a rise and fall that differed from the main bulk. Here we have time travel, the almost Biblical, and an epic poem in common time to rival Beowulf... get a metronome handy for that one.

The sheer amount of creativity on display in this book has been frankly staggering.

Right, I will stop waffling and let you dive into the watery depths. All that remains for me to do is thank everyone involved and thank *you*, the reader, for picking up what has been a labour of love. On behalf of the group and Nordic Press, we hope you enjoy the results of our work and hope to see you next time when we face... *The Whisperer in Valhalla.*

*Tim Mendees*

Our footsteps o'er the Doggerland
Chased retreating ice and snow
Left us breathing high and dry
Land's End to Scapa Flow
The seeds of Albion, wind-blown
Free, scattered to the moors
Dormant beneath the soggy heath
Where stouter oaks will grow

# An Arrow of Stone

Lee C. Conley

His blood surged, and he steadied his breathing. Even his breath seemed far too loud in this still place. He sighted down the arrow, just like they had practised, shifting his weight. His stomach tightened at the sound of rustling leaves underfoot—so loud in the stillness of the forest. Their quarry looked up from the undergrowth. It had heard something. It chewed lazily and after a moment it slowly lowered its head back down to forage.

"Now," breathed his father from his shoulder.

His pulse pounding in his ears, so loud he feared the beast would hear his very heartbeat. His chest tight with nerves, he slowly drew back the bowstring as his father had shown him. The sound as the string grew taught was horribly loud to him. The deer jerked its head up, its eyes darting around. It was spooked. Had it heard them? Had the gods of the forest called to it in warning? It looked straight into his eyes.

The bowstring thrummed as he loosed the arrow. The deer bolted. His arrow clattered off the stones and disappeared into the grass. He let out a sigh and watched the deer lope off into the forest as his heart sank.

"Bad luck, son." His father's hand patted him on the shoulder. 'Bad luck.'

His father strode into the clearing from their hiding place.

"What did I do wrong," asked Petri as he stood there, the feeling of disappointment and failure already weighing heavy.

His father turned. A consoling smile on his weathered face. Taelen scratched at his wiry beard. "Nothing, lad. Sometimes the gods grant us success… sometimes not. It is the way of things. There will be a lesson from them in all things, even the misses."

"What lesson?" he asked. His voice sounded so small to him compared to his father.

His father looked up into the eves of the surrounding trees. "That will be for you to hear. Perhaps, that all things have a time, and this was not the time."

Petri frowned at his father. It didn't seem like much of a lesson to him.

"Come on, lad. Let's find that arrow." Taelen began poking through the undergrowth with his own bow. "Look," he said with a gesture after the escaped deer, "he bolted downwind at least. We can still track him. He won't smell us coming if we are quick and quiet. Don't worry, perhaps next time will be the right time."

"Quick and quiet," Petri repeated and looked up into the light that dappled through the canopy of the trees. He muttered a silent word to the gods and joined his pa.

"I found it," said Petri. Holding up the arrow.

His father looked over and grinned. "Wait there," he examined the arrow. "Umm," she said with a frown, "we won't be losing this one again in a hurry. Look."

Petri's jubilation was cut short as he saw the arrowhead. The stone had shattered against a rock, splintering into a malformed shard. "Oh," he sighed. "I'm sorry."

"Happens," laughed Taelen. "Come on, it's obviously not his time. Let's get back to the fire, this is something you should learn." He slung the pair of limp rabbits they had snared that morning over his shoulder. "These will see us through."

They picked their way back through the trees. Petri listened to the bird calls and idly kicked at twigs as they walked, looking off into the sun-dappled forest around them. He watched the pair of rabbits bob gently on his father's back with each footfall. Eventually, they came upon the stream they had followed earlier, and Taelen looked both ways before trudging upstream. Petri traded idly kicking twigs for smooth round pebbles as he followed in his father's wake along the stream. The shallow water sprayed every time he sent a pebble spinning off into the bushes. Petri could see the ground begin to rise. He was glad of it—his feet were beginning to ache from the day's trek. He would be glad to get them dry again too. The water was cold, leaking into his hide boots, yet his father insisted on following the stream wherever possible to mask their scent.

Their makeshift camp was perched on a little outcrop on the hillside over the stream. The campfire they had lit the previous day was cold now and looked to Petri like it longed to be rekindled. They set to it, striking a flint beater onto his father's ferrun stone until it showered sparks onto the dry moss they had brought. The tinder caught and Taelen took up the smoking mass and blew until it kindled. The fire flickered into life and Petri busied himself building it up to his satisfaction— that was one thing Petri was good at, at least. He nodded to himself as the lambent glow lit up his youthful face, and then he kicked off his boots to dry by the fire and looked over at his pa who had prepared one of the rabbits on a spit and now rummaged in his hide pack.

"Well I guess now is as good a time as any," murmured Taelen.

"What is it?" asked Petri.

"I can't find the arrowheads," he replied with a frown. "It's no bother, time I showed you the finer points of it anyway."

Petri watched and listened as his father napped a piece of flint explaining as his own father had once shown him. Petri mimicked as best he could and managed to hit himself on the thumb more than once. His father explained how to find the best seam to strike, how to split the stone to find a razor-sharp edge, and how to carefully shape it to fit an arrow shaft. Taelen laughed affectionately and smiled at each of Petri's blunders. "You'll get it, keep at it," he said. The light spilling through the trees was fading by the time Petri had managed to fashion a half decent arrowhead. His father had made several in that time and was already busy binding and fletching the arrows. This at least Petri had done at home, many times, but it had never been his own flint heads he used. He held his arrowhead up to examine it in the fire light. It was by no means perfect, but he had done it. Petri smiled to himself, and it felt good to set his stone upon an arrow. Finally with a sense of triumph he held the arrow for his father to examine.

Taelen still chewed on a piece of roasted meat and the grease ran into his beard. He wiped his hands on his skins and reached up to take the finished arrow, trading it for a skin of milk-wine. Taelen examined it with a critical eye. "You know, lad. That's not half bad. You should have seen my first one." He offered Petri a proud smile, 'not half bad at all. Go on,' he said with a motion to the wineskin.

Petri hesitated, "But…"

"Go on, you're becoming a man now. Drink."

Petri unstoppered the skin and took a swing. The milky taste came with a kick of fire he did not expect. He nearly coughed. Taelen laughed and motioned to have another. Petri took another swallow before trading it back for his arrow. The milk wine lit a fire in his gut, its warmth coursing through him.

"A night for firsts," said Taelen. "It will keep the cold off you," he grinned. "And tomorrow, you will fire your arrow, your own first proper arrow, and if the gods are watching you, who knows, you could make your first kill too."

Petri smiled, but there was a nervous tightening at such an expectation. Could he find his mark, or would he miss again, like today? Would he really be a man soon, like his pa? It seemed a strange thought that he would ever be like Taelen one day, but he must. The milk wine burning away in his belly began to make his vision swim. His thoughts began to float away and settled beneath his rug and listened to his father's stories.

He awoke with a start. It was still dark. What was that? Something had made him start awake. He looked around in a daze, the milk wine still clouding his head. He found Taelen awake, crouched and looking out from the outcrop intently into the darkness.

"What was that?" asked Petri, rubbing his eyes.

"I'm not sure," replied Taelen absently. "It's nothing, lad," he said reassuringly, "go back to sleep." Petri settled down again beneath the blanket. What had woken him, some sound? On the edge of memory lingered the impression of a sound. Something unsettling that had disturbed his dreams. In an echo of memory lingered that terrible keening shriek.

* * *

He awoke to the warm sunlight on his face. His mouth was dry and he scrabbled around for the water-skin. He found his father crouched on the edge of the outcrop, staring off into the trees. "Ah, you're awake," Taelen said without turning.

Petri plucked a bone from the fire and sucked on it. He sat thoughtfully and stared into the embers. His father had obviously kept it going whilst he slept. *That sound.* "I heard something strange in the night."

His father turned and regarded him, "Aye, I wouldn't worry about it."

"What was it?"

"In truth," he seemed to hesitate, "I've not heard its like." He shrugged dismissively and turned back to look out over the trees. His father didn't seem overly bothered by it, although it seemed strange to Petri.

What could it have been?

Taelen pointed out to a shadow of dark hills to the north. "See those, we would do well to steer clear."

"Why?"

"I think I've heard of those hills. I didn't realise we had come that far east. If I am right, then beyond them to the north is the sea, and if the stories are true, they say those hills are a strange place, and few venture there."

Petri listened intently.

"They say that those hills are the home of spirits and gods… of dark things. It is not a place for men to tread. We should not stray too close."

"Is that what I heard last night, a spirit?"

Taelen shrugged. "I don't know, but it was an ill omen. We should heed the god's warning and make our way back south and west."

Petri nodded. He had no desire to walk in haunted hills. He had no desire to meet the thing that had made that sound. Taelen turned his gaze south and then west. "If we head towards the coast to the west there are good hunting grounds out that way and then we can swing south. We will stay well clear of those shadow hills."

"Should we not go back the way we came?"

Taelen considered it. "There was little sign of game on our way up, it's how we came so far. Let's try fresh grounds and get back on the good side of those hills."

They broke camp and headed west with the sun at their backs. Petri fingered the fletching of his newest arrow. A sense of pride warmed his heart, he had taken another step toward becoming a man. They stalked through the undergrowth looking for game trails and tracking signs. Petri walked with his bow slung over his shoulder and a fire-hardened spear in his hand which he found doubled as a handy walking staff. He had not yet fashioned a stone spear like his father's—another right of passage to manhood, which he suspected would soon be fast approaching. Now he had worked the flint, he wondered when he would be given the honour of fashioning his own spear.

His father raised his hand suddenly and they both sank into a crouch. Taelen examined the tracks at his feet. He beckoned Petri closer. In a low whisper, Taelen asked, "what do you see lad?"

Petri examined the ground, there was the impression

of a track there. The young hunter paced from side to side examining the grass to find the difference in colour that revealed the passage of a beast. The grass had been slightly flattened here and there, almost imperceptible to the untrained eye, but Petri could see something had come this way. He checked the wind, and it seemed in favour of the trail's direction. If the beast went that way it would not smell them coming. Carefully they picked their way along the trail, keeping one eye on the visible tree line ahead and one on the ground sign they tracked.

Petri felt a shudder and stopped to look around. *Something is watching us.*

"You alright?" whispered Taelen.

Petri scanned the surrounding trees. "Yeah, I just had a weird feeling. Come on."

They followed the tracks for perhaps an hour stopping now and then to check the signs. An oppressive feeling weighed on Petri's stomach, he just couldn't shake the feeling. Perhaps it was the nerves of another hunt after yesterday's failure. He knew he might have to make another shot. *What if I miss again?* He wanted to make his father proud. Perhaps it was the unsettling look in his father's eyes, the edge to his voice, as he spoke of those strange hills that morning. Something about this forest seemed unsettling. There was an odd silence to the trees.

His father slowly crouched and waved him to a stop, his eyes fixed on something ahead. Petri's eyes followed his silent gestures. He saw it. Antlers moving amongst a thicket up ahead. They stayed low and slowly strung their bows. There was more than one. Petri saw a doe and a buck moving cautiously through the undergrowth ahead, stopping to nuzzle the ground as they foraged. Taelen made a series of hand gestures. Petri nodded his understanding, and Taelen crept away to the right. A branch snapped from the direction of his father. Both animals shot up their heads, suddenly alert. Petri panicked and took aim and drew his bowstring, his special arrow between his fingers. The deer saw the movement and exploded into motion. Both creatures bounded away through the trees.

Petri heard his father curse, and Taelen made his way back to his son's side. "I'm sorry lad, that was my fault."

Petri smiled. "As you said, it wasn't their time."

His father grinned in reply. "Aye, but it soon will be, come on. They're still close." He beckoned Petri onward and they picked out a route to flank what Taelen suspected was the way the deer fled. The shadow closed in around them as they climbed up through a gully to a rise ahead. Again that strange feeling of being watched crept over Petri. Suddenly Taelen stopped.

"This place feels strange," murmured his father.

*He feels it too!* "The forest has eyes," breathed Petri as he looked around into the trees.

"Are you trying to spook me, boy?" grinned Taelen. Something in his eyes seemed unsettled, but he hid it as he always did—with a smile and a laugh. They emerged onto the rise and lay flat to survey the forest ahead. Petri spotted something moving. His heart leapt as he prodded his father and pointed. *There they are!* The two deer threaded their way between the trees. His father's instincts had been right, they had come back up on them downwind again. Petri felt great pride at the skill of his father's tracking, he hoped one day he would be that good too. He would make the ancestors proud.

They stalked down into the trees and approached their quarry. Petri steeled himself, determined. He felt a wave of confidence. He knew the gods were watching, he knew this was his time. They paused as the antlers became visible above the bushes. *They are close*. He waved his father back. The corner of Taelen's mouth twitched up into a smile and he nodded. Petri crept forward, bow in hand, his arrow nocked. He closed his eyes for a moment and breathed in the forest, the sounds, the smells. He could feel his place in the forest and felt the eyes of the gods upon his. When he opened them again he had those antlers in his sights, the bowstring taut. He caught a glimpse of hide. He loosed. The bowstring thrummed. His arrow flicked away and found its mark.

The bushes erupted as something thrashed violently. He dropped his bow, grabbed his spear, and ran forwards to finish his kill.

His heart froze and as he rose the spear to strike. He could not move, petrified mid-thrust as he burst out of the undergrowth. Before him sprawled a figure. His blood ran cold. Its antlered face snapped towards him. Before him was no deer, it was the figure of a man. The man's eyes locked onto his, a black glare of rage. Petri could see the arrow had caught him in the chest, and blood pumped out alarmingly. The figure struggled in pain and reached for a black stone axe at his side.

Taelen was suddenly there beside him. He thrust his spear down and savagely impaled the man through the eye. The figure screamed. A blood-curdling shriek burst from his lips. The sound was inhuman and turned Petri's blood to ice. Taelen staggered back in shock. The shriek turned into a howl, diminishing into a keening wail that echoed off through the trees.

Petri's heart hammered in his chest and seemed to stop as the realisation struck. *I have heard that before.* His skin turned to goose flesh and he took a step back grasping his father's arm to steady him. *What have I done?*

The figure stilled and became motionless, still pumping out an unnatural amount of blood. Something felt very wrong. The blood was thick and dark. The man's skin was caked in mud and blood. His teeth were bared and bloody, but they were filed to sharp points like some kind of terrible beast. The man's skins were old and tattered, and across his entire body, he was daubed with strange markings in what looked like old blood. Most striking of all was his strange headdress. He wore some kind of mask made of a stag's head, the wide antlers of the mantle spread out above his head and now lay in the dirt as his head flopped back lifeless. The mask enclosed his face all except his mouth and those terrible teeth. The man's head was so caked in mud and gore it was hard to tell which parts were the man and which were the mask, they seemed to be melded into one terrible visage. The body seemed impossibly broken, limps bent at gut-wrenching angles. Even dead this man was a horror to behold.

They both stood there staring at the corpse. *What have I done*, thought Petri, *I killed him*. He gave voice to his thoughts. "What have I done?" whimpered Petri.

"It was an accident," assured Taelen, his voice cracking.

"I killed him!"

"*We* killed him," said Taelen, his eyes touched with

a wildness Petri had never seen. He pulled his spear free, and a fresh pulse of thick black blood oozed out of its head. The remaining eye stared up at them, black and lifeless.

"Who is he?" stuttered Petri.

"I don't know," replied his father. Taelen prodded the mask with the butt of his spear, he frowned and driven by curiosity, bent to remove it with his hands. He recoiled in horror. "By the gods" he exclaimed and backed away in fear and revulsion.

Petri could see what turned his father's heart to ice. *That mask.* The man's face appeared merged with the mask, its skin grown over the stag's skull enclosing it into its own. *That is no mask...* Its eye leaked blood and the remaining one had an inhuman quality as it stared blankly up at him. Petri stood frozen in terror, watching the dark blood ooze from its wounds. *This thing is not human. By the gods, what have I done? I have killed a forest spirit. I have angered the gods.*

Suddenly a horn brayed through the forest, accompanied by one of those terrible shrieks which seemed to come in answer to the man's death cry. The forest around them erupted into a chorus of deathly shrieks and screams. Petri caught a flicker of movement from the corner of his vision.

Taelen turned to his son with a look of pure panic in

his eyes. "Petri, run!"

The trees seemed to rush towards him, then past him. He ran. Stumbling between the boles of trees, he plunged onwards. His heart was pounding, and his lungs burned. Wild panic clenched down on his stomach, wringing his innards to a cold ice. He could feel them behind him, the footfalls of pursuit hidden behind by his own thundering stampede through the brush. He could feel eyes burning into him, lancing into that panic-churned gut. He kept his father in his view. There were moments when he seemed to lose sight of him, the awareness of his surroundings wracked by spikes of terrible blinding panic until he, at times, found himself again, as if conscious awareness broke like waves on a cold shore. At times there was nothing but the tightening of his chest, it felt like it would burst with every ragged breath. As if fear were a flame, stealing every breath in its inferno of terror. *How far had they come?*

Petri drew to a halt beside Taelen. His father leaned gasping against a tree with both hands supporting him. He weakly fought to stop his hide satchel and bow from slipping to the floor. Petri grasped at his own tree, dragging deep breaths. The bark was rough. He turned to Taelen and saw his father frantically searching the trees behind them with an unreadable face of dread. *Are they there?* Petri had seen glances, snatches of movement after those terrible screeches exploded from the forest around them. Inexorable, these things seemed more beast than man. The ghostly figures melted into the trees somehow. He saw one sprinting with terrifying purpose. Then it was gone. He had run hard ever since, not looking back. Swallowing his terror he forced himself to swing a weary head, and raise his eyes to stare into those antler-headed terrors that bore vengeful death upon them. The hunters had become the hunted.

There was nothing.

He blinked.

Taelen searched and breathed, staring and breathing. "Where are they?" he said.

Petri couldn't talk, but terrified eyes darted between the trees. He found himself in a forest that had grown low and was scattered with pools and mire. The forest had become a swamp, still thick with trees, but no longer the firm dirt and bracken. Now the ground was damp. There was a smell of rotting vegetation and foetid water, but no deathly pursuit.

Petri expected a band of loping antler-headed ghost-men to burst into view, but there was nothing. "Did we lose them?" stammered Petri.

His father gave no reply, he just stared into the trees. "We should move," he said finally, "stay on the high ground and follow me." He tried to hide his fear in his voice but his father's eyes betrayed him—the sublime terror found in the eyes of the hunted. He led them onwards, picking a careful route between stunted hanging trees. Petri kept a wary eye on the trees, but they moved slower, less frantic. They moved quickly still, but it was no headlong or mindless rush, with death snapping at their heels. Now death stalked them. A menace which lurked out there, hunting them. They had to tread quickly but not recklessly. The urgency of their silent escape was oppressive. Still, there was a cold stone laid in his belly, and the prickle of a shock rippling over him, but he concentrated on breathing and keeping up with Taelen. He uttered prayers to the gods of the hunt, and to the gods of the forests, of the rocks, and the wicked sea, beseeching all that it should not be his time.

Time passed, he was not sure how long, but the sun grew low in the sky. Petri dared to think they had evaded them. There had been no glimpse of them since they wound their way into these swamps. They had lost those things in the forest. He found vigour to his step. He would see a dawn again. *Just keep going.*

Talen stumbled and tripped with a low cry. Petri, raised a weary head to focus blurring eyes on his father's collapsing form. Petri lurched to catch him.

His heart froze.

The antler man squatted right in front of him. The

black stone head of a savage club came to rest maliciously in the leaves. Taelen crashed to the floor unconscious, trailing blood from his scalp. Petri stared into inhuman eyes. They stared at each other frozen to the spot. Its pitch smeared face suddenly screeched from beneath the visage of a bloodied stag's head. A keening coarse shriek that sent a wave of sheer terror crashing over him.

There was a flash of light. Something struck him hard in the head from behind. He fell into the cold darkness as he felt his body collapse to the stagnant ground.

* * *

He opened his eyes with a jerk. Panic clutched his heart. His head throbbed and he could feel blood still trickling from his scalp. It ran down his hair and dripped into the undergrowth. He couldn't move, his hands were bound and he found the world was upside down. Petri was completely disoriented. He slowly realised he was suspended from a pole, trussed up like game from the hunt. He craned his neck to look. He saw his father suspended in the same manner. He was surrounded by strange figures. *Antler-men… Forest spirits.* These strange folk were like the one he had shot. Craggy rocks rose high around him, and a wind whistled through the cliffs and high places he found himself carried through. The panic rose and he fought to free himself. *We are at those shadow hills. We strayed too far!* He heard a shout in a harsh guttural tongue and felt something strike his head. Darkness.

He awoke as he was dumped to the earth. He groaned and found he could still not move his hands. He felt himself dragged into a circle of ruddy flickering light. Water dripped from above. They were in some cave. There were fires flickering. A cloying oily smoke made him cough.

He heard a woman's voice shout three strange words. Suddenly thunder erupted. Drums hammered. Dozens of drums hammered in unison. He saw shapes whirling and weaving amongst the flames. The naked forms of men and women were smeared in that same crusty pitch as the legs he glimpsed carrying him here. He caught sight of antlers and horns. For a terrible moment, he found himself in some insane carnival of woodland creatures, all dancing and wheeling to the thunderous pulse of the drums.

Petri could hear a strange sound. Chanting, but he could not understand the words. A series of guttural and sibilant utterances. Screamed from the throats of a menagerie of nightmare beast-folk. The words repeated in an unending cycle, slowly rising into a terrible crescendo.

Suddenly the drums stopped to reveal an eerie silence. He heard the woman's voice. She spoke in a strange accent but in words he somehow understood. He felt hands lift him and bind him to an upright stake. He glanced sideways squinting in the firelight to lay eyes on his father. There he was. Staked to the ground not far away.

The woman switched from words he knew to that strange guttural tongue akin to grinding stones. She spoke of the sea swallowing the lands, of the return. She spoke of the ones in the waters, the sacred ones. Terrible things. She spoke of a summoning of blood. Each drop brings us closer to the coming. She spoke of sacrifice. The suspicion of his fate striking true smashed home like a hammer. His legs grew weak. He cast a glance at Taelen. His father had twisted his head to stare helplessly at his son, his mouth moving wordlessly. Tears were in his eyes, alongside a desperate knowing terror. The shaman daubed them with blood and ash and forced strange pastes into their throats. Petri felt something wet and viscid on his tongue. A ferrous tang of blood. They held his face shut until some fouled fleshy globule slid down his throat.

The woman suddenly screamed something. The drums erupted to life and the silent antler creatures lurched into motion once more. The chanting began, those same ominous words. The pace quickened and the chanting became accented with the screeching of the woman, all entwining into a sickening cacophony that he could not bear any longer.

His consciousness blurred, warping. He looked around, his eyes darting from the glow of flickering fires and wheeling figures to things that were impossibly there. His head swam, dizziness seizing him.

He watched a great wave crash over the valley. The earth shook and cracked. A great chasm split the earth and he watched vast swathes fall away into a dark underworld. He stood on a high hill, at its very summit, and watched the wall of water, the wave's inexorable approach. The sky cracked with lightning and burned in a deep crimson, a tortured sky-scape of nightmare. The sound of water was deafening, a raging torrent tearing the trees from the roots and gouging rocks from the earth, all surging towards him. The wave broke over the hill he stood upon. To his dismay it enveloped him, it was a wave that seemed to scrape the clouds themselves. Monstrous and yet completely sublime. He stood frozen unable to tear his eyes from the doom that enveloped him. Against the sky, he noticed a black shape, gargantuan and impossible. He strained to focus, but his head swam.

He was back at the fires, the strange antler folk screeching and baying like animals. He faded once more to darkness.

He found himself sinking, drowning. He clutched

his throat, but his lungs burned to take a breath. There was no air. He sank. Above him, waves broke on a distant surface as he limply sank beneath the waves. A great lambent eye watched him through the murk. It blinked slowly and did not reopen, disappearing from view. He saw the trees and the hills all submerged beneath the waves. A world he once knew, drowned. He looked deep into a dark rent in the seabed. He sank slowly into it, as if swallowed by the maw of the earth, slowly sinking into a terrible abyss. There was something strange here. Hewn rocks and stones. Impossible cyclopean blocks of stone, hundreds of them. As if giants had piled them into some kind of bizarre dwelling or structure. Like nothing he could imagine. What was this place?

The shaman screamed and chanted strange words in his face. She seized him by his hair and lifted his head. His vision swam. He could see things amongst the antler-men, monstrous shapes stood there watching as if they belonged there, but how could they?

The shaman screamed in his face, terrible guttural words. *What's that in his hand?* The recognition punched him in the belly. *The arrowhead!* The Shaman brandished it in the air and shouted his strange words. *They took the arrowhead that had killed their own, and now it was their instrument of vengeance.*

With a flash she swung round upon Taelen and sliced

his throat. Blood spilled from the gash, a terrible amount of blood. Petri cried out in shock and then horror seized him. He fought as tears blinded him. He screamed, and if there were words there, they were not distinguishable, just a mournful anguish. *No!* Every memory turned to ash. He sobbed and cried. *Father!* His sanity snapped like a rotten chord. He screamed and screamed, a screech like the antler men. He was unable to comprehend what his eyes told him. Unable to think. The intensity of anguish stuck him numb. He watched his father sag slowly and with him all hope sagged from his heart.

He felt it before he knew what it was. The realisation slowly dawned as the stone blade slashed his throat. He choked; his throat full of blood. He drowned, unable to gasp. The ferrous tang on his tongue. He could feel the trickle of something flowing over him, dripping from his fingertips.

Eyes watched him. Round luminous eyes. Squatting on the slime slick stones were perching a gathering of strange leathery creatures, almost human but terribly distant, like some sort of amphibious mockery of man. They pawed at him with webbed claw-like hands and feet. Their needle-like fangs dripped and slavered. They were reaching for him.

He watched his father convulse, and then Taelen unleashed a terrible scream, a bubbling roar. His chest burst in a spray of blood. Terrible tendrils flickered out of him. Bones snapped and Petri watched in horror as his father changed. His neck elongated and cracked, to become some awful limb of its own crowned with his face. A scything construct of bone and flesh slowly forced its way free on the other side. The ribcage splayed open, everything was blood. His father melted and birthed at once, a hideous creature emerged in Taelen's place.

He felt himself lifted up amongst the chanting. His bonds were cut and he fell sprawling to the floor. The smell of blood was thick in his nostrils, cloying and sickening. He realised he lay in his father's blood. He tried to scream but he had no energy, no will. He could run, but he knew it was folly to try. He closed his eyes to escape the horror unfolding and was plunged into another vision.

Something pulled on his leg, a clawed hand grasped him tightly and dragged him deeper into the black void amongst the terrible carved stone. Yet there was something there in the gloom, something vast, something that squirmed and pulsed. Something that began to heave and rise.

His stomach squirmed and pulsed, something writhed in his belly trying to break free. *What was that sound? Screaming?* He shook the nightmare visions from his mind, as the cold reality of his fate brought him crystal clarity. He could see the fires again, the sound intensified. Petri realised with a cold horror it was his voice he could hear. He writhed and screamed on the cold floor. He felt his skin tear, felt things burst from him and grow. Something squirmed its way free of his abdomen and found the floor. He could feel it like a limb of his own, he could feel the damp earth, and it raised him up to stand monstrously at a greater height. He felt his bones crack as his limbs snapped into new angles, and his skin burned like liquid fire. He was changing, some horrific metamorphosis into a thing of nightmare. He could do nothing but scream and twist in agony as he became something utterly inhuman. The thread of thought that had been Petri, slipped away, replaced by insanity mingled with instinct and urge. His screams petered off into a sick gurgling croak and took a step with inhuman limbs.

A thing that had once been kin slopped down a blood-wreathed limb and settled its bulk upon a coil of writhing gelatinous tendrils. A mouth gaped from its torso, and a human face he once knew stretched and distorted on its strange appendage that jutted from a thorax of splintered rib cage. The lips of that second face peeled back to reveal hideous needle-like fangs that were certainly not human. A pair of eyes flopped around, one distended and enlarged but still sharp in a terrible like the eye of a fish. Its torso maw yawned again. He recoiled from the gruesome mockery of flesh and wondered in horror at his own mutilated visage and nightmare form. His mind span into an abyss of darkness, pain and terror. It would never return to this twisted flesh.

A cry rose up from the gathered antler-folk around them. They seemed to prostrate themselves before it. A leader chanted words, words that seemed distantly familiar. Beyond the glow of flames, perched familiar creatures, lambent eyes and webbed claws, creatures that looked to yearn to return to the darkness beneath the waves. Yet, he knew he was not one of them, he was a gore smeared horror of something else entirely. A presence was felt, something on the edge of sanity, something vast, something sublime, something ancient. These eyes, these hundreds of eyes from which he now gazed from behind, were still adjusting. His vision was new and untested, but he could see something. Something looming in the sky.

As the drums began, he killed. With terrible savagery, he revelled, they revelled, as things newly birthed from the darkness, they killed in a crimson fury. It knew not what it killed. Just that it was warm and living and then it was torn and cold. Blood glistened from scything claws. There were screams, such beautiful screams. The fires still flickered and amongst the carnage wheeled the strange man things, splattered in blood in a trance of oblivious ecstasy. Then, the red fury stopped. It felt a shadow fall over it. That presence, something old, something very old. It was here.

He paused in the debauchery of blood and carnage and raised many eyes to the sky. The other thing had stopped, dropping the slime of a skull to the ground with a splatter and peering into the sky also. The drums ceased and all eyes turned upward as an oppressive sense of dread crushed the souls of all who stood here.

Something moved, something hulking, something impossibly big. So big it blotted out the dark sky with a deeper inky darkness. A titan of shadow. An ancient bulk of eldritch consciousness, something too old to be evil or good, just indifferent to insignificance. It spread its terrible wings across the sky, obscuring horizon to horizon. Something ancient had risen. It had come from the sea, and it knew, everything in its malign presence would soon return there.

# Distant Beckonings

Vincent H. O'Neil

Akilna slid the stone knife into the moist dirt without looking at it. Her mother used this particular root to brew a pain-killing drink, and Akilna had harvested many of them for her.

Her eyes were watching the shadows where thin sunlight fought its way into the marsh. Small trees rose up amid the tangle of vines, bushes, and thorns, all possibly shielding an attacker from view. She inhaled the jumbled scents of the verdant lowland, not detecting a predator's odour and hoping for the return of the bird song that had ceased while she'd been working.

Akilna's searching fingers found the narrow

segment of the root, and she slowly sawed at it with the knife's chipped edge. Sound and motion attract attention, so survival depended on making as little of either as possible. Every living thing is food for some other living thing, and she was too far from the village to run. Her eyes shifted away from the shadows to her planned escape route, a thicket of thorns with a hole just big enough for her thin frame. Every step of the way there she'd identified the closest obstacle or potential sanctuary, a habit so ingrained by her foraging trips that it was almost an instinct.

A real instinct came alive within her just then, the awareness of being watched. It grew across her back like the heat from the sun when clouds part, swiftly changing from observation to malice. Releasing the root but clutching the knife, she dropped and rolled just as an angry growl rippled behind her. Akilna's free hand pushed off against the damp earth while her bark-soled feet fought for purchase in the mud. Branches snapped where she'd been digging, a heavy body landing in the space she'd just emptied.

Seeing the gap among the thorns was smaller than she'd thought, Akilna brought both hands over her head and dived. Long sharp points scratched her bare arms, but her hide shirt and tied leggings took the rest of it as she plummeted through the branches. The space inside the protective walls was just large enough for her young body, and she landed hard against more barbs.

Her strong legs immediately hopped her into a squatting position, the knife extended just as the brown and black cat, twice her size, landed on the brush. Its snarl showed white teeth in jaws that could have snapped her leg, and the sagging mass of tangled thorns carried the beast toward her.

Akilna swung the stone blade, swatting at a reaching claw, but the thorns finally penetrated the dark fur and the cat cried out. It was flailing at the barbs when the stalks resumed their original shape and tossed the beast away. It landed upright, roaring in anger, and crouched as if to leap again. Just as Akilna saw the sinews of its shoulders tightening, it let out a yelp and lifted a foreleg off the ground to shake it furiously. Hissing, the big cat settled to the dirt and started biting at the pads of that paw, trying to extract the thorn that was paining it so. Its eyes stayed fixed on Akilna until she sank to the wet ground and the vegetation concealed her.

The sanctuary was not perfect, though. The beast knew it could wait her out. The water in the lowlands was still and murky, and Akilna's mouth was already dry. Still hugging the earth, she gradually moved her head to see where the thorn bushes met the ground. She spotted a space between two of them just wide enough for her shoulders   and shifted away from where the cat tended its wound.

With the patience of a spider, she started inching toward the gap. The slightest tremor in the foliage would alert the predator, but she'd evaded danger this way before. Her cheek slid over green moss, and her fingers gently separated the creepers that blocked her path. Motion so subtle that it seemed to be no motion at all, progress so minuscule that it felt as if she were merely lying there.

* * *

The latest vision came while she was crawling out of the thicket. Akilna was surprised, as they usually made their appearances when she was at rest. Her concentration seemed to split at first   as if one eye was studying the dirt while the other one focused on an utterly different scene. Then the unfamiliar sights took over, and she was transported elsewhere.

This was a new one, and its vividness surpassed all the others. Her nostrils inhaled salt even as her eyes beheld a seemingly endless sea. The dark blue water was still, its tiny waves slapping the sides of the ship. Akilna stood in its rear, marvelling at its size. Made of finely shaped wood, it dwarfed the bowl-shaped, one-man boats she'd seen at the shore during the annual pilgrimage to harvest salt. What appeared to be a carved tree trunk rose from its centre, with a cross-piece holding a stretch of tan fabric bigger than any hide she'd ever seen. Twisted cords held this curiosity to the cross-piece while others tied its lower corners to the ship, and a strong breeze filled it.

Her gaze dropped to the men and women on the boat. They seemed bigger than the people of her village, although it was hard to tell because they were all lying down. Shoulders and heads rested against the boat's inner sides while their legs extended past wooden platforms that lined the boat in a double row. Akilna couldn't identify the material of their clothing, but it looked similar to the fabric that was propelling them across the water.

A face appeared next to her, a man with skin much paler than her own and hair the colour of dead grass. He seemed to know her, and when he spoke it was in a dialect she'd never heard before but recognized and understood immediately.

"We'll be there soon," his lips curved in a confident smile as if to say more. Akilna's attention was pulled away by a sensation in her fingertips, and she looked down to see they were resting on the ship's rail. A vibration was running through the wood, and she sensed it came from the water.

So many of the visions were like that. Details and senses that suggested she was actually there. She looked over the side, wondering what in the vast water around them could be causing the tremors in the hull. The rocking waves were dark, but she intuited something far beneath them, something alive. Something enormous. It was starting to take rough shape in her mind when she was torn from the vision.

The cat outside the thicket had let loose a terrified and confused shriek, shaking Akilna back into awareness. It leapt up and went crashing off through the foliage.

* * *

The trails leading to the village were wide and dead against the greenery. Akilna avoided them for as long as possible, hating the way that human feet had killed what once grew there.

Slipping through the trees became easier as she got closer to home because foraging parties had trampled the underbrush long ago. Her eyes and ears stayed alert, but it was her nose that detected the human who was waiting to surprise her. Recognising the scent, Akilna glided around the lichen-covered rock that concealed the prankster and tapped him on the shoulder.

Borka merely shook his head in defeat. He leaned his tall frame against the rock and grinned. "I should have moved when I lost sight of you."

"Wouldn't have helped," she looked down at the body of a large bore the hunter had killed. "I thought I was smelling *you*, but now I'm not sure."

"Pretty much the same," he laughed while lifting the kill onto his shoulders. "I've been carrying it for some time."

His spear was propped against the rock, so Akilna took it and followed. Older, approaching manhood, Borka was lean and slim. Despite the load, he moved gracefully through the trees. She studied the spear's stone point, a new kind with notches at its base that protected the leather wrappings from wear.

"You get this from your friends?" She extended the lance so he could see it.

"I wouldn't call them friends. With so many of them in camp, it's hard not to mingle. Although you've managed it well enough."

"I don't trust the antler folk. I wish they'd stayed by the sea where they belong."

"They know things," he tapped the tip of the spear. "Better weapons, better tools."

"Their god gives them these new ideas. Don't you listen at their ceremonies?"

"I don't go to many of those. You don't have to join them if you don't want to."

"Too many of us want to."

They entered the camp as the sun was setting. Simple pole-and-bark dwellings sprouted among the trees, their main supports lashed to the trunks around them. Hide-clad men and women worked everywhere, preparing food, repairing tools, or supervising the young. Multi-point antlers from the forest's deer and elk sprouted from the tops of half the huts.

"Enjoy your walk, while the rest of us were working?" A stout woman named Leeno sneered at Akilna as they passed.

"You visit my mother whenever you're sick, just like anyone else," Akilna didn't stop. "Can't make the medicine without the ingredients."

* * *

"You'd never had this dream before?" Akilna's mother Pertil stood in the back of their hut, examining roots hung there to age. She was preparing to brew a special drink for Mata, a neighbour who was struggling to give birth.

"It wasn't a dream. That cat was still hunting me, so I wasn't asleep."

"Dream. Vision. Almost the same. But this was new, yes?"

"I've never seen a boat like that one. Or the clothing.

And the people … they didn't look like us. Pale skin and some had yellow hair." She shook her head.

"What?"

"It should have been strange, but somehow it wasn't. I understood their words."

"Say some of them now."

"I don't *remember* any of them!"

Her mother smiled. "See? Just like a dream."

"So it wasn't a vision?"

Pertil started chopping ingredients, and Akilna joined her. They worked in silence for some time before her mother answered.

"Everyone has visions. Me, I sensed your father was dead the night he didn't return from that last hunt. He'd been late before, but that time I knew. Then I dreamt of him, surrounded by spears and knives, fighting outnumbered. When I awoke, it was with the certainty that he was gone and we'd never know what happened to him."

"You've interpreted every one of my dreams. Why didn't you tell me this before?"

"I didn't want to put anything in your head. As soon as you could walk, you wanted to explore outside the camp. You were always touching the leaves and the trees and imitating the birds' songs. That's why I renamed you Akilna."

"Watchful."

"And that was you," Pertil paused. "But you could also remember your dreams, and felt driven to understand them. These can be signs of someone who is receptive to visions."

"When I was younger my dreams didn't feel real like these do," Akilna paused. "I think they are real."

"Perhaps. Perhaps not. Sadly, we find out which ones are real after they come true."

"These are different. Special. I feel like I'm *there*, same as I'm here right now."

Her mother stopped working. "Just when did these special dreams start?"

"When I got old enough to walk to the sea with you and the others. Not the first time, but the second."

Pertil frowned. "That was when we met the antler people."

Akilna was about to respond, but the camp's normal sounds were abruptly broken by the shrill cries of a newborn. They exchanged happy smiles and went back to work in a hurry. For some reason, the cries reminded Akilna of the cat's shriek that afternoon.

"Why do we scream like that, Mother? When we're born?"

"It's not a scream, child. It's a shout. Every one of us takes in the air for the first time, and we all yell the same thing: I'm breathing! I'm alive!"

* * *

The drums called Akilna to the centre of the village later that night. She could go unnoticed in the crowd because almost everyone was there. As much as she disliked the newcomers, somehow she couldn't stay away from their ceremonies.

Followers of the oceanic god donned the antlers on these occasions, and she noticed with alarm that more of the villagers were wearing them than not. The devotees wore the horns upside-down on their backs, to signify the titan's tattered wings.

A circle of barbed acolytes danced around a large fire, spinning and beating out the rhythm on hide drums. Their leader, a large man named Tuku, finally quieted them.

"As always, we begin with the blessed event that revealed the water-dwelling god to us," his voice was deep and pleasing, and the crowd pulled in closer. An elbow brushed Akilna's arm, and she jumped in concern that it might be the point of a horn. Instead, she looked up into Borka's smile. They both turned to listen as Tuku continued.

"One man, alone in a tiny boat, set out to fish one day. He stayed close to shore, but then fell asleep. When he awoke he was in a dense fog, and when it parted he saw nothing but water."

"That's why you stay on land," Borka whispered to Akilnar. Trying not to laugh, she jabbed him with an elbow.

"A day and a night he drifted. With no water to drink, he was soon near death. He prayed to the wind and the sky, but it did no good. Late on the second night, almost too weak to raise his head, he felt he was no longer alone."

"No longer alone," the crowd murmured in response. Akilna saw the firelight bounce off Leeno's round face, and it made her shiver. The unpleasant woman's eyes and mouth were wide open, as if she were completely enthralled.

"No voice did he hear, and yet he understood. A deity he did not know had come to his aid. He was no longer faint, and searched the dark for his rescuer."

"His rescuer," the people breathed, as if seeing the enormous aquatic saviour themselves. Their bodies swayed like tall grass in a breeze, and the drums gently resumed.

"The stars disappeared, blocked by a figure taller and wider than any hill. Its back was to him, but he saw the outline of ragged wings, arms like a man's, and a head the size of the moon. The god walked off through the waves, its wake pulling the boat toward safety."

"Safety!" Now, the villagers were shouting, their rapt faces frightening Akilna.

"And just as the rays of the sun were about to appear, the sea god vanished. The man did not know its name, but knew he was supposed to tell all the people of its existence and power. To prove this, the deity gave the man knowledge that no others possessed, skills that would help believers prosper and hunt. And when the darkness was gone, the man saw the shore and began to spread the word."

"The word!" The end of the tale sent the believers into a frenzy, moving around the fire and starting to dance. Arms flailed, feet stamped, and the pointed horns jerked back and forth.

"If I went out there, I'd lose an eye," Akilna said to Borka. Although the night was filled with drumming and yells, she kept her voice low.

Borka struggled not to laugh. "You can speak normally. We're alone."

Akilna looked around, dismayed to see he was right. In the shadows beyond the throng she detected several villagers hanging back, but their numbers were few.

"Is that your father?" She asked, pointing. The man was slightly shorter than Borka and had no adornment, but was dancing with a woman who wore the horns.

"Yes," Borka answered, his head bobbing slightly with the drums. "Her name is Wetani. She makes my father happy."

"She's new."

"The antler villages near the sea are getting crowded. No harm in their coming here."

Somewhere inside Akilna's skull, pain leapt up as if she'd been stabbed with a thorn. The blazing fire dulled for an instant, the jumping forms blending together, and then a scene appeared in front of her eyes that simply could not be.

It was the seashore she'd visited twice before, but it was nothing like she remembered. The skies were composed of swirling grey clouds that poured rain and belched thunder. The sea was surging higher than she would have believed, slapping the land and booming forward over sand and rock. The wind howled, but still, she heard a collective wail, as if hundreds of humans were screaming for help.

The scene disappeared, replaced with blackness and then Borka's face directly in front of her own. His hands squeezed her shoulders, holding her up, and at first, his lips moved with no sound. His voice slowly grew, as if he were approaching from a distance.

"—what's wrong? Are you not well? Did you eat?"

Akilna pushed his hands away and took two wobbly

steps back. Her mind was still on that tortured shore with its unseen, terrified multitudes.

"I'm fine. Fine. I'm all right," she stammered, and then passed out.

* * *

The drums were in her dreams. Pulsing, pulling, driving. Dim shapes against an orange glow, their antler wings standing out. A mass of bodies prancing, twisting, writhing. The drumbeat quickening in a way that it never did during the antler ceremonies.

She was outside the throng, as always, but this time she was alone because everyone there was now a believer. There was safety in her isolation, though. Even in a dream state Akilna could think and observe, and knew she was of no importance to the celebrants. Their attention was shifting inward, toward the fire that was rising tall above them.

Their whoops and shouts fought the drums, arms rising in expectation—or was it greeting? Her own eyes were drawn to the fire as a cloud of smoke formed above it. Dark, shifting, thrilling the dancers. The smoke took the more solid form of a shadow and continued to ascend. She watched it grow, imagining it blotting out the stars in the night sky above and then seeing it was no illusion. Not smoke, not shadow.

Her struggling vision tried to match it to something she knew, but the only thing close was the etchings of the long-vanished mammoths she'd once seen on a cave wall. The form solidified into massive shoulders and a bowed head, bigger than any tree in the forest and still growing.

The drumbeat was completely blotted out by the shrieks and shouts as the worshipers reached a peak of ecstasy. The monster's back arched and then separated into two wings that couldn't possibly have lifted something that enormous off the ground. Its rounded head started to turn in her direction, utterly ignoring its celebrants, as if abruptly sensing her presence.

Just as the very corner of one eye became visible, a glowing coal larger than a boulder, the image snapped into a completely different scene. It was the deep woods, lush and alive, but instead of comforting her, it sent Akilna's sleeping body into tremors.

Lying on the green ground was her father, pierced by at least a dozen wounds and fighting for breath. Tuku, wearing his antler wings, stood over him with spear raised.

"Our god demands sacrifice. You should feel honoured." He said.

Just as Tuku drove the stone spear point downward, her father's body turned into Borka's.

Akilna sat up screaming.

* * *

"Daughter! Daughter!" Pertil was holding her upper arms. "What's wrong?"

Her eyes raced around the confines of the small hut, not believing she was there. She couldn't be. Just a moment before, she'd been in the woods at the ghastly scene of Borka's murder. Her mind twisted in confusion, and then Akilna saw that the sun had already risen.

"Why was I still asleep?" She demanded.

"You don't remember? Borka brought you back last night, in a daze. You were mumbling and tossing for half the night."

"Borka?" She grabbed her mother's hands. "Is he here?"

"Of course not. He has to hunt. He left just after you finally went to sleep."

Akilna struggled to her feet, even as Pertil tried to stop her. "You shouldn't be up. You're running a fever."

"Which way did he go?"

"Back to his father's hut. Where else would he go?"

"Did he say where he'd be *hunting*?" Akilna tried hard not to scream, fighting to escape her mother's grasp.

"Daughter, you must lie down again. You're making no sense."

"Mother!" She brought her nose close to Pertil's. "The antlers are killing the people who won't join them. They killed Father."

Pertil's mouth opened, and her hands went slack. "You saw this?"

"Yes. And now they want Borka. I have to find him. *Now*."

* * *

Akilna ran through the woods, heedless of her own safety. She didn't swat at obstructing branches or crash through the underbrush, but she wasn't taking the normal precautions either. The years of surviving in the wilderness had taught her to weave through the obstacles, and she moved with a speed that was remarkably quiet.

That wasn't good enough, though. Sound would announce her approach, but movement would attract hostile eyes. The admonitions of her mother from her earliest memory rose up and told her to stop running, to blend back into the lethal environment, but she couldn't do that. Running through the village, her first thought had been to summon the help she'd need to save Borka— only to realise such assistance would have come from Borka himself.

After a time she was in the deep forest, fatigue finally slowing her down. The territory where Borka hunted was enormous, and she'd seldom come this way. Her head snapped left and right while her nostrils reached out for any sign that he was near. The futility of the effort made her heart thump harder, and she turned in place in utter frustration.

She froze upon seeing a trio of large trees nearby, their bases obscured by bright green ferns. She'd never been on that spot before but recognized it instantly. Akilna's instincts started to reassert themselves as she moved around the trio. She frowned at the sight just beyond, a water-filled depression covered in yellow pollen. Completely alien, but quite familiar.

The sensation from the boat vision returned, that feeling of being at home in a place she'd never been. Of knowing the people on the deck, and even understanding their language.

The dream. She knew this place because, as impossible as it was, she'd actually been here in that vision. Looking past the stagnant pool, Akilna already knew there'd be a fallen tree so large she'd have to climb over it. Past that was a stretch of more open ground she'd have to skirt, and after that she'd find Borka.

* * *

The scent of male sweat came on the breeze, sending her into thick brush because it was too strong to be Borka alone. Akilna crouched beneath the overlapping fern leaves and watched with despair as Tuku and several other antler worshipers passed. They carried spears and hide bundles from which, here and there, sprouted the points from their ceremonial ornaments. She'd never seen them take the items outside the village.

Though clearly fatigued by whatever they'd just done, their bodies showed a relaxed mood like predators after a good feed. She studied each of the men as best she could, now seeing that one limped in pain while another held a compress of moss against a cut in his side.

Her woods instincts now returned in full, Akilna slipped away through the fronds. Toward the spot where Tuku and the others had been.

It wasn't hard to find. A heavy odour of recent blood hung in the air as she entered a small clearing ringed by stout trees. The trunks were adorned with sets of antlers, tied upside down like their deity's wings. Arcane symbols had been carved into the bark, but she dismissed them while circling just outside the clearing. The blood smell grew stronger, pulling her toward a fallen tree limb covered in dead leaves.

It looked like it had been there for some time but moving some of the camouflage showed her the loose dirt beneath. They'd disguised it well, but she knew it contained Borka and stopped digging. Tears rolled down her cheeks, distorting her vision even as she looked around to make sure nothing was sneaking up on her. Akilna's gaze passed through the clearing, the liquid in her eyes making the antlers deform and the trees seem to dance. That's what the antler worshipers had done after killing Borka. They'd danced in a circle around his murdered body.

Her vision swam again, but it was accompanied by a tensing of her muscles. Akilna gradually raised a hand to wipe away the tears, sniffing without making a sound because this was the same sensation she'd had when the big cat had almost caught her.

Curiously, there was nothing on the wind that hadn't been there before. Her attention returned to the clearing, and it abruptly became important to go out there. Not understanding her own movement, she rose and walked into the centre of the awful place where her friend had been sacrificed. The horned decorations she so loathed now held her attention, and vibration passed through her like a chill.

The drums from the night before began pulsing in the back of her mind, and Akilna recalled the enormous form in smoke that had risen in her dream. Although she saw nothing that shouldn't have been there, Akilna felt the presence studying her. Warmth spread through her limbs, accompanied by a soothing feeling of acceptance.

No words formed in her ears or her mind, and yet it was clear that this thing, this god of the antler folk, admired her in some way.

Knowledge flowered into her awareness as if it had always been there. Like the dew in the morning, its arrival could not be observed but its presence was undeniable. The being wanted her to know these things.

Tuku and his people by the shore had a ridiculously limited understanding of the creature they called their god. They didn't even know its name, although that had been revealed to the first man adrift in the boat so long ago. Unschooled in the simplest invocations, they were straying farther and farther from what it wanted. The symbols scratched into the bark around her were a sham, meaningless scrawls designed to give the preachers of the religion a more mystic aura.

For no apparent reason, an old village saying came to mind.

The sound of raindrops hitting branches and stones is not the rain itself.

"What … what is it that you want?" She stammered.

Pain welled up inside her head, the same stabbing thorn from the night before. The clearing vanished, and she returned to the storm-lashed shore with its angry clouds, howling winds, and wailing voices.

Now she saw them, and Akilna's cry joined theirs

even though they were almost a mile away. The huge rocks of the shore, scraped clean of sand by the battering sea, were covered with bodies that struggled against cords holding them in place. The surging water pulled back just long enough to show hundreds more, their lifeless bodies flopping against their bonds before the next onslaught slammed into the shore and covered them again.

The rain slapped her like an endless volley of pebbles, but she strained to see what was just inland of the mass sacrifice. It was a multitude of sodden humanity, kneeling and crying out words she couldn't hear above the gale. Just beyond them, a circle of men and women wearing ceremonial antlers stood on a rise shouting useless invocations into the maelstrom. Arms and hands rose and fell, pleading, begging, but the storm only gained intensity.

Akilna's eyes stretched wide when an unnaturally prolonged series of lightning flashes illuminated the rain-choked sky. At first, it looked like more of the grey clouds, but then she saw its motion and recognized it as a gigantic wave. It climbed higher as it gained speed, and the mass of supplicants broke with a hideous cry in a vain attempt to outrun it and the sea that followed in its wake.

The sacrificial victims were gone in an instant, and

then the wave landed directly on the antler-festooned celebrants before cascading across the land to consume it and everyone on it.

Akilna was on her knees, panting, the lightning flashes still bursting in her vision as she slowly realised she was back in the clearing where Borka had died. She dropped onto her palms, her mind unable to stop the vision of destruction that kept reappearing. The thing that would someday cause that catastrophe was still with her, and even though Akilna heard no voice she knew the vision was the answer to the question she'd asked.

That is what I want.

* * *

The trek back was almost impossible. Akilna stumbled along, her limbs robbed of strength and her brain spinning. The apocalyptic images provided by the antler god streamed through her consciousness over and over, refusing to stop or depart. The presence had disappeared as soon as she'd left the clearing, but its intentions grew clearer as she shuffled toward home.

It was displeased with Tuku and his entire people, but not for their self-serving embellishments to its worship. It hungered for destruction and death, and their expansion into other tribes was too slow and too small. The sea deity would show them the scale and severity of its hunger when it washed them from existence and started anew.

Akilna had never been so happy to tread on one of the paths leading to the village, and the nearness of the temporary sanctuary drove some of the visions from her head. Tuku had converted most of the people, so seeking vengeance for her father and Borka would only get her and Mother killed. She would find Pertil and quietly tell her everything. Sometime that evening they would slip away from the village, leaving it to the antlers.

That plan evaporated when she reached the outskirts of the camp and heard the noise. A low murmur of hostile disapproval sent her sprinting for the centre. Well short of that, Akilna ran into a crowd that appeared to contain every adult in the village. They formed a ring not unlike the antler ceremony the night before, but no bonfire held their attention. Pertil was just visible beyond them, holding a spear with both hands as if trying to drive something very tough into the dirt. Akilna pushed her way through the forest of bodies, seeing that many of them held knives or spears or even stones.

"Where is my daughter?" Her mother shouted, and then Akilna saw that Pertil had Tuku flat on his back with the spear point at his throat. "You think I can't smell blood on you?"

Cries of "let him up!" and "stop her!" rose from

different points in the crowd, lone antler acolytes trying to direct the throng. Reaching the inside of the circle, Akilna knew that merely returning alive and unharmed would not save her mother. As soon as the chipped stone was away from Tuku's throat, his followers would swarm her for this affront.

"Kill him, Mother!" she cried, stepping into the open space. "He murdered Father, and he just murdered Borka!"

Her friend's name sent a shudder through the throng, and she didn't wait. Turning in place, searching for the eyes of those villagers not yet under the antlers' spell. "That's what they've been doing to anyone who doesn't join them. How many of you lost loved ones, and then the antlers gave you someone else? It's their plan!"

The circle widened as the villagers looked left and right. Akilna drew breath to continue, but her reason flickered like a flame struck by the wind. A dark wind no one else could feel.

The presence swirled around her, a cold wave that quickly spread outward across the assembled bodies. Expressions of confusion and concern twisted into suspicion and malice, and she saw the fight coming even as the thing kept her from speaking. Akilna turned in time to see Tuku swing a heavy arm at her mother's spear, knocking it away. Pertil merely widened her grip, taking the shaft across her body before dropping on it with her full weight. Tuku just managed to catch the pole before it could reach his throat, but Pertil's knees landed hard on his belly, winding him. She straddled his chest, arms locked, furiously forcing the wood down. Tuku released the spear with one hand, reaching under his body.

Robbed of speech but still able to move, Akilna dashed across the open even as the first blows were struck. The crowd erupted into shouts and screams, a thrashing hedge of stone and wood and muscle and blood all around the clearing. She'd almost reached her mother when Tuku's hand came up holding a stone knife. He drove it into Pertil's side as Akilna screamed and then leapt.

Her mother's eyes bulged with pain and effort, but her arms still pressed the wood down onto Tuku's neck. The big man had just pulled the knife out for another strike when Akilna's feet landed on the spear, crushing his throat. She and her mother both fell off his thrashing body, and then Akilna had Pertil in her arms.

A rock smashed into Akilna's back, but all she registered was the dark red blood spreading all over Pertil's side. "It's all right, Mother. You're cut, but we can fix it."

"I was so worried when you didn't come back." Blood appeared at the corners of her mouth. "I'm glad to die here with you, Daughter. I couldn't bear to live without you."

Pertil's eyes lost focus, and her hands slid off Akilna's arms. A maelstrom of shouts and shrieks and groans now sailed into her ears, and she looked up to see Tuku's lifeless form was just one of many bodies on the ground. Rocks still flew, but the antler folk greatly outnumbered the others and the day was already lost. Spears rose and fell, fists pounded against flesh, and a vibration began to hum through Akilna's body.

The sea deity was back. It thrilled at the bloodshed, and its joy tried to enter her. It had used her to reach this spot and launch this carnage, and now it wished to claim her for its own.

"You bitch! I'll kill you!" The words came from a wild-eyed Leeno, just as the older woman swung a stone that struck Akilna in the side of the head. The village centre spun out of control, a windstorm of violence, and then she was lying on the dirt next to her mother. Her eyes found the bright sky just in time to see Leeno's rock rise again. This would be the death blow, and the thought pleased her.

"You don't get me after all," she whispered to the presence, and then Leeno's arm and hand and the stone it carried elongated in her vision and her head swam and Akilna felt an overpowering need to sleep.

* * *

"Jorina." The name was foreign, and yet she knew it was hers. Akilna turned to see one of the men from the boat dream. They were on the dragon ship again, and even though she was Akilna she was also Jorina and had sailed many times on this vessel of war.

"Yes, Frode?" She responded in a language that she'd never heard in the village, but that she spoke fluently. Akilna glanced down at her raiment, recognizing it as a thick wool dress with a leather belt and hide boots.

"We're losing the wind," Frode's words made her look up at the mast where the great sail was furled, just as she'd requested. A seer's wishes weren't commands, but they carried weight and the Northmen had complied, along with the other two ships of their party.

Party. A war party, the latest of many she'd initiated. Akilna's memory summoned the images of a burning stockade and the raid they'd conducted the night before. The warriors on this ship, men and women, had wiped out that entire settlement at her behest. She recalled the wondrous sight of a set of gigantic antlers, carved from tree branches, that had decorated the settlement's main gate. She smiled, having watched those antlers burn to ashes.

Now remembering the rock that had hit her back as

her mother lay dying and the blow to the side of her head, she stretched her shoulders and reached up a hand. No pain, just the awareness that she was several years older now with a woman's shape and long hair tied behind her head. She leaned out over the still water to see the same face she'd known as Akilna.

The dreams had been real, after all. She'd briefly visited this ship in her vision, and had somehow leapt to this life from what may or may not have been her death in the village. She'd lived this existence too, every moment of it from her birth among a people called the Frisians. In their tongue, Jorina carried the same meaning as Akilna. Watchful.

Remembering the night when, very young, she'd been stolen by an antler raiding party. Their cruelty to her and their other prisoners as they'd sailed north to the land of the people on this boat. Her years as a slave to the Northmen that had only ended when the strange dreams that had begun with her kidnapping had turned into visions. The Northmen, awed by people with the sight, apprenticed her to an aged clairvoyant so she could harness this unnatural talent. Those skills eventually earned her a place with this roving band, raiders who cared little that the rich targets she provided them were always the hidden settlements of the antler people.

A vibration gently thrummed through the carved

wood of the ship's rail, calling her to look down into the waters. That was why she'd had them stop.

The death of her old home had also been real, but instead of the future it was now somewhere in a very distant past. People still spoke of the land beneath the waves that had once connected the Frisians' home with that of the Saxons to the west. The legend said it had been swallowed by the sea as the vengeance of a terrible god long dead and forgotten.

"We cannot lose this wind," Frode spoke more firmly. His brown hair was twisted into fine braids on the left side of his face, and a thick moustache drooped over his mouth. "We've been summoned, and must make haste."

"Then let's make haste," she grinned, knowing it made him uncomfortable, and he quickly turned away to give the orders. Still smiling, Akilna looked back down into the water that now blanketed the territory that had been her home so long ago. Moments ago.

"I'm breathing, Mother," she spoke to the water in the old tongue, enjoying the unease in the nearest warriors on their benches. "I'm alive, Mother."

The vibration under her hands abruptly vanished, as did her smile. She raised her eyes to the unbroken horizon to the north, where they were headed. News of a new antler threat called them there, panicked reports of a veritable army of winged warriors. Their deity had concealed their presence while their numbers grew but had obviously decided it was time to unleash them. A god not forgotten, and certainly not dead.

Her eyes narrowed. "I'm coming for you too."

A rogue gust of wind struck her cheek, and it was difficult to tell if it was a slap or a greeting.

# The Temple of the Toad

Robert Poyton

The creatures attacked again last night," the woman's voice brought Tal's head around, away from his scanning of the hazy horizon ahead.

"Again?" he asked, drawing the woollen cloak aside to place a hand on the axe at his hip. The woman stopped and nodded, two small children clinging to her skirts. "Again. We've heard the stories of the elders, we thought them mere tales. But now we have seen them. Three times this past moon." She brushed back the hair that blew across her pinch-cheeked face and scowled, gesturing back across the marshes. She was one of a group of fisherfolk walking the narrow track that led away from the coast to join up with the larger pathway inland.

"And the warriors?" Tal growled.

"Taken. With a dozen of our people," a flicker of pain across her face.

"Including your man?"

She nodded. "He fought. We all fought. But what mortal can stand against such devils?"

Tal shrugged. "Perhaps we shall find out."

She took in his resolute mien; the scarred forearms; the lean, dark face framed by tangled black hair that fell to broad shoulders. At almost six feet tall he towered over the fisherfolk, obviously a fighting man.

An older woman called. "Come, Ega, tarry no more, we must be far gone by sundown."

The woman resumed her trudging and Tal turned again to the low rise ahead and the pearly mist that gently spilled over it. By the time he crested the ridge, the refugees had already vanished from sight. Pausing, he peered ahead. Visibility was poor here at the best of times, despite the open flatlands that characterised this part of the coast. That was largely due to the clinging sea frets that rolled in from the cold, brown ocean whose leaden waves lapped dully upon the shingle shore. That sound came to his ears now, the eternal whisper of the sea; a whisper that spoke of mystery and the terrors of the deep. Men of lore spoke of the Old Race; those who came before, devils from the sea, who might one day rise to reclaim their birthright. Many scoffed at such nonsense or used the stories to scare their children into good behaviour. Yet those who scoffed, Tal grimly noted, dwelt on hilltop homesteads, protected by palisades, far from the lapping waves.

He strode through the abandoned huts until his feet crunched on loose pebbles. The fog had lifted a little, though there was nothing to see, other than listless waves ahead, the beach stretching into the distance on each side. Then, a movement, off away to his right. Tal strode towards the figure of a man who glanced up at his noisome approach. An aged fisherman sat beside a small boat outside a hut, his weathered brown skin even darker than Tal's, twisted fingers repairing a net. He grunted and continued his work.

"You stayed where the others have left?"

The elder shrugged. "Leave to go where?" He waved a gnarled hand at the sea. "This is my place, this is my life. What else do I know?"

"And the sea creatures?"

"I live here alone, out on the edge of the village. They've no interest in me."

Tal ran a hand over the edge of the boat. A simple craft, but well enough made. "And those they took?"

"Ah, so that is what you are here for. To rescue the taken?"

"It is a task assigned to me. Besides, there are those of my kin amongst them."

"Kin you say? And what if you are too late? What if they are already… gone?"

"Then rescue becomes revenge." Tal curled his fists.

The old man gave a wheezing laugh and spat into the shingle. "Revenge won't fill your belly, boy. It won't keep you warm at night." He paused, pain flashing across his lined face. "And it won't bring them back."

Tal cast his gaze back out across the chill ocean. "Nonetheless, such is my task, given me by my Chieftain. For word reached us of raids and attacks along the coast."

"That explains the group who arrived yesterday. The warriors. Your kin?"

"Aye. My sister among them. My leaving was delayed."

"But you are here now. What is your plan?"

"Rescue the taken, destroy the sea demons."

Another rasping chuckle. "Do you even know what they are?"

Tal shook his head. The fisherman sighed. "They appeared some moons back. Negg, out way beyond his usual fishing grounds, spoke of an island - an island that had not been there before. Most thought him touched, yet he changed not his story and boasted that on his next trip he would set foot on the island, would explore it. We never saw him again. And so it began. Odd sightings at first. Other fishers not returning. Then the first being taken from the village. A child here, a crone there."

"And last night?"

"A group of them, at dusk. Lurching from the waves, the sea behind them blood red in the setting sun. The beach was red soon enough, too."

"I saw no bodies."

"They took all the dead. Their own and ours."

"And you? Where were you?"

"Here. There was nothing I could do" He lifted a withered leg. "In the time it took me to stumble to the village, it was done."

"I see," Tal scowled and looked out again over the waves. "An island you say? Where?"

The old man raised a gnarled hand. "Out that way," Negg said. Just beyond the horizon."

Tal eyed the boat. The old man read the gesture. He put down the net and stood slowly, wincing.

"You are set on going, then?"

"Aye. I'll swim if I have to."

"You'll drown. She looks placid but there are dark currents here, lad. Currents that will sweep you out beyond, or drag you under and turn you into food for the crabs."

"You know the currents."

Another wheezing laugh. "You want me to take you? Out there? To them?"

"Drop me at the island, wait a while. That is all I ask."

"That is all, eh? Very well, lad." The elder tossed a gig pole into the stern. "Those devils have scared away the fish in any case. I'll take you. What the hell, it will be a quicker end than starving."

The elder lowered the small sail and handed Tal an oar. The pair began paddling towards the rocky outcrop ahead. All was still, the sea a mirror, the only sound the drip of water from the paddles. As the fisherman had said, there was indeed a small island, out beyond sight of the shore. Viridescent weeds shone out against the dark rock to which they clung. Tal nudged the old man and pointed, the fisherman nodded, altering course towards a small inlet now revealed between looming boulders. Small waves lapped gently against a ledge, onto which had been dragged what Tal took to be fishing boats from the village. "They used them to take the captives," the elder explained.

"They wanted live captives, then?" Tal stood, stepping out onto the ledge, turning to lift and drag the prow of the boat out of the water. "Wait here," he told the fisherman. "If I have not returned before the light fails, then go back to the village, or wherever you will. I will be beyond caring."

The old fisherman nodded and grasped the crude amulet at his chest. "The luck of the gods go with you, boy."

Tal drew the axe at his hip and trod carefully up the slippery rock. A rough path led up from the inlet  into a narrow way between high rock walls. The odour of sea-rot filled his nose, multi-legged creatures scuttled away from his tread. At last, the way opened out and the warrior found himself on the rocky plateau that sat atop the island - though what at first appeared to be a flat pain soon revealed itself as a series of gullies, jagged spires and limpid pools that did much to slow his progress. On the other side, they also did much to conceal his approach from potential sentries or watchers. Tal had little concept of what manner of  foe he might face. Stories from the coast spoke only of *creatures from the sea*. Vague, man-like shapes seen dimly through the dusky haze; lambent eyes in the gloom, flashing white teeth. None had got that close to the monsters and survived to tell the tale.

Tal hearkened back to the old stories, the lays of the bards, the legends and lore of the cunning men. He had said as much to his uncle, the Chieftain. Lomi had laughed and drained his drinking horn. "Raiders, boy," he'd belched. "Raiders, that's all.  And what do raiders always want? Gems, sheep and arse. Go. You and Dena. Take six of the Guard with you. When you find the raiders, put an end to them. If you need more arms, send word."

By the time Tal neared the centre of the island, the sun was high. Not that he could see it clearly, the miasma and haze raised from the steaming ground rendered it little more than a pale disk above. Still, his efforts were rewarded by the sight of a more regular shape amongst the serrated peaks ahead. A dome made of greyish stone showed between the dark, twisted spires and he found, once again, a narrow path that led to it. Down, the trail took him, through a black stone arch that put the warrior uncomfortably in mind of the maw of some great sea-beast. Down a further dip, then the dome loomed above him, pocked and pitted, streaked with the crusted slime of the deep. It sat atop a squat edifice, likewise grey, windowless and without apparent entry or exit.

Tal approached and laid a hand on the stone. It was cool to the touch, the sea-rot odour was even stronger here. He followed the track to where it ended in a blank wall. Hanging the axe back on his belt he began running his fingers around the smooth stone. He smiled as the thinnest of lines revealed itself to him. A door, then, but how to open it? His unspoken question was answered by the grinding of stone as the section of wall swung inwards, revealing a low, wide aperture, beyond which lay only darkness.

An unholy reek issued from within, yet Tal plunged forward without hesitation, the image of kin and the fisher-folk in the grip of sea devils overcoming any primal fears. He detected a slight downward slope in the passageway. The ceiling sat barely a hand's width above his head, though the walls were beyond the span of his reach. Axe forward, one hand covering his nose and mouth against the foul stench, he glided forward in a hunter's crouch, eyes straining against the gloom. A faint glow showed ahead, a violaceous phosphorescence that was as uncomfortable to the eye as the odour was to the nose. Tal moved towards it, sensing too late the movement that came from his left. There was an increase in the stench, a vague impression of a humanoid bulk topped by limpid, globose eyes, then only darkness.

Tal awoke, head throbbing. He made to sit up then cursed at the restraining thongs that bit deep into his arms. He lay in the corner of a dank cell, lit only by the lambent glow of a gemstone set in the wall. The room was unfurnished, a single heavy door the only exit. Its hinges screeched as it was pushed open, prompting Tal to struggle to his feet. As he lurched against the damp wall, a figure was shoved through the opening that brought a name to his lips.

"Dena!"

The woman ignored him, spun and hurled herself back towards the door, which slammed in her face. With an oath, she punched it then turned back towards Tal.

"What are you doing here?"

"I came to rescue you," he replied.

"And how is that working out?"

"You got captured first," Tal grumbled.

Dena growled. In looks, she was not dissimilar to her brother and was clad in the same style of simple cloak, tunic and leggings. Though lither of build, her eyes were as blue as his, and currently flamed with an inner rage that Tal knew only too well was best avoided.

"Any chance you could cut my bonds?" he turned, raising his hands as high as he could.

"They took all my weapons." Dena moved forward and pulled at the thongs. "This looks like some sort of seaweed. It's damned tough."

"Do your best. I can scarce feel my hands. They obviously want us alive, do you know why?"

Before Dena could answer, a small hatch in the door opened, revealing a face, its skin pale green in the gem light.

"You," the voice was flat and croaky. "Her. Lay together. Now."

"What the hell!" Tal was across the cell in three strides, launching a kick at the door. The face did not so much as flinch at the boom of foot on metal. Closer, Tal noticed some odd features. The man's skin was pale as fungus, slick and smooth. The eyes were far apart and protuberant, they didn't blink. They regarded Tal now with some amusement, the wide, almost lipless mouth spreading in a toothless grin.

"You. Her. Babies. Not lay, not feed. You starve."

"She is my sister, you fiend!" Tal roared.

The grin remained. "Do not know what that is. You lay now. I bring food later."

The hatch was sharply closed leaving a fuming Tal struggling against his bonds. Dena assisted, removing a bone comb from her hair to saw at the rubbery vines. Eventually, they were cut, Tal massaging his arms as he paced the cell. His sister, by contrast now the calm one, sighed again.

"Sit down, will you? Pacing is no use. We need to think of a way out."

Tal grumbled but crouched in the corner. "He, it, whatever it was, said he was returning with food. We wait until then. What are these things?"

"Difficult to say. The raiders looked even worse than him. Larger. Less human. They came at dusk, the light was poor. They surged onto the shore, armed with tridents and nets. As we charged them, a stinking net was thrown over me, I was clubbed to the ground. I came to in a cell much like this one. Then, not long ago, that thing dragged me out by the arm and brought me here."

"The others?"

"I have seen nought of them. Though I heard screams that chilled my marrow."

"Why would they want us to breed?"

Dena shrugged. "And how could he not understand the concept of kin?"

Tal moved to press an ear to the door. "Nothing. No wait, someone approaches. Be ready!"

The hatch slid aside revealing the same face. "Water, food," he rasped.

Tal extended a hand to just inside the door. As he hoped, their captor reached through to hand over the small bowl. Tal grasped the man's wrist and pulled, leveraging it against the edge of the frame. He grimaced at the peculiar flabbiness of the arm, the moistness of the skin. Dena was already at the hatch, bone comb pressed to the gaoler's throat.

"Open the door," she hissed. The bowl was dropped with a clatter as the man twisted and squirmed but to no avail. Tal wrenched the limb, eliciting a gasp of pain leading to a scrabbling at the door bolt. The door swung in, bringing the guard with it. He cried out as Tal released the grip and Dena shoved him across the cell into the far wall.

"Don't hurt!" he whimpered, slumping against the wall, hands held up before his face.

"Leave him," Tal muttered, his sister following him out, slamming the bolt back in place behind her.

"They brought me from there." She pointed along the corridor, gem-lit but no less damp and foul-smelling than the passageway Tal had first entered. They unbolted other doors as they went, releasing captive fisher-folk and three fellow warriors. One cell disgorged a wild looking figure, a squat, hairy individual who bounded over to Dena, cackling.

"Who's this lunatic?" Tal scowled.

"This is Garogh," Dena nodded to the grinning elder. "He's a cunning man. He joined us on the way here."

Tal rolled his eyes and cursed under his breath.

"Knowledge!" squealed the old man. "Knowledge is key! Through knowledge we can defeat these invaders. Look!" He extracted a small clay tablet from within his stained tunic and thrust it toward Tal. "I learn. I write. Then others learn. See?"

Tal recoiled as if confronted by an adder. Everyone knew that runes and writings were the work of devils. "Keep him away from me," he muttered, moving swiftly down the corridor. Steps led up to a circular chamber, passageways leading off in three other directions. Dena appeared at his shoulder.

"The fisherfolk are terrified," she whispered. "They will be of little use to us."

"Tell them to take that way," he pointed right. "I am sure that is the way I came in. It leads to a door. Once outside they should go straight ahead, there are boats there, and the old man who ferried me over."

"And us?"

He gestured, grinning to the floor. Their weapons had been left in a pile. "We wipe out this nest of snakes."

Armed and feeling more confident, the quintet of warriors trod steadily further into the building. They had first found a large chamber wherein lay their companions - or, rather, the remains of the three. Each lay on a slab and had been... *opened*. As a slaughterman might carve a pig, though whether the purpose be butchery or curiosity, they could not say. Still, the sight of comrades hewn and sliced so, while obviously still alive, lit a hot coal of vengeance in each breast and none now thought of retreat.

The response from the enemy came swift and silent. One instant the group were exploring another chamber, an open space lined with statues of a disquieting nature, the next they were being assailed by a group of men of similar appearance to the gaoler. Soundless they came, wielding short blades of coral, slashing at the intruders. Numbers they had, and lacked not in bravery, or perhaps compulsion, but the experience of the warriors soon told. This is what they were bred to do, the finest fighters of the tribes, selected and trained for the Chieftain's personal Guard. Tal whooped and bashed in a skull with his first strike, whipping the axe back to crush a temple. Dena howled and whirled at his side, short bronze sword in one hand, dagger in the other, stabbing with rapid, precise strikes.

The stones underfoot were soon slick and slippery with blood, as red as any he had seen, Tal noted with some satisfaction. Then, as quickly as it had begun, the assault was over. Dena, panting, took stock. About them lay the pale dead. One of their own number lay slain. Another had received a stab to the torso, he sat clutching the wound, bearing his pain in tenacious silence. Dena moved to him, then instructed the remaining warrior, "Help him back up and out of here. We shall continue on."

The man nodded and assisted his comrade to his feet. Tal was already moving ahead, through the portal from which the attack had come. With an oath, he disappeared into the gloom beyond. He had caught a glimpse of colour, the flash of a yellow robe. With the tenacity of the wolf, he plunged immediately towards it, crossing the narrow chamber in four steps, then under the archway beyond.

The cowled and hunched figure ahead paused, raising its arms as if in invocation. This chamber was large, lined by large metal bowls, from which flickered lurid green flames that gave a sickly light but no heat. The figure stood at the room's centre before an onyx altar, atop which sat the carven likeness of a denizen of nighted hell. Wide and squat, the statue perched life-like on the dark altar. The thing's curved talons gripped the stone, certain parts of its gross anatomy hanging over the edge. In shape, it was like some monstrous toad, though certain proportions and aspects of its features marked it as no earthly creature. Tal glanced up to the sightless, bulging eyes, with an unnerving feeling that the thing was leering at him, seemingly in jest, or hunger or lust, or perhaps even all three. The sensation prompted a vague itch in the dim recesses of his mind, a sensation that brought him up short.

Then Dena was at his side and he leapt forward again, snatching the shoulder of the yellow robe in his fist. The figure turned, and Tal Twas once again shocked into immobility. Whereas the faces of the gaoler and their previous attackers had been human, if rather odd, the visage within the cowl lacked most of what could be termed human, most even of what could be termed mammal. The eyes were as pale and bulbous as the attackers but were set much wider apart on the misshapen head. The skin was fish-belly pale, glistening in the glow of the flames. The mouth was a wide slash beneath a snub nose, thin lips opening to reveal small, serrated white teeth. Gills pulsated at its throat. The thing raised a webbed hand and Tal took an involuntary step back, he heard Dena gasp at his side.

"Foolish humans!" came a croaking voice. "How dare you defile the temple of our Lord! You shall suffer the consequences!"

"As our companions suffered?" Tal replied. "Slaughtered like animals!"

The response was a guttural cacchination. "But you are animals. That is all you are. Hairless apes. A blight on the land above."

"Then why raid our settlements? Why not leave us in peace?"

"Peace? Peace?" the priest-thing replied. "What do your kind know of the serenity of the deep? Of the rhythms of the tides and the great pulse of the planet? Your lives are the flash of sun on a wave, the briefest mote of light between aeons of darkness."

"Yet you take us captive," growled Dena, hefting her blades.

The priest gestured back through the archway they

had pursued him through. "Yes. For hybrids. And for more. Those you slew were born to us through your kind. They serve a purpose. Not so long lived and somewhat more fragile than pure-breeds but they can spend longer on land. And so, with ritual and sacrifice, we raise the temple in order to increase our stock."

"But your servant told us to mate!" Tal spat.

The priest-thing's maw yawned in a mocking croak. "Yes. Breeding human hatchlings that we will raise as our own."

"To what purpose?"

"To send aloft. To mingle with your kind. To infiltrate and prepare the way for the *Great Rising*."

"You would make spies of human children? But that would take decades!" Dena, growing impatient, drew back her hand to strike. The priest stamped his foot, uttered an unearthly syllable and made a curious gesture. Both Tal and Dena found themselves frozen, muscles locked solid, unable to move.

"Idiots! Did I not already say our lives span generations of yours? Decades to us are as the passing of a day. Our machinations stretch back into your dim past, even unto the days of marble-spired Commoriom. The arcane texts of the archmage Eibon speak of us, before the coming of the White Worm."

These names meant nothing to Tal, besides which

he was now straining every fibre of his being in an effort to move. Sweat ran down his face, his teeth ground as he fought the enchantment. The priest-thing, secure now in his confidence, stepped back and waved a be-robed arm to his side.

"Lands rise and oceans fall. But our time is coming again." He gestured to an opening in the floor beyond the idol. It had the appearance of a large well or shaft, twice the height of a man across. Even from this distance, Tal sensed an unearthly chill emanating from it.

The priest-thing nodded. "You feel it, don't you, human? For far below, in the deeps, slumbers a being which, once awoken, will spell doom and ruin for your kind. With its aid, we shall resume our rightful place as rulers. Your kind will be as livestock and vassals to us. You will learn to obey."

At that moment there sounded a horn-blast from above, as if from some great conch-shell. The priest-thing's head twisted upwards, breaking his concentration for an instant. It was all Tal needed. With a primal surge, he pounced forward, lashing out a murderous swipe with his axe. The priest-thing moved with serpentine speed, yet still caught the blow on his shoulder. He tumbled back, hissing, as Tal and Dena both unleashed a barrage of blows. Their quarry twined like an eel, and with surprising speed, fled their attack, disappearing through another archway beyond the pit. Dena made to pursue but Tal stopped her.

"No sense chasing him in the dark. He knows this place, we do not." His gaze was drawn to the opening in the floor and he walked towards it. The smooth stone ended in a tiled edge around its circumference. Tal knelt, peering down into the yawning dark before him. The chill increased, but there was something else, too. A sound, he thought, faint, on the very edge of his perception. He leaned forward a little to better listen. Yes, there was a definite noise, a low whistling… no, a fluting, echoing up from the vast depths. A sinuous melody, unknown, yet oddly familiar. He leaned forward a little more, and with the haunting tune came images, pictures as memories of dreams. Of Cyclopean buildings set amongst icy peaks. Of men, or things that would become men, grunting and howling as they capered around a jet black megalith. Of a vast intelligence that slumbered yet brooded in immeasurable depths of space and time. Under it all, Tal sensed an intelligence that called to him, the fluting enticing him to lean forward… forward…

Dena yanked her brother back by the hair, leaving him sprawled on the floor in dazed confusion. He shook his head and got to his feet.

"Sorcery!" he spat. Then he glanced up at the faint sounds of strife from above.

"Let's get out of this hellhole" Dena suggested, Tal nodded and followed her back to the main passageway. In a short time they emerged blinking into the sunlight, the din of battle growing louder. The pair raced up the slope at the side of the temple, back onto the plateau, from where there sounded shouts and the clash of arms. An amazing sight met their eyes. Two lines struggled, stabbed, fought and slipped on the dark rock. One, warriors from the clan, Chieftain Lomi at their centre. The other, a line of sea demons, the yellow-robed priest at their midst. Wielding tridents, they fought the humans and, though severely outnumbered, were taking heavy toll of the invaders. The sight roused the blood of the siblings and they charged, screaming their war cries, into the rear of the sea creature line. They hit like a thunderbolt, stabbing and hewing with a long-repressed fury, their appearance both surprising their foes and lending renewed vigour to their kith and kin.

The monsters from the deep were large, powerful creatures, an unholy amalgam of man, toad and fish. They wore no armour but their hides were tough and scaly. Their tridents were fearsome weapons, but at such close range their use was compromised. Still, they died hard, sweeping out with webbed claws that sprayed crimson across the rocks, or crunching into shoulders and arms with savage bites. Yet numbers told and, one by one, the devils were hewn down, the priest last to die, spitting curses at the humans. Lomi, tunic torn, spattered with both his own blood and the green gore of the creatures, strode over to them laughing.

"As well we charged when we did," Dena observed wryly. "Looked like those things were beating you."

"No," Lomi grinned through his beard, "All was in hand. We were merely toying with them, waiting for you to arrive. Besides which, we only sailed out here to rescue you idiots."

"How did you know where to find us?" asked Tal.

"Further word of attacks came in after you left. Then we met villagers on the way here, they told us of events and this strange island. Luckily there were boats enough to get us all across. The old fisherman below told us you had trod this way. As we got up onto the plateau here, there was a horn blast and those demons charged us. What lies below?"

"A temple," Tal answered. "Empty but for more dead."

"Any plunder?" Lomi's eyes gleamed.

"None that we saw," Dena replied. "Though if there were any, I wouldn't touch it. Cursed, no doubt."

"Perhaps." The Chieftain took a swig from the flask at his hip and handed it to them. "All this way for nothing, that's a shame. No treasures to loot or prisoners to burn. Still, we rescued those who we could, and have seen off those devils. That will suffice."

He was about to speak again when a shudder ran through the rock beneath their feet.

"Perhaps the priest's enchantments die with him?" Tal suggested. "Time for us to leave?"  The survivors were rallied, the wounded assisted and loaded into the boats. The old fishermen led the way back, across the sea now red in the setting sun's crimson glow. Behind them, the reeking island sank slowly beneath the glimmering waves. Tal was glad to feel the shingle beach beneath his feet again, to be back on home soil. He glanced around as the rest of the group trudged past. Frowning, he tapped Dena's shoulder.

"That old madman. What was his name?"

"Garogh, the cunning man?"

"Aye. Where is he? I don't see him?"

Dena scanned the twilit beach and shrugged. "I don't know. I don't think I saw him after that first fight. Perhaps one of those things got him. Perhaps he went down with the island."

Tal scratched his chin. "Oh well. You can't save everyone. And that's the last we'll see of those foul creatures. Let's get home."

The group began to silently form up, preparing for the march back to the homestead. None of the villagers, it seemed, were disposed to remain here. Even the old fisherman joined the group, limping and cursing under his breath. But as Tal's eyes ran across the faces before him, some old, some young, he experienced a curious lurch in his stomach. *Human hatchlings, to mingle with your kind, to infiltrate and prepare the way for the Great Rising.* Those had been the words of the priest-thing. How long had that plan been in operation? Were they, even now, welcoming a viper into the bosom of the tribes? Doing his best to shake away these nagging suspicions, Tal fell in with the column, matching his stride to that of his sister.

Garogh had quickly tucked himself away in a corner at the first sign of violence. Following that, he followed the male and female warrior as they moved through the archway, moving quietly into the shadows as they spoke to the thing in yellow. His ears pricked up at the words *arcane texts*, and when the priest fled, Garogh came out of the gloom and stood before the idol, staring up at it with a mixture of horror and reverence. Snapping out of the semi trance state, he began to search around - for what, he wasn't sure, though in an antechamber he found a solid, sealed chest. With mounting excitement he fumbled at the bronze clasps. The heavy lid creaked open, revealing yellow vestments, atop which lay a curiously shaped smaragdine gem affixed on a wrought golden chain. It pulsed slightly in his hand as he plucked it forth, tucking it into his tunic before rummaging further. His weathered face crinkled in a broad smile as his fingers closed around something else at the bottom of the chest, bringing forth an oilskin sack which contained something of bulk.

Cackling, Garogh tucked the sack under his arm and sought the temple exit. By the time he reached the ledge, the warriors and rescued captives had already left. Fortunately, two craft remained and, straining, he dragged one into the sea as the ground lurched beneath him. With scant time to spare, the shaman leapt into the small boat and paddled furiously as the island sank behind him, fearful of being taken down in its maelstrom. Yet, by grace or luck, he pulled clear and rowed, pondering, as the sun sank on the horizon. Where to go? Back to the village? No, there was nothing there. To his brother cunning men, perhaps, to share this trove? He quickly dismissed the idea. His treasures would be removed from him, passed on to the Great Council, no doubt,

Back on land, Garogh squatted on the shingle, removed the sack and examined its contents. The object was rectangular, made of a material that felt odd in his hands. Clammy, soft to the touch, like hide but smoother. Ignoring the shudder that ran the length of his spine, he opened it. Within were a small number of loose-bound parchments of a type the shaman had not seen before. Yes, the cunning men carved runes onto clay tablets, they were taught the secret ways as part of their initiation. And Garogh had once seen a scroll, shown to him by a trader from far-off lands which, when unrolled, revealed rows of small symbols or pictures. But this… no, this was something different, something beyond the ken of mortal man. *From the Gods, perhaps?*

As his shadow lengthened across the strand, Garogh wrinkled his brow at the curious, dot-like script that covered most of the sheets within. He could recognise only a few runes at the top of the first, though the word they formed meant nothing. Still, scripts could be translated, and Garogh had a feeling that the gem might assist him in some way. *Yes, the gem, that might be the key.* He glanced at the parchment again, silently mouthing the rune-word at its top before closing the cover and replacing the item in the bag. As the rays of the dying sun illumined the cliff path up which he now wound his way, Garogh whispered that word into the growing dusk. *"Cthäat… Cthäat."*

# The Abomination from the Deep

E.L. Giles

Khal Trobor the shaman was standing in the middle of the wide circle of villagers, his fur garments flapping in the cold, rainy morning wind. His bulging, stary yellow eyes scanned the congregation of brooding townies. The ground was muddy, and a large puddle of water had formed around Khal Trobor. The townies were all shivering, their leather clothes soaked, and an expression between hopelessness and frustration drawn on every face. Everyone except the shaman.

*The bastard is enjoying this,* thought Zoraz the Hunter. A subtle grin lit the shaman up with a smile of contempt, accentuating the sharpness of his cheekbones and large, square jaw, rendering his toad-like face even more reptilian, more demoniacal.

Zoraz' gaze was continuously driven toward the village entry where his flint knife and spear had been left. Carrying weapons at a village council was strictly forbidden, and it was with reluctance that the hunter got rid of his gear. His hands itched with a compulsive need to hold them, to use them. He felt diminished, weakened, at the mercy of the Khal Trobor. How bad did he want to thrust his spear into the shaman's stomach and free the village from his evil shenanigans once and for all.…

"My friends, the situation is critical," began Khal Trobor. The denizens had stopped shivering, and they stared with rapt attention. A film of water covered their faces. The rain was unstoppable. "Where the verdant isles of Gador once rose, there is now but only a vast expanse of water." Khal Trobor, pivoted slowly, his arms raised high. He was holding the infamous antler crown, looking for a head over which to place it. "How long, my dear friends, before our huts fall, our gardens drown, and the river engulf us all?"

Khal Trobor stopped his rotation when he met Zoraz' gaze. Zoraz had his arms crossed over his chest and he was standing one step farther into the ring. His own gaze was defiant, his posture intimidating, and the wide, pink and white scars crisscrossing his naked arms and face told anyone Zoraz the Hunter was not the kind to fear anything nor anyone, even less an old man whom nature in some way must have loathed enough to give him such odd, detestable physical appearance. Weapons or not, he would not let another sacrifice happen.

There was a problem though. The villagers were gullible enough to believe Khal Trobor was a demi-God, and his words were taken as prophetic, bearer of truth, the Gods' interlocutor for those    mortal beings. For Zoraz, Khal Trobor was simply nothing more than a *charlatan*, a man devoured by his ambitions for domination. Even Azor Ozora, the village's chief, was but a sheep in front of this little, shambling parody of man.

"The Gods appeared to me in my dreams last night," said the shaman. He dropped his arms theatrically, pressing the crown now against his chest with one hand and pointing one greyish digit toward Zoraz. "By the end of the day, when Aton, the God of the Sun sets, Kalha, the Goddess of the sea, Vooris, the God of the sky, and Horaz, the God of all Lands meet in the darkest hours of the night, we'll sacrifice one of you, hoping the Gods feast joyously over this offering and provide us with warmth and plenty on the morrow."

"Enough!" shouted Zoraz. The hunter made one step inside the circle, turned his back to the shaman and addressed the villagers. "No deaths have    ever brought back the lands we have lost. No deaths ever stopped the sky from raining, or the Gods from hammering and lashing out the heavens with their blue wisps of death. This is not the way."

"How dare you speak out against the Gods' wish," cried Azor Ozora. The chief was switching his sight between Khal Trobor, the skies, and then Zoraz, as though fearing some holy reprisals.

"If the water rises, then why don't we just leave this place and seek the higher grounds of our great-grandfathers?" said Zoraz, staring at the chief. Azor Ozora was frowning.

"And abandon what they have built for us? A home—"

"A home meant to disappear." Zoraz made a complete turn around himself. All the villagers had their gaze turned toward Zoraz. All but one: Khal Trobor. The shaman was already going from one villager to the other, sniffing the air around them, deciding upon the next victim of his sadistic game.

"You seem to forget something, Zoraz the Hunter," said the chief. Zoraz briefly looked away from the shaman. "To leave the village, we must traverse the forbidden territory."

Zoraz was about to retort something about it when a strong, nauseating fishy smell pervaded the air around him. Khal Trobor was standing right in front of him, sniffing around the hunter, an evident grin of satisfaction tearing his alien face in half.

"You!" shouted the shaman, forcefully placing the antler crown over Zoraz' head. The crown sat much too tightly around Zoraz' prominent head, applying a pressure which instantly sent waves of sharp pain into his temples, forehead, and all around his skull. "Zoraz the Hunter, may your sacrifice honour the village and bring us all prosperity and plenty."

Zoraz screamed with rage. He stepped ahead, fists clenched, readying himself to jump off the shaman when a strong grip on his shoulders restrained him from doing so. A new wave of fishy odour attacked his nostrils, emanating from both shaman's henchmen.

"Don't let him do it," Zoraz implored the villagers as he was being dragged out of the circle. "Don't let him take your lives. Resist. Fight."

One of the henchmen, a tall, bulky grey-skinned individual with a short forehead and narrow, cone-shaped head, placed his large hand over Zoraz's mouth and nose, closing his fingers around Zoraz' cheeks, renewing the hunter's torments with fresh new levels of pain. The henchman's fingers were long and slender, each connected by a loose web of tissues like that of seabird toes, and ending with sharp, acerated claw-like nails. Their grip was as powerful as a lion's maw, as inextricable as a snake's constriction.

Zoraz tried to unlock himself from the mighty clench, fighting for his life. The awful grimace of contentment never left Khal Trobor's face, and Zoraz' gaze never quit it. He thought to himself *My time has not come yet. I will come back for you, and I will kill you.*

The prospect of vengeance insufflated Zoraz the will to redouble his attempts to free himself. The henchmen grunted, struggling to keep Zoraz under control. The hunter wriggled, punched, kicked. But in the end, their grip only tightened, momentarily cutting his air. And yet, despite the pain, Zoraz continued.

The villagers stared with horrified eyes at the show of the first man to ever resist his capture and refuse his fate. The first man to oppose the Gods' wish. The first man to oppose Khal Trobor.

Zoraz quickly tired. He suddenly felt sick, his brain was under-oxygenated. His entire head prickled painfully and the pressure inside his skull augmented to the point black spots sprinkled in the corner of his eyes and he struggled to breath, to stay conscious. The cold rain and wind hit his burning skin like thousands of sharp spear heads. Zoraz summoned the very last strand of his energy to let out a loud scream, the kind he let out when fighting with the great mammoths or facing sabretooth lions. Such screams never faltered to frighten its listener. But the only one being frightened right now was Zoraz himself.

The sight of the villagers, the top of the huts, and the wooded area surrounding his home slowly faded, their outlines disappearing behind gently sloping grassy hills. The topography then drastically changed to give place to the swampy lagoons, the inlets, and the archipelagos populated by flocks of screeching seabirds and voracious reptiles. It was also the land of the red deer, the kingdom of the mammoth, the verdant prairies of the aurochs. It was Zoraz' playground, and he knew those mudflats like the back of his hands. He could have easily outrun the henchmen, hunt them, kill them, and they'd never see him coming. But Zoraz was far too exhausted to keep on fighting. He had realised the uselessness of it, so Zoraz decided to save his energy. There was no escapee possible right now, which did not mean no occasion would present itself to Zoraz though.

A sheet of fog has risen, and the rain intensified. Overhead, the ceiling of clouds hung low, casting a shadow which spread over the land like gangrene. The land suddenly seemed to have no borders, no end, no beginning, only the continuation of this sheet of opaque and damp air. The sensation was oppressing, claustrophobic, even for Zoraz.

Flanked by the two henchmen who carried him across the land like a child. His feet barely touched the ground. The henchmen should have grown tired after such a march and without a single pause. Zoraz had followed the course of the sun, and he counted at least three hours had flown by since the council. But of their tiredness, they showed nothing, as though the wretches were impervious to fatigue, or even pain. There seemed to exist no weaknesses in their guard, no carelessness any, until they suddenly entered a particularly agitated and unnerving speech, the matter of which Zoraz knew not, for they spoke in a dialect Zoraz did not know. It resembled Khal Trobor's own language when he "spoke to the Gods", but with a more pronounced croaking and guttural intonation to it.

They had just passed the four tall, grossly sculpted limestone pilasters representing the four Gods and delimiting their lands from the forbidden territory, heading straight toward a narrower, higher column of black flint where the execution happened when the two henchmen momentarily released their iron grip of Zoraz. Surely, they were too used to people being obedient, and, Zoraz having been quiet for quite a long time now, had forgotten how sneaky the hunter could be and therefore dropped his guard.

Pivoting his torso in a quick, sharp movement,

Zoraz headbutted the left-side guard, thrusting one of the crown's huge thorns into his wide-open, yellow bulging eye. The hunter then snapped his head back, knocking the other guard behind him, severing his face. Their screams of pain were abominable to hear, a cacophony of gargles and throaty noises neither animal nor human but simply evil.

A thick, dark blue liquid oozed between clenched fingers as the first henchman hid his wounded eye. Head down, antlers pointing ahead, Zoraz jumped off him, severing his face, stealing the flint knife off the guard's hand, and thrusting the blade wherever skin came into view. The nasty sounds of tearing flesh and agonising cries haunted the hunter's ears, the smell of dead fish polluted the air surrounding him as the grey demon fell down under the incessant blows. Zoraz then quickly turned around and ran toward the other guard, dodging his slow, clumsy blow, blood smearing his awful reptilian face, sliding his own blade across the henchman's huge bulging throat. Blue blood cascaded down the gash, flowing over Zoraz's hand, leaving a pestilent goo over it. The hunter rubbed his hand clean over the guard's filthy garments. There remained a stain of inky matter which prickled and heated Zoraz's skin.

Zoraz quickly forgot about the annoying sensation on his hand. The orgy of pain and the ecstasy of victory exhilarated him, as did the relief when he finally removed the bloodied antler crown onto which hung small bits of dark flesh. Zoraz let out a long, victorious growl, sat down, and then thought. The hunter hesitated. He was high on adrenaline, euphoric, and vengeance boiled inside of him. Zoraz burned with a desire to come back undercover to the village and free its people from Khal Trobor's reign of terror. But he knew better. Azor Ozora would personally bludgeon him to death and in front of everyone if he'd do so, or even if he'd dare come back. Such was not an honourable death. Not for a hunter, a warrior like him. No. Zoraz needed proof that Khal Trobor was an imposter, and that their own survival lay in the lands of their great-grandfathers, somewhere beyond the dark, heavily wooded area of the forbidden territory.

Although Zoraz rebuked entering those shadowy alleys between the tall, sentinel trees, he nonetheless braved the unknown territory, moving stealthily, his eyes averted. He hated the predominant tranquillity, felt more prey than predator, observed, followed. He saw not, he heard not, but behind every tree or bush could hide a woolly rhinoceros, or a lion, or even other hunters like him. The concept of "forbidden" started to take form in his head. Maybe something lurked in those unfathomable woods, something Zoraz was disturbing.

So invested in his speculation, he neglected his therefore minute inspection of every square inch of terrain and vile pools of green water he went by. Zoraz did not notice at first the sheet of fog had followed him into the woods. Quickly though, it surrounded him, attracted to him, and, raising waist high, bathed the world into diaphanous tendrils of cold vapour. Overhead, the canopy of black leaves completely blocked out the sky, the hunter's only true beacon. Zoraz heard no river, no inlets, and his acute sense of orientation could not save him.

He could not believe it, but Zoraz the Hunter was lost.

Stopping by a large tree, Zoraz paused, his back leaned against the brittle bark, his head invested in the forging of a plan. The sound of water suddenly broke the monotonous noise of his own respiration. A hundred yards away from him laid a wide lake that the fog had somewhat circumvented. Zoraz could see no source to it, no stream, no river. But he thought of fish, and he was starving.

Approaching the lake, Zoraz sat on the damp grassy shore, staring below, trying to catch sight of his next meal. Ripples circled on and on, although no wind could have stirred them into motion. Frowning, Zoraz leaned closer to the glassy surface, at first mesmerised by his own distorted reflection, and then terrified by the pair of yellow blinking orbs amidst the ripples. They were not his eyes, but someone, or something else. For a short moment, Zoraz closed his eyes and shook his head. He'd swear he had just seen Khal Trobor or one of his henchmen under the water!

When Zoraz opened his eyes again, an abominable face welcomed his sight, sprouting out the water like a malformed baby being violently extracted from the womb of a dead mother. Huge batrachian bulging yellow eyes, around which a purple ring of saggy tissues hung    loosely, stared at Zoraz, the skin of its head a paler, more sickly tone of grey than Khal Trobor. Wide and deep wrinkles crossed its toad face, the top of its hairless, skid-like head, and down its squarish jaw. The beast had extracted its entire head and part of its broad, scaled shoulders when it finally let out a low snarl, its thin, dark-blue lips receding over black gums and rows of acerated, flint-like teeth. All over the lake, the horror kept spreading. Tens of similar black shapes broke the water, and their eyes shone in the dark like that of nocturnal predators.

Zoraz let out a scream, recoiling, brandishing his pathetic weapon. He wished he had his spear with him and avoided any form of close combat with any one of those wretched things. If they were the same size and strength as Khal Trobor's henchmen, Zoraz was lost.

Webbed fingers suddenly sprouted into existence, gripping the grassy shore with long, lion-like claws, pulling the body of the closest beast out of the water. The similarities with the shaman and his henchmen were even more striking now that the creature was standing out of the water and up on two legs. It was evident that Khal Trobor and his henchmen pertained, to some extent, to the same species of aquatic bipedal creature, for the general physical features spoke by themselves. But the specimen standing up in front of Zoraz looked much more bestial than civilized, more aquatic than terrestrial, more alien than human.

The creature was completely naked, its skin gleaming oddly under the weak light, the colour of it changing from light grey to ruby-green and amethyst-purple depending on the angle with which the weak, clouded light reflected on it. Three narrow slits crossed the monster's broad neck on each side, one above the other, opening and closing following the heaving movement of its bulky chest. On its forearms and calves sprouted sharp, studded fins Zoraz believed were acerated and dangerous.

For a moment, the creature in front of Zoraz, as well as its demoniac pals behind it in the lake, stood absolutely still. Their glowing eyes were locked on Zoraz. Neither of them talked, so Zoraz could not tell their intentions toward him. Outnumbered, Zoraz hesitated whether to attack or run away.

"Who are you?" asked Zoraz. The creatures remained still and silent. Their huge, bulging eyes barely moved, barely blinked. Zoraz wondered if they understood him. Raising his free hand, Zoraz said, "I want you no harm."

A great commotion suddenly stirred the creatures out of their lethargic observance. All at once, the beasts in the lake plunged below the water surface, then resurfaced, undulating now their bodies writhing like eels, moving fast toward the shore, instilling Zoraz to take a few steps back. Only the specimen facing Zoraz remained immobile. Something evil and malignant lived in its eyes, and, as though the beast found a way to penetrate inside Zoraz' head, locked the hunter in a series of psychic nightmares showing submerged cities, annihilated populations, immense pain and agonies, storms of cataclysmic outcome, and worlds dominated by the same half-men, half-marine detestable creatures. The visions of destruction were awful enough, but the greatest of Zoraz' inner terror truly took form when a pair of blank eyes pierced through the dark tapestry of the deep sea, looking at him malignantly.

When Zoraz, with great trouble and by sheer strength of will, finally extricated himself from the dark, vicious corners of his subconscious, the horde of creatures had already reached the shore. Some were grunting, others were emitting a series of distressing noises Zoraz believed were intended to threaten the hunter. The creature closest to Zoraz grinned, then raised one veiny    arm, pointing one of his crooked, clawed fingers toward Zoraz. A single syllable *word* exited his large reptilian mouth, too unintelligible to be understood, even less repeated, and much too frightful in its hearing not to be of bad omen.

Obeying the obscure order, the group of wretched beasts sprang forward, moving with disconcerting agility when compared to Khal Trobor's shambling, clumsy gait. Their long, muscular legs propelled themselves ahead in long strides, large hands slashing the air as they went for the hunter. They yelled and croaked like a bunch of demented folks, and so did Zoraz. For the first time in his life, Zoraz the Hunter took flight to save his own life, going against his own principles, throwing away a lifetime of unfaltering courage and boldness. Zoraz the Hunter became Zoraz the Coward.

Zoraz ran across the fogged land, the tightly clustered trees, the thick, thorny vegetation, the mud puddles, stumbling over the uneven, difficult terrain, losing faint in his chance to outrun the creatures. They knew the land, Zoraz did not, and, if anything, they could see much better than Zoraz in the omnipresent gloom. He could simply not distance them, only keep pushing forward, praying the Gods this place had an end, a threshold past which its inhabitants could not follow him, a forbidden land they could not breach like Zoraz breached this one.

All around Zoraz, the branches cracked, the screams reverberated against invisible walls, and the stampeding of dozens of feet haunted the darkening day. The fog was omnipresent, every inch of this place resembled one another; an evil agglomeration of pestilent, ankle-deep ponds, muddy untamed trails, wild patches of man-high grass, and tangles of branches down which hung gripping vines. Zoraz could have well been turning in a round without him noticing it. Slowly though, Zoraz became aware of some changes in the landscape. The trees grew sparser, the vegetation; thinner, and there came a cold, salty, and fishy wind as was often found by the seaside. The sound of breaking waves could even be heard under the mad crescendo of insanity-ridden roars. Zoraz was saved.

His lungs burned, his legs wobbled, his gait became erratic, but Zoraz pushed forward to almost passing out. His instinct did not betray him. After tens of yards of painful manoeuvre through thorny bushes and a ground so uneven and unstable that Zoraz stumbled and nearly twisted his ankles at least three times, he finally managed to reach a strip of beach covered with black gritty sand which led down to the sea.

Unfortunately, that was all he could find. Water, and no more land across which to escape his pursuers' grasp. All around, the sea stretched out of sight, its leaden colour merging almost perfectly with the monochromatic heavens, creating the illusion that Zoraz had reached the end of the world. The sun was nowhere to be seen, and the wind carried effluvium of rotten fish and dried-out kelp. Behind, the rustling and creaking branches told of the creatures' arrival. Their silhouette could be discerned across the trees and tall bushes.

"Zoraz the Hunter!" finally came a croaking voice, coming from his right side. The creatures stopped their mad course, standing in a line at the border of the beach and the woods.

Zoraz spun around, holding his stone blade with white knuckles. His hand hurt and throbbed so the weapon was embedded tightly, and it trembled with a renewed desire for vengeance, even though it was his last commitment in this life.

"Khal Trobor," shouted Zoraz, pointing the knife toward the shaman while heading toward his mortal enemy. Khal Trobor did not utter a single movement. He was holding an antler crown in his hands, and his face showed the same contempt, despicable smile Zoraz would gladly slice out.

The closer Zoraz got to the shaman, the more agitated the water became, starting with a faint bubbling at its surface, then ripples succeeding to one another, growing bigger and closer to each other. The wind suddenly switched, bringing with it the cold carrion breath of the sea. Ripples turned to waves, rising higher now than the height of a man. A dark, mountainous shape slowly exited the cover of the liquid veil, opening a pair of white, translucent orbs.

Zoraz finally halted, obsessed by the monstrous, shadowy shape taking form in front of him, raising the waves ever higher, blowing gusts of wind, always more pestilent, colder, and more destructive. The trees behind him leaned to almost breaking, rain plummeted the land like arrows breaking the dawn and descending unto enemy shields. The waves now licked at Zoraz's feet. The sea rose.

*Khal Trobor was right,* thought Zoraz, finally persuaded that the wrath of the Gods was unfurling.

"I implore you to pardon me," Zoraz knelt, dropping his knife, and raising his arms to the heavens. He wept noisily. Had he condemned his village, the people he foolishly tried to help and deliver from the very man who ultimately tried to save them?

Khal Trobor shuffled toward Zoraz, rubbing his

long, booted feet onto the black sand. His awful perfume quickly invaded his space, snatching him a retching impulse.

The shaman dropped the crown of antlers over Zoraz's head, then put his thin blue lips to his ear. "Your Gods won't hear you, Zoraz the Hunter. They've been dead a long time now," said the shaman.

Zoraz frowned. A sizzling breath echoes in the hunter's ear, preceding a sudden, sharp burst of pain irradiating from his side, right under the ribs. The pain accentuated as the shaman twisted the Zoraz' blade into his stomach. "Dagon is the only ruler, our father, our saviour ."

The shaman pulled out the knife, stabbed the hunter a new time but under the chest, pulled the blade out and struck another time. It happened with such suddenness and intensity Zoraz didn't have time to react.

"One day, when Dagon has replenished himself and grown sufficiently powerful, he will drive this world into a new era. There will be no more land, just endless seas and regions of eternal ice. And us, the Deep Ones, will build cities, and reign underwater for the ages to come. Our time has come. Yours is coming to an end."

A rivulet of blood streamed down the corner of Zoraz' mouth. He coughed, his vision tunnelling. The hateful silhouette of Khal Trobor materialised in front of

Zoraz. He now occupied all the space.

"It seems like your sacrifice will serve its purpose, Zoraz the Hunter. Dagon is hungry."

Gritting his teeth, Zoraz gripped the flint knife, pulled it out his chest and thrusted it into Khal Trobor's throat, right under the chin. The shaman's eyes fogged; his mouth twitched. He blinked in disbelief, gargled, and slowly leaned forward.

"And I will bring you down with me, Khal Trobor the Deep One."

# The Flame That Burns Underwater

## S.O. Green

The thing in the swamp had a mouth where its face should have been. It had eyes all around it, like petals on a flower made of teeth. It had arms—dozens of them—but no hands, no fingers. It spoke to her. Not with a voice and not in words, but in images and emotions. It wanted her to slip into the water. It wanted everything to slip into the water.

"Go away," Shade-of-Leaf growled and tossed a rock at it.

The thing glided away, avoiding her throw, and slid deeper into the murk, until only one of its bulbous, glistening eyes remained. Then that vanished too, leaving nothing but a glow like a flame burning underwater and bubbles on the surface. Pop-pop-pop.

Shay scowled and hugged her knees. The swamp always reminded her that she was different. No one else could see the toothy horrors in the water, and they *definitely* couldn't hear them in their heads. Given the choice, she'd never come here.

But they needed *somewhere* far enough from the village that no one in the tribe would see them. Cast-to-the-Wind was different too, and not in a way her people would forgive.

Shay heard rustling in the undergrowth and her heart jumped. Cas never cared to move silently. 'Sneak up on what?' she always asked. She walked tall and proud, and almost everything in the forest left her alone  because she left them alone. Shay moved like a predator—it was in her blood—but she admired this strange, untroubled woman in her outfit of woven grass, with flowers braided into her flaxen hair, willowy, sharp and tall, and basically everything Shay wasn't.

"Hello, beautiful," she said, slipping into a crouch on her perch.

She heard the breath catch in Cas's throat, one of her favourite sounds, and dropped from her branch to land right in her path. Shay smiled at the wide-eyed expression on the other girl's face as she stood and swept back her unruly tangle of red hair.

"I'm glad you came. I was starting to think—"

"Shay, don't you know what's happening at your village?"

She frowned. "No, I left at first light. I didn't want anyone to see which direction I was heading in. Besides, it doesn't concern me. I told you, Cas. I'm not going to hunt anymore. I'm going to live right, like you."

"It's not a hunt," Cas said, grabbing Shay's hands. She hated being restrained, but she tolerated it for her. "They took the dogs and the horns, yes, but it was more like a mob than a hunting party. I think… I think they're going to make another sacrifice."

Shay blanched. "So soon? But… The moon hasn't even waned yet! How could they…?"

She trailed off. She knew what would drive her tribe to make another sacrifice, before the last one had even sloughed the rotten flesh from its bones. The Antlerman. Whatever he demanded, the tribe was bound to give. For prosperity. For progress.

"I'll stop them."

"Shay, you can't—"

"I have to try. And if you're right… Well, we'll deal with that later."

She pulled Cas closer, crushed their lips together, broke breathless. If it was in her power, she had to try to stop the tribe from doing what they were about to do.

Or a lot of innocents were going to die.

* * *

Some of the tribe said Shay moved like a wolf. Others that she was a falcon that had traded sky for earth. Only she ever likened her movements to the gliding of something through water. Not a fish, not a bird, but something sleeker and slimier and hungrier by far.

Her father had taught her to hunt, but he'd taught her how the tribe hunted, with bows and spears and flint knives, with dogs and hawks, with traps and snares. She'd always hunted with nothing but her own body, stalking silently, running down prey, worrying it apart with teeth and claws. Something lived inside her—a dark, terrible hunger—and it had been a boon at first, the way the tribe prized and revered her, like it did the Antlerman. Until the day she'd met Cas and seen the monster reflected in the other girl's eyes.

No. She didn't want to be that anymore.

She tore up the hillside towards the killing fields. She could smell the hunters on the slopes, downwind of the Great Horns that would be their prey. They stalked the woods, streaked with mud and wearing hoods of leaves, prowling with dogs at heel, feral lust rattling in their chests. Man and beast, beast and man, and who could tell the difference? Maybe just her.

She could smell the Great Horns too, clean and clear, fearless and mild. Whatever terrible thing they were planning hadn't happened yet. Which meant she still had time to stop it.

When needing to move quickly, she took to loping. It felt sickeningly effortless, though she knew humans weren't built for it. It helped her gain ground on the hunting party, then shoot out ahead.

Turning off her predatory instincts left her disoriented for a moment. The world was always so much brighter when she was both more and less than human. She slid to a stop and rounded, watching the dark shapes of the hunters emerge from the trees. The dogs saw her first, hackles rising and ears lying flat, jowls lifting from drool-soggy teeth. They wanted this kill, and they wanted her gone.

"Go away," she growled, just like she'd done at the creature in the swamp.

Even upwind of them now, she could smell their sudden anxiety. They wheeled and yelped, unwilling to get closer. She crouched in their way, giving them a clear choice, and they were smart enough to turn tail and run. Animals could sense danger better than humans. Maybe that was why the hunters kept coming.

"Out of our way, Shay," the hunt leader ordered.

"The Antlerman demands another sacrifice."

"How many are you going to kill this time? There'll be nothing left for you to eat if you keep this up."

"Maybe we can just eat leaves and dirt like you," one of the others scoffed.

He paled when her eyes fixed on him. She'd been named for their colour—the vivid green of springtime—but when she looked at prey, they darkened to black. Cas had told her it was an adaptation, whatever that meant, like most of her gifts. Everyone else just seemed to lose control of their bladders.

"You can't stop this, Shay," the leader insisted, and she could see him shifting his feet, clutching his spear tight like he thought she wouldn't know what he was planning. "It's already done."

She heard the blast of the horns and the baying of hounds on the other side of the hill too late to react. Of *course,* this group had been a diversion. They'd spread their scents all around the killing field, all to confuse her, to keep her from interfering. She'd made her opinions too well-known, and her father had acted accordingly.

She shot them her filthiest, most murderous look and bounded away, hoping against hope that there'd still be something she could do. She heard the sharp barking of the Great Horns from up ahead, the thunder of their hooves as the dogs harried them and the hunters chased them up the hillside.

Even at full speed, tearing through grass and shrubs and a carpet of brittle leaves on hands and feet, she wouldn't be fast enough. She couldn't draw level with the herd, to chase them away from what she knew awaited them beyond the trees.

The edge.

She burst from under the canopy, just in time to see the first of the magnificent, towering Great Horns plunging over into nothingness. The rest followed, too panicked, running too hard and fast to stop. Shay skidded to a halt at the very edge of the precipice but turned her head away. She already knew what she'd see at the bottom.

The cliff didn't end at rocks or flat ground. It ended in the swamp. Every single Great Horn would drown. Slip beneath the water. Pop-pop-pop.

She couldn't watch.

More hounds emerged from the trees, barking and snapping with excitement. Some of them had bloody muzzles. They'd be well-compensated for their lost meals back at the village. She knew the dogs were blameless—just tools, like the spears and horns—but she couldn't help the vindictive urge to turn and snarl at them, sending them scampering away, back into the forest.

"Your father said you would interfere," the hunt leader said   when he finally caught up.

"He knows me pretty well. But then, he is my dad."

Once upon a time, they'd known everything about each other. She was a different person now, but still so predictable, apparently. And as for him, well, he took his orders from the Antlerman, and who knew what *he* was thinking.

She sighed. "What a waste."

"The sacrifices are necessary."

"Because the Antlerman said so?"

"He hasn't steered us wrong thus far. And your own mother—"

There were few ways to get at the heart of Shay's savage side. The thrill of the hunt was one. Mentioning her mother was another. That was why Shay, at least, wasn't surprised when she found herself sitting astride the hunt leader's chest with her teeth in his throat.

"Don't talk about her," she whispered, as she released his quivering windpipe with only the lightest of wounds.

But she tasted his blood on her teeth and her stomach snarled for more. She thought of Cas and let him go.

"I'm going to speak to my father," she said, stepping over him, and past the spears the others aimed in her direction. "And maybe I'll see the Antlerman while I'm there."

* * *

The mood soured the moment she set foot in the village. The hunters who'd already returned, flushed and ready to celebrate from the thrill of causing so much death, turned their faces away when she stalked through the ring of huts they'd fashioned from sticks and grass and pelts, past the fire pit, towards her father's home.

Once she was gone, they'd rave and revel long into the night, drinking ferment and howling like wolves. They'd rut and scream, overcome with bloodlust and with the promises of the Antlerman's favour. The Great Horns were a stepping stone to their prosperity. Good hunts, healthy young, power over their enemies in the hills and forests.

What were a few dead elks in the face of everything they desired?

She found Eye-of-Hawk outside his hut, sitting on a log with a spear balanced on his knees. He'd been the tribe's finest hunter until a boar had shredded the muscles in his thighs with its tusks. Now, his energy was restless, a weapon always in hand. He longed to stalk the plains once more, longed to lead his tribe in more than just words.

He had always looked at Shay with something

between pride and unease. His gaze only held disappointment these days.

"More sacrifices?" she demanded, swiping a hand at the horizon behind her, the miserable scene she'd left behind.

"Necessary," he insisted.

"A whole herd, wasted."

"Not my decision, Shade-of-Leaf."

"Of *course,* it was your decision," she hissed, leaning close. "You lead this tribe, not the Antlerman. Show some stomach."

"Do not judge your father harshly, child."

Her glare fixed on the shape emerging from the hut beside her father's. It wore a cloak of animal hides, stitched together yet distinct, trimmed with fur that might have come from a wolf. Its skin was the murky blue-green of the swamp, of bog water, and Shay couldn't tell if it painted itself or if that was truly its colour. The antlers on its head were a crown. She'd seen the shorn scalp beneath. That, at least, made it seem human. The too-long fingers and black eyes and pointed teeth did not.

The tribe saw it as divine. They'd seen Shay that way too. Her mother's child, equally blessed.

"He does what is needed, for the sake of his tribe. These sacrifices will make you great. The greatest in this valley."

"How many more will it take?"

"As many as necessary. I cannot predict it. I am merely the conduit through which the demands and the balance of existence flow."

"That's a steaming pile of Great Horn shit, and you know it. You're a charlatan. You're not divine, just a beast in a fancy headdress."

"That is enough, Shade-of-Leaf!" her father snapped, rising to his feet. If it came to a fight, his spear wouldn't avail him.

"He's using you," she insisted. "I don't know what his game is, but all these sacrifices… They're not for the tribe. Not even a little bit."

"You are wrong. Ever since we began to honour the sacrifices, our hunts have become more fruitful. Our enemies tremble before us. No mother in our camp has known the grief of a lost child."

"And how long do you think that will last?"

"I hoped you'd come around. I wanted you to lead the tribe, as you were meant to. Instead, you ran afoul of that outcast…"

"It isn't her fault she's an outcast," Shay growled. "Her tribe exiled her for speaking out. For choosing a different way. A *better* way."

"A pity you feel that way," the Antlerman said, "but then, it is hardly a surprise that your mother found you wanting and departed this tribe for—"

Hawk knew what was going to happen before the Antlerman did. Maybe existence hadn't chosen to impart that choice bit of knowledge to it. He threw a hand out to ward Shay off, but it was too late. Her claws sliced him across the face, shredding the flesh of his cheek, maybe even taking his eye. He reeled away, and Shay looked at the blue blood dripping from her fingers.

"Don't talk about her," she snarled.

"Go, Shay!" Hawk thundered. "Leave now! Return only when you are willing to honour our guest and his wise advice."

"I'm leaving. But I'm not coming back. As far as I'm concerned, I'm cast to the wind now too."

She caught the Antlerman's remaining eye as she turned to leave, saw the filthy murder in his gaze as he held his torn face together. Blood ran into his mouth from the grooves in the meat of his cheek and dripped off his narrow, pointed chin.

"I'm not going to stay in the valley," she said. "You're going to kill this place. I won't let you kill Cas as well."

* * *

"And then I clawed his face off," Shay explained, as she and Cas held each other in the light of the rising dawn.

They curled around one another on a reed mat Cas had woven, on the floor of the hut they'd built together, far distant from the tribes that had shunned them. Shay had split her time between her      and her village, but it looked like she wouldn't be doing that anymore.

She couldn't say she felt good about everything that had happened in the village, even if being alone with Cas felt better. Unlike her cuckoo of a mother, she'd felt love from her father. She'd felt like she mattered. Their relationship had been tenuous for months. Now, it finally felt broken.

But from that came a kind of freedom. Her father hadn't just named her for the colour of her eyes, but for the way she flitted with the winds. She could finally just fly away.

"You really left?" Cas asked. "Just left your tribe behind?"

"I wanted to believe they could change, but… I don't think they will. The valley is going to suffer, I know it. We should go, Cas. Somewhere far, far away. I don't like any of this."

She'd been burning up with the need for them to flee, but other needs had taken over. The moment her hand had found Cas's, in the forest outside the village, she'd run with her back to their home. They'd stoked a fire and then found heat in other ways for the better part of the night.

Now, cooling in the morning, they turned to the future, as dismal and grey as the timid sunrise.

Cas nodded, her voice soft. "I think you're right."

Shay heard the space where the unspoken words lived. "What did you see?"

"It's…better if I show you."

Shay watched her dress from the bed. Cas was different from the women of her tribe—softer, milder, sharper around the eyes and peaceful in the spirit—and even now she fascinated. She seemed to sense Shay's eyes on her and flushed across her chest. Once she was clothed, Shay rose, unashamed, and searched the hut for wherever she'd thrown her hides.

Outside, Cas took the lead, pulling Shay by the hand. In that moment, she thought she might go anywhere Cas led her. She was also gripped by a sudden urge to turn and flee, dragging Cas behind her, until they were far, far away from the valley, her tribe, the Antlermen, and the things in the water.

They took a winding, overgrown path through the trees and into the wetlands where the rivers widened and swelled and the ground became boggy and unfriendly. The swamp lurked beyond, but they took a path that skirted the edges. Shay kept Cas close, watching the lights flickering on the surface of the water, a growl in the back of her throat.

"I found this place after my tribe turned me away," Cas said, pointing out a low cave mouth choked with water ahead.

They had to duck to enter, wading through the shallows at the edges of the passage. Shay expected it to be dark inside, but the angle of the fading sunlight glanced off the water, casting rippling undulations of light across the walls. Blooms of incandescent fungus lit the far corners, reminding Shay of the scattering of stars across the night sky. They hoisted themselves onto a rocky shelf, and Shay sat in wonder at this secret, private place that had been Cas's and was now theirs.

"Why did you come in here when it's so wet?" she asked, wringing out her sodden hides.

"It wasn't like this when I first found it, a few winters back. Actually, it was mostly dry."

Shay looked at the water below them, and a slow-dawning horror began to edge into her mind.

Then where did all this water come from?

"Here," Cas said, clasping Shay's hand and matching their fingers. Her touch was warm and soft, and Shay felt a flush creeping up her neck onto her face.

She moved her hand into the water, pressing them to the slimy rock below their perch. Shay didn't know what was happening at first, then felt a ridge under her fingertips, then another and another as they went lower and lower until they were submerged up to their elbows.

"What are those?"

"I made them. To mark the water line. Each new moon."

Shay jerked her hand out of the water. She seized Cas's face, pressed her lips to her mouth, and held them there, just *feeling* her. When she released her, she could see the confusion on her face, even in the unusual light.

"We need to leave," she said. "Right now."

"Do you…want to warn your father?"

"No. I've already tried. This won't change anything for him."

She seized Cas's hand, pressed a kiss to her knuckles, then pulled her to the edge of the shelf. They clambered back down into the water and made their way to the cave entrance, clinging, supporting one another. Shay turned to duck out of the cave and felt Cas's fingers slip from her grasp.

When she turned, nothing but a glow like a flame burning underwater and bubbles on the surface.

Pop-pop-pop.

"No!"

She plunged into the water, reaching out vainly for Cas's hand, something she could grab to bring her back.

The light moved away, gliding through the water, leaving her in its wake and taking her heart with it. She started swimming after it, detesting the way it felt so natural to power through the murky depths.

She swam for minutes, navigating the narrows in the dying light, following the path she was certain the thing had taken. She found nothing. No creature, no Cas. She burst to the surface and collapsed against a tree, sobbing in frustration. Before she could waste more valuable seconds, she scrubbed her fist over her watery eyes and clenched her teeth.

She needed to approach this like Cas. Rationally. She needed to climb the tree, look for landmarks, get her bearings. Then she needed to hunt, like she'd been born to do.

She turned to clamber into the tree. Something pulled hard on her ankle. At first, she thought it was a root she'd stepped in. Only it wasn't pulling her down. It was pulling her *away.*

Her leg shot out from under her as it yanked her off her feet. She plunged back into the water, glimpsing the glow of it shining beneath, and tried to pry the grasping tendril off. Its rubbery flesh distended and bulged under her fingers. When it wouldn't let her go, she slashed it with her claws.

It bled like the Antlerman had, a gush of thick, hot,

clotted filth. It let her go for a moment—long enough for her to burst to the surface and *breathe*—and then it seized her with another gelatinous limb, heaving her into the air. Its other limbs swirled through the air around her, coiling like snakes, afraid to strike because it realised she had teeth too.

Teeth seemed to be what the creature was made from. Teeth and eyes and wriggling tentacles, multiplying into infinity. It pulled her towards the jagged vortex of its mouth, its throat working greedily, ready to shred her into scraps for its waiting stomach. She wondered if this was the one she'd seen that morning.

She imagined how her eyes must have gleamed when she spied the soft, vulnerable flesh inside its gullet.

She slashed again, this time when she was close to being consumed. Her arm sank to the shoulder in its waiting maw, and her claws sawed through the wall of its throat. It let out a keening wail that left her half-deaf and rattled her bones, then tossed her away.

Water erupted around her as she splashed down. She fought herself upright, crouching low in case it came at her a second time. Instead of attacking, it fled, cutting a trail through the crust of filth on the water's surface, its tendrils dragging limply behind it. Toxic ichor floated like pond scum in its wake.

She thought about chasing it, thought about tearing

it apart with her bare hands. Then she remembered Cas, and nothing else mattered.

She pressed on, ignoring the blood soaking her clothing and pouring from the shredded flesh on her arm. With each laboured step, her strength seemed to flee from her. She could feel her heart pulsing against her ribs, slowing, struggling.

A mound rose from the swamp. She crawled out of the water and lay on the bank, trying to muster the strength to stand.

Something stood over her, watching. Shay forced her head up, forced her eyes to focus.

It wasn't something. It was someone.

A woman. With thick, red hair.

* * *

It might have been night or the next morning, or maybe even the night after, when Shay reopened her eyes. She couldn't see the sky because she was lying in a cave on a bed of reeds like the one she'd shared with Cas that morning before they'd made their ill-fated trek.

She sat up. Pain viced up her arm into her shoulder and she curled her fingers around it, finding a dressing of leaves and roots there. She couldn't imagine what her flesh looked like underneath, or that it would ever be the same again.

"You're awake."

The woman was sitting in the corner of the cave, watching her. In the darkness, her eyes glittered, fiery as her hair. It moved in the air around her as though she were underwater, glowing softly. It reminded Shay of the tendrils of the water monsters, reaching out for prey.

"You saved me," Shay said.

"Perhaps."

"Why?"

"Why not?"

"Who are you?"

The woman didn't answer. She rose from her seat and strode across the room, her strange hair flowing in her wake. Shay realised this wasn't a cave. The stone of the walls and ceiling had been carved into its shape, too precisely to be natural, and every surface crawled with engravings that seemed to move under the weight of her eyes like spiders scuttling into the corners.

And she realised she could see, despite there being no fire.

"You should leave," the woman said. "This place is not for you."

"I can't."

"Shall I lead you to the border? You should be able to find your way back to your tribe from there."

"It's not that. The monster I fought…took my heart."

The woman looked her over. For someone with eyes that burned like embers, they were cold as the depths of winter. "And yet, you are still alive."

"No, I mean it took the girl I love. I need to get her back."

"Love?" The woman's mouth articulated strangely around the word, like she tasted something foul. "The swamp is dangerous. If you go further in, you will die. Surely nothing could be worth that risk."

"She is," Shay insisted, pushing to her feet and meeting her eye. "I'm going to cut my way to the middle of the swamp and find her. I don't care how dangerous it is, and I don't care what stands in my way. I'll tear them all apart if I have to."

The water monsters, the Antlerman, even her own tribe—they would all die if that was what it took. She would trade their lives for Cas in a heartbeat.

"You feel that strongly about her?"

She didn't flinch under the burning gaze. Her answer was important. She felt the woman waiting for it.

"Yes. More important than anything. I'd die for her."

Something that might have been a smile danced across the hard line of her lips. "Then we hunt."

* * *

The woman was to Shay what she had been to her tribe. She was faster, stronger, sleeker, quieter. Her grace went beyond the animal. It flowed like water, free like the air, as intense as flame. Shay had to hurry to keep up, dragging herself in the stranger's wake, cursing her injured arm with every misstep she made.

"You will heal stronger," the woman said, suddenly next to her, though Shay hadn't heard her backtrack, "if you survive."

That was the closest they got to conversation. Shay had gotten used to her own company. The others in the tribe avoided her because they feared her. In her younger days, she'd been happy with that. They made too much noise and the overpowering stink of them chased away the prey. After she'd met Cas, her every waking moment had been filled with their gentle babbling, whittling away hours together. Shay had never heard so many words as from Cas, had never spoken as much to any other.

Without her, everything was silent. Dead.

They chewed through the swamp, the woman ever in the lead. Amorphous forms in the mist shrank out of sight, their faint glow rippling on the water's surface. None of them dared come closer. Shay would have liked to believe it was her they were afraid of after she'd mutilated one of them. More likely, it was the woman.

In the deepest part of the wetland, they found more hewn caves, like the one where Shay had awoken. They were half-submerged, strung with vines and creepers.

Some had trees growing from them. As she clambered into the boughs of a sprawling cypress to sit beside the woman, the vantage brought the truth home to her.

The carved stone was everywhere, beneath the water, under every heap of moss or grassy bank. She wondered if they had once been homes, like the huts of the village, but if so, this village would have been immense, perhaps as big as the whole swamp. How many people was that?

Had they even been people?

The water creatures were here, oozing through the gullies and channels, their lights betraying their position. She saw more Antlermen too. She had never thought the two would live in harmony. Now she was more certain than ever that her father had been tricked.

"If your heart is anywhere, she is there," the woman said, placing a hand on Shay's shoulder and pointing to the largest of the smooth-sided rock formations. After what Cas had shown her, she wondered how deep it went beneath the water, how tall it had once been. It was like a mountain, shaped like clay by an immense hand. "But your enemies gather. Will you turn tail and run?"

Shay swallowed down her fear. "No."

Without waiting for the woman to make the first move, she slid out of the tree, ignoring the nagging pain of her wounded arm. She sprang from island to island, her heart climbing her throat at the thought of Cas, so close and yet still so distant. The Antlermen didn't notice her. They believed they were unassailable in the heart of their territory. She would show them otherwise.

At the foot of the steps, one of the Antlermen patrolled, carrying a length of carved wood bristling with teeth. The fangs of the water creatures, Shay thought. Serrated and nasty. She wanted it.

He wasn't alert, didn't think there were any dangers to face. That was why the small noise he managed to get out before Shay tore out his throat with her teeth was one of surprise. He slumped onto his side, kicking and twitching, clutching at his neck, as she relieved him of his weapon. With a final convulsion, he slithered into the water, leaving only a streak of viscous blood behind. Lights began to converge where he had slipped beneath.

"Eat up," Shay said, and hurried to the top of the mountain.

The climb was easy thanks to the stone ledges carved at regular intervals all the way to the top, hampered only slightly by the swamp slime sticking to them. Shay was sure-footed by nature. The loss of traction didn't slow her.

When the other Antlermen saw her and attacked, she was ready.

Two of them challenged her on her ascent. They tried to stop her with words, but blood was the only thing that would satisfy her now. She slashed one across the belly, feeling the fangs saw through his abdomen. Steaming viscera slopped between his feet and cascaded down the stone behind her. The other reached for a long, curved knife—not made from flint, but something shiny she didn't recognise—on his leather belt. She hacked off his hand, and as he fell screaming to the floor, cleaved halfway through his neck. His head fell back, dangling from the remaining flesh.

A horn blew somewhere in the stone village. She heard more Antlermen shouting. An arrow plinked off the stone near her. No time to waste.

She plunged into the darkness of the tallest structure, eyes adjusting rapidly. Even on the hunt, she had never been able to see so well. Was it the swamp? Were things different here? Was *she* different?

Inside was the largest cavern she had ever seen, and still just as sculpted as the other. More of the insane symbols spiralled into madness on every wall. Stone bowls held flickering fires. Walkways and islands jutted from deep, murky water. When she looked harder, Shay realised they were the tops of walls that descended so deep she couldn't see where they began.

More of the Antlermen gathered, watching a wicker basket floating in the water. They chanted and ululated and threw their arms up in ecstatic worship.

Inside the basket was Cas, bloody and bruised, clutching herself and weeping.

Something inside Shay cracked.

She sprang from one island to another, one walkway to the next, until she reached the cavorting Antlermen. The first to die lost his head in a spray of blue-tinged gore. The second, she drove the saw-toothed weapon through his gut. When she tried to pull it free, it tore him through the navel and down.

The third slashed her with a dagger made from bone. She wheeled away, pitching his companion into the water, where he floated face-down. Her opponent lunged at her, aiming for her heart. She twisted away, trapped his hand, snapped her head back into his nose, felt the crunch of cartilage and a gush of something hot on the back of her neck. Then she bit off his thumb. It meant he lost his grip on the dagger.

She seized him by the face, her claws sinking through his flesh like it was mud. He gurgled as she ripped him. Then she threw him to the floor and ran to the basket, dragging it back to shore before it could drift away.

"Shay?"

"Cas, I'm sorry. I let them take you. I should have kept you safe. But it's okay. I'm here now. I'm going to get you out, and then we're going to go far away from this place. Somewhere safe."

She threw open the hatch on the basket and realised Cas could barely move. Without hesitation, she clambered inside, wrapping her arms around the other girl and lifting her to carry her out.

The hatch snapped shut over her, trapping her inside. The strange, red-haired woman stared down at her, eyes still smouldering inscrutably.

"What are you doing?" Shay begged.

"Nowhere is safe, child. No matter how fast or far you run, this land is doomed. This is only the beginning, what you see here. It is a foothold. This land belongs to those that dwell beneath, and they will have what is their due."

Shay let Cas down and reached for the hatch, trying to force it open. The woman stamped on her hand so hard that the pain made her scream. She collapsed beside Cas, clutching at her arm, her fingers mangled, splayed in odd directions, her claws broken. Blood oozed into her palm.

"Why not let us leave, if it doesn't make a difference?"

"Haven't you learned yet? There must always be sacrifices."

"Why us?" Shay demanded, but the woman said nothing. So, she asked, "Why did you help me?"

"Because a human sacrifice is worthy, but the

sacrifice of two who are bonded? So much *more*. I wanted to see the lengths you would go with my own eyes, and now I see, I was right to bring you here." She leaned down until her pitiless eyes were level with Shay's, but too far for her to strike at her. "Why did you *think* I helped you?"

"Because…" Shay had wrestled with this moment her whole life. If she was going to die, she had to say it. "Because I'm your child."

"I have many children," the woman said, without a flicker. "They all serve their purpose."

She seized the dying Antlerman by his head. A sharp crack rang out as she twisted it between her hands. Then she pulled his antlered headdress off and settled it among her flowing, fiery locks. Like Shay, she stood between worlds, half-human, half-something else. The antlers made her look so much more natural than she really was.

"If they take this land below," Shay said, desperation seizing her, "you'll sink too."

"I am the Flame that Burns Underwater, child," the woman said. "I am the Chosen Daughter. I am the Emissary. I am the Tongue that Drips Poison. My purpose is still yet to be served."

She planted a webbed foot on the wicker basket and pushed it out into the open water. As Shay and Cas drifted out onto the dark lake filling up the inside of the carved mountain, they clung to one another, sobbing into each other's hair, as the Flame that Burns Underwater took up the chant of the dead Antlermen. Her voice carried, filling up the chamber, the overlapping echo of it agitating the maddening symbols on the walls.

"It's okay," Shay whispered, pulling Cas into a kiss that tasted of their tears. "We're together. That's all that matters."

Below them, deep beneath the surface, a light began to shine. Slowly, it began to grow brighter. Nearer. It filled the lake from wall to wall. Shay envisioned a mouth large enough to swallow her village. Tendrils thick as tree trunks. Eyes larger than caves.

"Don't look," Shay begged, clutching Cas's face to her chest and holding her there.

The water began to churn.

"Whatever happens, don't look."

# Soldier of Dread

Chris McAuley & Claudia Christian

Kail's eyes narrowed as he attempted to look ahead into the underground chamber. His nostrils flared as he took in the scent of the dirt which lay on the ground and the stink of the creatures that approached him. Grimacing, he threw the torch at his feet and drew the two-handed axe from the rough animal-hide sheath on his back. His ears pricked as he heard the stop-start skittering of feet across the floor. In moments his mighty arm muscles strained as he hefted the axe towards the first of the chitinous beasts that seemed to pour from the darkness of the tomb. They moved with a stooped gait; their spindle-like legs caused the warrior to remember his recent fights with the giant spiders of the forest. Impossibly sharp teeth snapped at him as he became surrounded by them. In the scant light, Kail could see that a thick mucus substance drooled from their gibbering mouths. He suppressed a shudder as he watched the dark pink liquid dribble from their swollen lips and onto their full breasts. These things seemed a mixture between spider, crab and voluptuous woman.

The axe glanced off the monster who faced him, it dislodged some of the dark grey plating on its back but failed to cause the instant death blow that Kail had hoped for. Kail felt a sharp pain in his back, one of the creatures behind him had used its bladed arms to cut into him. Momentarily distracted, Kail failed to defend himself from the counterattack mounted by the creature in front. Enraged by the damage Kail's axe had caused, it slashed into his unprotected stomach. The razor-edged arms tore at the warrior's flesh and caused dark red blood to splash across the dirt and stone of the floor. In a desperate attempt to defend himself, Kail rolled away from the creatures.

He came to a stop and brought himself into a crouched position. The light of the torch which he had discarded in favour of the heavy weapon continued to burn. This afforded him some vision with regard to the enemies who were a few feet away. Watching their forms as they moved across the torchlight, Kail breathed deeply, remembering the techniques he had learned as a knight-in-training. Calming his body and controlling the sensation of fear that threatened to overwhelm him. From somewhere deep in his mind came the resonant and strong voice of his Swordmaster. The memory stirred him to action once more.

"Come on lad, look for the weakness. Every enemy has one whether man, beast or dragon!".

It took less than a few seconds for Kail to see the oncoming creatures protruding leg joints as one and the soft tissue of their stomachs as another.

Gritting his teeth, Kail charged from his crouching position. He kept his body low and focused all his strength on his legs and arms. Speed and brutality would win the day here and he was determined to emerge from this battle victorious. The axe's sharp blade found its mark as it cut into the first creature's leg. Yellow liquid emerged and Kail rejoiced as he heard the snap of its brittle joint. The beast let out a horrific mewing sound. Its moans of agony goaded the others to skitter forward and attack. Through the snapping of their jaws and the slashing of their arms, the warrior rolled and dodged. The creatures attempted to surround him but now Kail had their measure. Alternating his attacks, he cut upwards and the axe shredded the next creature's pale bloated flesh. The blade punctured the stomach lining and bile duct, Kail's face soon became a mess, splattered with stinking internal fluids and the remains of ruptured internal organs.

Eventually, the creatures began to retreat. They were losing too many of their kind to this invading human. He was unlike the easy prey who stumbled into the barrow unawares, lost or seeking some mythical treasure. Besides, his body had the look of too much sinew and muscle for there to be much meat anyway. Kail caught his breath as he listened to the chittering of his foes retreating. The injured ones trailed broken or severed limbs after them. The warrior allowed himself a small moment of satisfaction. Since he had been brought to this strange place, he had been assailed by all manner of demons and monsters. But still, he stood, still he was undefeated. If ever he returned to his tribe in Ireland, he would have many stories to tell in exchange for meat and comfort. Maybe he could even hire bards to tell his stories in the kingly halls?

These happy thoughts gave him strength enough to once again holster the heavy axe in its mooring on his back and regain his torch once again. Thankfully, the scuffle with the creatures had not dulled it or extinguished its light as he had feared. He would have need of it as he ventured on. In search of the woman who had been taken in the night.

It had been several weeks since Kail had been swept up in the Shaman's curse and brought to this strange place. He should have decapitated the old wizard while he had the chance. As he wandered the wastelands of this new land he had been found by a friendly tribe. They had recognized him as a stranger and welcomed him, providing food and shelter. They had treated him as one of their own. As Kail sat by the heartsome communal fire and was handed a bowl of broth, he realised that there were those back home who would call themselves his kin who would not do as much. In time he learned the name of this place. Doggerland. An island that was slowly sinking beneath the waves. With this knowledge, Kail had given it another name, Tir Far Thoninn, meaning 'the land being lost to the sea.'

Its people were aware of this fate, some prayed to their gods for salvation, others merely accepted it with stoic determination. Although he found the latter attitude admirable, Kail could never contemplate going to his death without a struggle.

Then there was Estrid, the woman who had brought him food. They shared an easy friendship and eager to do his part, Kail volunteered to go hunting with her. The game was different from that which he was familiar with in the Celtic isles. Estrid showed him how to set clever traps for those animals who were intended to be their supper. Over time, Kail came to care for her and even considered that life would not be so bad living here. Even if this place was doomed, he would have the comfort of Estrid to face that eventuality when it came.

Then last night, as the moon had reached its peak, he had awoken to her screams. Gathering only his axe, he rushed from his tent to see her naked form being dragged away by tall, thin red-skinned creatures. In the dim, silver-tinged light, Kail thought that he saw gleaming red jewels peppering their backs, it was only when one blinked at him did he realise that they were eyes. The screams had also woken the headman of the tribe. Kail heard his voice call after him as he ran onward, tracking Estrid's kidnappers. The old man's surprisingly strong voice carried into the forest after the young warrior.

"She is being taken to the Ghoul King's temple deep in the Forbidden Lands. Find her before she is swallowed by the ground."

It had taken many hours of trailing long-limbed ghouls and encountering and defeating many beasts before Kail found this unholy place. It was an underground tomb upon whose entrance contained many carved symbols that seemed to glow with a dim green light. This was where Estrid had been taken and although Kail detested magic, he was determined to find her and kill anything that stood in his way.

Bringing his mind back to the present, Kail stepped over the dead carcasses of the spider creatures and continued on his quest. As he moved from the large antechamber to a narrower entry, he noticed that the rock wall had been smoothened. As the torchlight shone upon the glossy surface, Kail could make out more strange symbols intricately carved upon them. He had seen the glyphs of the Celtic shamans and druids before but these seemed different. As he held his gaze upon them, tracing their circular shapes and sharp angles with his eyes he began to feel dizzy. He began to hear the impossible sounds like sea waves crashing onto the beach. He was nowhere near the ocean. He shook his head in an attempt to gain sense once again and determined that he should not concentrate on these evil symbols in case he became possessed. There was the stench of evil magic in the air. Kail growled in defiance of it and spat an oath that its originator would soon meet his axe.

Moving onwards, the small stone-lined corridor emerged into a square room. It was lit but barely. The scant torchlight flickered from some unknown breeze which had penetrated the tomb. As hissing, wheezing sounds in front of him caused him to pause. Moving forward cautiously he found that a loathsome slug-like beast stood between him and a large wooden framed door. No doubt this was another one of the undead wizard's guardians. It reared its bloated body upwards, all six of its questing pseudopods tasted the air.

The beast moved towards the warrior slowly, unfolding its undulating and pulsing body. Once again Kail unsheathed his axe. 'At least this monster is not armoured' he thought. Glancing around the room's floor, Kail did not underestimate the creature's skill when it came to killing. The copious amount of human and bestial skulls with littered its lair was testament to that.

Kail yelled defiantly and charged forward, he attempted to move to the side of the creature. The warrior was aware of the sharp teeth which protruded from its maw. Kail also calculated that its size would hinder its movement. If he could stay away from the mouth and gain some kind of advantage based on agility, he should emerge victorious once again. The warrior kept close to the right side of the wall, pressing his shoulder against the cold stone. As Kail watched the beast advance awkwardly, he continued to comfort himself. 'Its lack of turning speed would hamper any chance of a sideways counter attack' he thought. As Krail raised the axe above his head, he realised his error in judgement.

The Dhol's keen senses detected Kail and lashed its mighty head to one side knocking the warrior off-balance. The creature then let out an ear-piercing shriek which rattled Kail to his bones. In moments, the warrior felt claws dig into his side and slash his face. Weakened from his previous battles but determined, the Irish warrior forced his arms upwards.

The steel axe knocked the creatures' jaws upwards. This gave Kail enough room to swing the axe once more, this time towards his left side. The sharp blade sliced into the Dhol's tentacular protrusion and severed it neatly. Kail heard the monster's fury as he rolled to the side, this time avoiding its hooked claws. His sides and face ached, he was sure that the creature had punctured several internal organs. He couldn't think about that now, however. As Kail pulled his frame up to a half-crouching position he realised he had had no time to strategize as he did with his previous foes. The Dhol was pulling itself towards the warrior with frenzied speed. Kail had been the first creature to wound it and challenge its dominance. It was determined to finish this battle quickly and suck the marrow from this human's bones.

Using the last of his strength, Kail performed the fabled Salmon leap, a technique taught to him as a member of the famed Red Branch Knights. A group of Irish warriors of renown who, it had been said, had been personally blessed by the goddess herself. Using it, he could leap twice as high as an ordinary man. As he sailed over the Dhol's head, he smashed his axe downwards and sliced through the creature's thin membrane. As Kail tumbled over the creature he caught a glimpse of its exposed brain. The warrior then slammed into the cold, hard, stone ground as the monster desperately twisted its body to try and intercept him.

The Dhol's senses reeled, an unpleasant burning smell was pervading its nostrils as it sought the human who had ended its life. It knew that its wounds were fatal but would make sure that he took this upstart warrior to hell with it. The beast caught a sense of Kail struggling to raise himself up. It hissed in anticipation and satisfaction. The human was seriously injured, not mortally wounded but damaged. The Dhol moved quickly, remaining conscious as it travelled across the mucus and brain matter which spilt from its head to the floor.

Kail shook his head, his vision was blurred by the impact. He was still bleeding from the deep slices which the creature had inflicted with its claws. He knew that his axe had struck a mortal blow but yet, he could hear the creature hissing and moving towards him. Kail's arms trembled as he readied his axe. Suddenly the wooden door behind him burst open. The warrior felt a gust of warm air fly past his head and heard the shrill death cries of the Dhol as it exploded into flame. The smell of the burning flesh touched his nostrils and once again he recalled his last hunt with Estrid. How they had captured the wild boar and cooked it for that night's supper. He had sung to her then, an old Irish ballad, soft and sweet. She had smiled.

The recollection of her smile and soft hair teased him as the warrior felt rough and gnarled hands drag him across the stone floor towards the open wooden door. In the moments before he lost consciousness, sweet memories of Estrid were replaced by the sight of a rotting face leaning over him. It had curved horns erupting from the side of its head and wore the perpetual smile of a corpse. It leered at him as the world went black.

Kail awoke to find himself chained against a stone wall. His arms were manacled and when he tested his strength against the bonds, he was dismayed by the quality of the metal. The links were evidently well crafted and it wouldn't have surprised him if there lay some enchantment upon them for double measure. Deciding to save his strength for later battles, he concentrated on examining his surroundings. A large table sat a few metres in front of him. It was filled with bottles containing murky-looking liquids and the heads of various creatures.

One of these seemed to be caught in mid-transformation between dog and man Peering ahead in the dim light, Kail could discern bookcases filled with large tomes of books.

From the inky darkness, a voice thick with bubbling rot and decay addressed him.

"I'm glad that you are awake."

Kail heard a movement in the darkness towards his left as the grotesque voice continued to address him.

"No doubt you came here after the girl? I'm afraid that I cannot let you leave with her. She is vital to the next stage of my experiment".

A robed figure emerged; its covering was crimson with a hem made of spun gold. Thin, skeletal hands pulled the hood back and once again the warrior found himself looking at the rotting face of the Ghoul King. Kail grimaced and pulled on his chains again.

The Ghoul waved his thin corpse-like hand and gestured to Kails' manacles.

"Do not struggle, as you may have guessed those links are not forged from ordinary metal. A precaution against one as…skilled as you. I see that you may find my appearance offensive? I was not always like this. Once I was a soldier of the tribe which you live among. I fought many battles and protected my people. However, there was one thing which my mighty arms and strong steel could not protect them from. The growing threat of the tides. The sea will soon swallow Doggerland up and us all with it."

The skeletal figure turned and moved into the darkness. Its voice grew distant but Kail could still make out the words issued from the collapsing muscles in its throat.

"Following the knowledge of the Atlermen, I sought communion with their Gods. I wished to entreat them to save our land. I would offer my services as a warrior to whichever cause they wished me to join. This was, as you may suspect…an unwise course of action. The deities which replied to my offer had no intention of saving us from the water. They come from there, you see. Mighty Dagon and the lord Cthulhu himself. But there is no need to talk of things which you have no understanding of."

As the undead creature continued to talk, Kail could hear him return, his footsteps resounding against the stone floor. There was also another sound which came after his steps, something softer, like the trailing of feet.

"They gave me the knowledge of the ancient arcane arts. I admit that my initial grasp was clumsy. The disastrous results of my second experiment continue to eat my flesh and muscle. Leaving me as I am today. I soon realised that I would need fresh bodies to experiment on before the great work was complete. You see, in order for any of us to survive, we must change. You have seen this in nature with the caterpillar and the butterfly? Well like that, we must transform in order to survive."

Kail felt a trembling in the pit of his stomach, his mouth suddenly felt very dry. What had happened to Estrid?

"You must be wondering what happened to your friend? Yes, I am coming to that. In the short few hours that I was left alone with her, I managed to assist her in achieving her greatest dream."

The shuffling figure joined the Ghoul King in the softness of the light, Kail could make out the features of the woman that he loved. At the sight of her, the trembling feeling in the pit of his stomach turned sour. He choked on the rising vomit which threatened to explode from his mouth. What was left of Estrid's beautiful golden hair had turned grey. Her skin had transformed into a bluish-grey tinge and her face was misshapen. Kail could clearly see gills on the side of her neck which pulsed against the thick trunk which was now her neck. Estrid's lips were thick and encrusted with a shell-like material, as she smiled up at the warrior, a streak of thin green slime dribbled from her mouth.

Estrid shuffled closer and it was then that Kail noticed in place of her feet her enlarged frame was being supported by writhing tentacles. Sagging breasts limply rested over her bloated stomach. Noxious clear liquid dripped from their nipples. Kail's mind reeled from horror and anguish, he screamed. For the first time in his life truly tasting terror. The abomination in front of him reached up to his naked torso with elongated webbed fingers. Her once welcome touch was cold and clammy.

The Ghoul King let out a small laugh.

"You also have a part to play. I mentioned fulfilling the girl's deepest desire did I not. Oh, I know what you are thinking. Unfortunately, I no longer possess the … equipment to fulfil that end of the bargain. I believe that it rotted and fell off a few weeks ago. My masters however… well not to be too indelicate but they do. So, you see, Estrid here is about to become a mother."

As if on cue, Estrid's stomach writhed. Her lips stretched out in ecstasy as her flesh began to split. As Kail looked down transfixed, he saw eel-like creatures chewing their way through Estrid's body erupted as the pressure of birthing her children became too much. Among the viscera and ruptured organs, Kail could still see her smiling face and the gills twitching.

"Oh dear." The Ghoul exclaimed. "That was unexpected. However, I expect the breeding process will go smoother with the next one."

Kail lurched forward with all his strength, hoping that against all the odds his chains would shatter. Despite his efforts he was still held fast.

The Ghoul gazed up at him. "Now we come to you. Your purpose in all of this. Well, not to put too fine a point on it. Is to be lunch. I can't have these little ones going hungry, not with their mother dead."

The ravenous creatures began to make their way towards Kail. The warmth of his body attracts their senses. The Ghoul regarded the scene for a few moments and with a nod of satisfaction disappeared back into the darkness of its sanctuary again.

As Kail's screams fell silent, the Ghoul communed with the Old Ones of the deep. They were pleased with the soldier's progress. He had proven that humans were compatible with their blessings. When Doggerland was welcomed into the Chthonic embrace, its inhabitants would join in communion with the waters. They would take their place as the first worshipers of the Old Ones. They would live forever and populate the oceans with progeny.

As for the Ghoul, well, there were other plans for him and other lands to visit.

# Crom-Ya and the City of False Seeming

Gavin Chappell

## I

## *The Ambush*

*Doggerland, 15,002 BC,*
*April 12ᵗʰ, 8.00 AM*

Crom-Ya flung himself back to dodge the thrust of a flint-tipped spear. His own weapon, forged from a fallen star, glimmered dully in the watery sunlight as he swung an overhand blow at his skin clad warrior opponent. With a splintering crunch, he split the attacker's skull to his teeth and a welter of blood and brains flooded out. The man dropped to the boggy earth where the pink paste of his unseated brains oozed into the mud.

Wheeling, Crom-Ya caught sight of Shuggthrod, who had led them into these swamps in search of the raiders. He was sprinting away from the fierce struggle where Crom-Ya's tribal warriors fought against the yelling Men of the North. Crom-Ya's colourless eyes narrowed. He had been a fool to let Shuggthrod lead them into peril.

He snatched up the spear from the man dying at his feet, turned, and used the impetus to send it whizzing through the wet air. He cursed, invoking the Toad-God as the spear sank into the mud on the spot Shuggthrod had just quit.

Frightened by this unexpected attack, Shuggthrod put on a sudden burst of speed, vanishing into a thicket of blackthorn, its white blossom an incongruously cheery sight. Crom-Ya would have followed, but his men were hard pressed. Seven already lay in the mud, brainpans crushed by the flint axes of the Men of the North, or with the blue snakes of their guts slithering from spear-ripped bellies.

Two men of the Tribe were fighting back to back, but even as Crom-Ya watched, one fell to a Northman's savage axe blow. The last, a sinewy warrior with a mane of hair as black as jet, who wielded a feathered spear that was bloody along the haft, was now surrounded by four Men of the North. Elsewhere amongst the thickets, Crom-Ya's folk could be heard fighting for their lives. But this combat was closest.

He struck the Northmen like a bolt of lightning, his sorcerous weapon whirring like a woodcock, faster than an arrow from a bow. Two warriors fell back, clutching at scarlet spouting throats. At once the numbers were equal—two Men of the North confronted by two men of the Tribe.

Crom-Ya knew the warrior who clutched at a spear-gored side. Tsath was a cousin of his, younger by several winters.

"Crom-Ya!" he called out, leaning wearily on his spear haft. 'By the Toad, we will die together!'

Crom-Ya gave a bark of laughter. "I shall not die this day, kinsman," he assured him. "Nor will any of my tribesfolk." But he boasted in vain.

A reckless Northman tried to hamstring him, but without seeming effort Crom-Ya's wizard blade slid through the greasy, wattled neck of the hairy man, biting into his spinal column. As he did so, the last of the Northmen lunged at Tsath, piercing his belly with a spear so that it stood out a handspan's length from the man's back.

Looking up, Crom-Ya snarled to see Tsath clutching at the weapon that pierced him. All around him Crom-Ya's men were falling to the axes and spears of the Northman raiding party. Two more Northmen, blood staining their beards crimson, ran towards them. Not heeding them, Crom-Ya swung his glittering blade at the victorious Northman, slicing into his ribcage with a wet thud.

Out of the corner of his eye, Crom-Ya caught movement, but before he could react, something exploded in his mind as a stone axe struck him on the side of the head. That instant of awareness had been enough for Crom-Ya to begin to move, so he escaped a split skull. But the resultant blow was enough to knock the wits from him.

He fell to the mud like a dead man, and knew nothing for a long time.

* * *

It was the full throated croaking of ravens that awoke him. He lay full length at the foot of a blackthorn bush, face sticky with blood from a scalp wound. For a space, he lay on his side, still dazed, gathering his scattered wits.

The rank smell of spilt blood hung dankly in the

wet air. Crom-Ya knew it well, had known it since he was a boy, when he went with his father on his first hunts, his first raids. Blood and death had been constant companions for this chieftain of the Tribe.

Still the ravens croak-croak-croaked. He could hear them squabbling over the fallen. One landed on his own unmoving form, drawn by the smell of blood. Crom-Ya summoned up all his reserves of strength to roll over, flailing ineffectually at the raven as it flew off, flapping low to the ground as it croaked imprecations.

He sat up, head spinning, and a chiding flock of black birds flew up immediately to circle overhead. Nearby lay the bloody length of his sorcerous weapon—a *sword* was what it had been called by the wizard who had forged it. He had dreamed of such weaponry. The men of old had wielded its like before the western island vanished beneath the waves.

Why had not the Men of the North taken it as booty?

Next to it lay a stiffened corpse, pecked at mercilessly by the ravens who now settled on the bushes, watching disapprovingly. On his hands and knees, Crom-Ya crawled forwards through the mud.

He uttered a wolf bark of laughter. The fingers of the man's right hand lay in a sticky pool of blood. They had been neatly sliced off—when, Crom-Ya guessed, the would-be thief had seized his sword by the blade. His credulous comrades had left him here to bleed to death, perhaps believing that he had angered the gods by his presumption.

The blade had descended to the earth in a storm, flung down by the sky god in his wrath. Only Crom-Ya himself knew how to wield it.

With the sword's aid he helped himself to his feet. Ravens croaked their displeasure, watching him beadily from the bushes. Unsteady as a new-born fawn, Crom-Ya gazed around.

Other than the man who had tried to take the sword of star metal, no bodies were to be seen but those of the Tribe. The raiders had borne away their own kind for interment within the ice cold caves they called home. He saw a clear trail leading northwards through the undergrowth. But they had left the dead of Crom-Ya's Tribe for the raven.

Crom-Ya roared as several bolder birds flew down to peck at the gory remains. One plucked the eye from a sightless man's socket, gulped down the white and pink gobbet. Crom-Ya flourished his blade and the raven flew off, followed by its fellows, to scream and jeer from atop a nearby tree.

Moisture gathered like glittering jewels on Crom-Ya's thews, dripped from his long, swart hair, trickled down his face as if his colourless eyes were weeping.

But the men of the Tribe did not weep for the dead—they sought the soothing balm of vengeance.

Crom-Ya remembered Shuggthrod, fleeing the fight. He had led them into this narrows, claiming it would be a faster route to the caves of the Northmen. Shuggthrod had led them into this ambush, and he had not been slow in his flight.

Now Crom-Ya knew the man for a traitor. Shuggthrod came from a clan whose territory lay upon the margins of Northman country. Often enough had he protested his hatred for the Men of the North around the council fires. But it had all been a sham, it seemed. Somehow and at some point he had been suborned by the Tribe's traditional enemies.

Crom-Ya crossed over to the spot where he had last seen Shuggthrod. Here was the spear he had thrown, jutting up from the turf as if it were a sapling bowed by the wind. Casting about, Crom-Ya saw a footprint here, a broken twig there. A trail was clear to his keen eyes—the spoor of Shuggthrod. Startled by Crom-Ya's spear cast, the traitor had bolted and run, fleeing friend and foe— and which was which?—alike.

The trail led away through the thickets. Crom-Ya followed it with his eye. Alone as he was, even with the aid of his sorcerous sword, he stood no chance of gaining vengeance on the Northmen. That pleasure must be deferred until he returned to the lands of the Tribe and mustered more warriors. But in the meantime, he would slake his thirst for revenge by hunting down the treacherous Shuggthrod...

## II

## *The City*

Across the plain strode Crom-Ya, sword in hand. For many leagues the land rolled, flat and featureless apart from thickets of blackthorn and gorse, for many leagues towards the Western Hills that were a blue, serrated line on the far horizon.

Shuggthrod's trail was not hard to find. It seemed that he had fled southwards in panic without thinking even to conceal the tokens of his passing. Here his footprints were clearly visible in the wet turf, there a broken twig and a wisp of barkcloth fluttering on a bush told its story. To Crom-Ya, each sign was a clear message.

He pursued the traitor across the dismal landscape as he would hunt a deer, following a distinctive spoor. And as he went, the land began to change. No longer did it consist of endless flat expanses of thicket grown turf. Now folds and hummocks became visible, the beginnings of knolls that, though dwarfed by the immensity of the far off Western Hills, still broke up the monotony.

Spinneys of birches replaced the blackthorn and gorse, heather swallowed up the turf. Crom-Ya moved through scrubland now, where slender trees shivered in the breeze and moisture oozed down the branches to drip on the passing Tribesman's head.

His iron endurance kept him going, his strong legs devoured the leagues. Now he saw that Shuggthrod's footprints were more evenly spaced. The fugitive had no longer been running by this point. Weariness had assailed him, Crom-Ya surmised. Now Shuggthrod would be looking for somewhere to lair, like a bolting beast that had spent itself in its flight.

Kneeling, Crom-Ya watched how water oozed back into a footprint in a patch of mud. He nodded to himself and grunted in satisfaction. He was very close now. Shuggthrod must be only a short way over that rise.

Crom-Ya rose in one lithe, fluid movement, and strode away through the birches, ascending the slope.

Beyond the rise was a fold of land. In the middle of this valley, green with moss and white and yellow with lichen, overgrown with trees, was a vast array of stones, all heaped upon each other. These constructions took up the whole floor of the valley like a veritable forest of stone, towering into the dank, mist hung air.

Had it been any other hunter of Crom-Ya's Tribe, they would have been unable to understand that these stones had been heaped one on top of another by the hand of man—or some other being. But Crom-Ya differed from his fellow Tribesmen: he had spent some years of his life dwelling in strange visions of another place, another age.

He had inhabited the body of a cone-shaped being, one of countless multitudes dwelling in a vast city of stone in another land, another time. At the same time his own body had been possessed by the spirit that had hitherto inhabited the cone-shaped body.

All this had been numberless aeons ago, yet it was but two winters since Crom-Ya had woken from his dreams. These visions had opened his mind to other modes of being, although he could never find the words to explain his spiritual peregrinations to the Tribesmen he ruled.

The sprawling constructions of stone were the edifices of a strange city.

City. A word that did not exist in the primitive Tribal tongue. Crom-Ya only knew it from the language of Yith, the alien folk with whom he had dwelt, or dreamed that he dwelt with. It was a city that stood before him. But an old city, a dead city. Crom-Ya shivered. His people knew naught of cities, and yet they had lived in this land ever since they came here as exiles from a drowned island in the West.

This city was old and dead. It must have been dead long before Crom-Ya's folk had come to this land. And it was here, going by the plainly marked trail down the slope, that Shuggthrod had gone to ground.

Hefting his sword of star metal, Crom-Ya descended the slope.

Half ruined buildings reared on either side of him like stone crags. Moss bearded them. Bushes grew from cracks in the stone. It was very unlike the city in his dreams, where the Great Race of Yith had dwelt, a place of vast towers and deep, dark vaults. These buildings were made of stone blocks, heaped one upon another into great walls. And yet each stone fitted the others perfectly.

By what sorcery it had been fabricated, even Crom-Ya with his understanding of the worlds beyond could not fathom. As for who or what had built this city, and in what long vanished aeons, he could not guess.

The echoes of his footsteps rang out from the stone walls as he forced his way down an overgrown street. Momentarily, he froze into stillness, the stillness of a hunter who may have sighted quarry. Was that movement he had detected up on the tower of stone blocks ahead? He gazed in silence, whole attention focused on the edifice. But nothing else moved. Growling to himself, Crom-Ya followed the stone street.

Now he saw no sign of Shuggthrod's trail. The prints had petered out as he entered the city, there being little scope for them on the aeons-worn cobbles that lined the streets. Although the woods had almost swallowed up the stone city, it was barren of those small indications that are a hunter's meat and drink. Were he a lesser man, Crom-Ya might have despaired of finding his prey.

It opened out into a broad plaza, similar in some ways to those he remembered from Pnakotus, city of the Yithians. Bushes grew amongst the stones here too, but on the far side of it stood buildings that seemed better preserved. No moss or lichen swathed their stones, no vegetation had taken root between the cracks. It was as if this section of the city still lived, when all about it was dead and rotting. Would he find Shuggthrod here? And what else might he find there? Was the city still inhabited? By whom, then? Or what?

Crom-Ya's dreams had given him an advantage over his Tribe. A dim sense of other planes of existence haunted him. Not for him was the daily round of hunting and fishing, trapping and grubbing for roots that formed the narrow confines of his comrades' lives. He looked to the far horizons, peered into the mist, tried to fathom the mysteries of his world. Although a savage warrior and a ruthless hunter, in his own way this barbaric man was a visionary. A seeker after wisdom.

But there was much that remained hidden from him.

As he took another step out into the plaza, heeding only the enigmatic edifices that rose from the vegetation swathed ruins, his ears caught the clatter of a living being moving in the mist above him. Then something came whizzing down out of the fog that hung round the tops of the ruinous towers and Crom-Ya was struck a glancing blow. Knocked off his feet he staggered dizzily into a thicket of blackthorn, fell backwards and hit his head against a rock.

He lay amongst the broken branches, skin lacerated, gazing up into the misty air. Whatever it was that had hit him had struck his shoulder, his right shoulder. His arm was numb. His head was dizzy. Gasping for breath, he used his other arm to force himself up into a crouch, then kneaded his numb shoulder while scanning his surroundings.

There lay his sword. There was the stone block that had struck him. And there, leaping down from a stone wall and forcing its way through the undergrowth, was a familiar figure.

Shuggthrod! Crom-Ya growled wrathfully to himself. He watched as the fugitive vanished into the stone building through an open archway. He would not find sanctuary there, Crom-Ya vowed to himself. But then he slumped back to the stony ground.

For a long time, Crom-Ya could not stir. This was the second time that day he had suffered a blow to his head. But once life began to seep back into his arm and his head had ceased its pounding, he rose, seized his sword and began crossing the plaza. Striding up the steps that led to the archway, he saw that this building was indeed intact. A strange, rank, musty odour drifted on the air. The arch opened out into a courtyard, where a fountain played, spilling fresh water into a circular stone bowl.

Crom-Ya's natural instinct would be that of any man of the Tribe, to throw himself down at the edge of the water and lap at it. But caution and cunning still dwelt within his skull despite his recent knocks. He halted as a figure appeared in a stone doorway on the far side of the courtyard.

It was Shuggthrod. And he was smiling in welcome. He beckoned Crom-Ya.

# III
## *The Traitor*

"Why did you betray us?" Crom-Ya spat, gripping his sword firmly in readiness for cutting the man's grinning head from his neck. "I shall slay you for it!"

"Chieftain," wheedled Shuggthrod. "you're wrong. In the Toad's name, I betrayed nobody."

"How can you say that?" Crom-Ya snarled.

Shuggthrod came to stand beside the bowl of the fountain. "Come with me," he said. "Come with me, and I shall show you them."

"What are these words?" Crom-Ya demanded.

"It must have been the blow to your head," Shuggthrod said. "You have been behaving very strangely, my chieftain. Seeing things that are not there," he added, moistening his lips with a fat, pink tongue, "and hearing things too. Evil spirits possess you."

"I do not believe you," Crom-Ya said. "I saw you lead my men into a trap. I saw you flee as the Men of the North butchered men of your own Tribe, flee when you knew that I would come after you, hunt you down. Now I have tracked you to this place of stones, and vengeance shall be sweet."

He drew closer. Shuggthrod waited by the pool. "All

I ask is that you come with me, into that… cave." He indicated the doorway from out of which he had come. "You will find all the men you think killed waiting for you in there."

"A trick," said Crom-Ya. "A trap. You would beguile me. No doubt more Northmen await me in there?"

"Why would I trick you or trap you?" reasoned Shuggthrod. "If the Men of the North wanted you dead, surely they could have slain you at this ambush you speak of. But there was no ambush. You are unwell, chieftain. Oh, you have led your folk long. We all honour you highly for it. But you grow old and tired and unwell. Perhaps it is time for you to stand down, let a younger man take your place as chieftain of the Tribe."

"I saw Tsath slain, plain as I see you now," said Crom-Ya. "I saw Tu'vog slain, and Shan-Zar. Only you and I remain of the men who set out to seek the Northmen who had burnt our outlying settlements."

Shuggthrod uttered a laugh. "You have been dreaming, chieftain," he cooed. "In your illness you have had a fever. The blow to your head—men have suffered like this before. And you have suffered from malaise before now. I beseech you, chieftain. Come with me, let me show you. Your men await you."

"Why should I believe you…" Crom-Ya broke off, distracted by a shimmer from the pool. He nodded slowly, his eyes narrowing. "Aye," he muttered. "Very well, if you say that things are not as my mind recalls them… perhaps I should stand down."

"No need," said Shuggthrod. "When you see the truth you will grow more reasonable. Come with me."

"I will come with you," Crom-Ya agreed. "I will come with you and learn the truth."

Giving a delighted smile, Shuggthrod turned and went ahead of him. Up the steps Crom-Ya followed him, entering the shadows beneath the archway. Shuggthrod had called it a cave, speaking like the primitive brute that he was, as Crom-Ya had been until he had spent so long amongst an alien people. But Crom-Ya knew that it was no cave, but the entrance to a building made by people of some kind.

He saw how worn the stone steps were, eroded by how many feet over numberless ages. This place was old, very old. Although it had remained intact while the rest had fallen into decay, it was in itself ancient, far older than Crom-Ya's Tribe that had come to this land many lifetimes ago. Long before the sea levels had begun to rise this city had stood. Perhaps it had languished in ruins all that time. How long had passed since it reared its towers whole and unblemished to a savage, prehistoric sky?

Within, Shuggthrod led Crom-Ya into a high vaulted chamber, lit by burning cresets on the frescoed walls. In the midst of it a stone table was heaped with fruit and meat. Sitting on benches beside it was a group of bearded, skin clad men who looked very familiar to Crom-Ya. The musty smell was stronger now in the dry air.

"Chieftain!" Tsath called, rising to his feet to greet Crom-Ya. "Chieftain!" chorused the others. Crom-Ya saw the bearded faces of Shan-Zar and Tu'vog, and Klaar, and Khel, and more. "Chieftain," Tsath repeated, and Crom-Ya saw that he bore a spear, leaning on it as if it were a staff. "We feared you slain."

"Why did you think me slain?" Crom-Ya asked, a puzzled look on his face as he stood at the head of the table, his sword at his side. "It was you, aye, all of you, who I saw slain."

Shuggthrod shot Tsath a look of irritation. "Our chieftain remembers seeing us all killed."

"By whom?" asked Klaar with a laugh. "By the Painted Folk?"

Calmly, Crom-Ya shook his head. "No," he said. "By the Men of the North. But it seems that I was wrong. I see that you stand before me, all of you who I feared dead at the hands of the Northmen. Perhaps I dreamed. I have had strange dreams of late. Dreams of other worlds, other ways of being… Perhaps life is all a dream."

Shuggthrod clapped his chieftain on his broad back.

"This is no dream," he said, gesturing to the smoking strips of meat on the stone table. "Eat your fill, and drink too. Life is very real, and all is as you see it."

Crom-Ya gritted his teeth. "Will you strike me with your clammy hand?" he growled. "I know you for what you truly are. I know all of you!"

"His sword!" Tsath shouted. "You should have taken his sword!"

Crom-Ya thrust his blade at the Tribesman who had greeted him so heartily. Shuggthrod dodged lithely out of the way, locks writhing on his pate like serpents. Tsath surged to his feet, spear outstretched, but he did not sink it into Crom-Ya's chest. Rather did he touch it lightly to the chieftain's wrist. There was a flash, a waft of strange smelling smoke, and the sword fell with a ringing clang to the stone floor of the high vaulted chamber.

Clutching at his hand, which was swiftly returning to the numbness he had known in the courtyard, Crom-Ya bared his teeth in defiance.

"Now you are almost revealed," he ranted. "Now you are close to being seen for what you truly are."

Rising up, his men surrounded him, seizing his arms and pinioning him to the table. Meat and fruit was knocked to the floor in the struggle. Men fell back, clutching at ribs or chest where Crom-Ya struck them. Shuggthrod reached down and retrieved the fallen blade.

He studied it sardonically.

"Good workmanship," he commented. "We have heard much of this miraculous blade." He used it to point at the struggling Crom-Ya. "Take him to a place where he can do no harm—to himself or others."

He stood over Crom-Ya, looking down into the chieftain's eyes.

"You have been unwell," he said. "You must be saved from yourself. You will be transformed before you can be allowed to rule over your Tribe again."

Down a long and winding passageway, helpless in the iron grip of the warriors, Crom-Ya was dragged. Light fell from periodic openings in the stone roof, but other sections were left shadowed in darkness. The echo of their tramping feet echoed from the stark stone walls. Crom-Ya could feel only a spreading numbness.

He was a prisoner. That was clear. What he could not understand was why they had not killed him outright. Did Shuggthrod have ambitions to rule the Tribe? Was this the real trap? The man followed the others, still examining the sword in sardonic fascination. "Out of its time," Shuggthrod was heard to whisper. "Out of its time. Such promise!"

The words meant little to Crom-Ya. All he knew was that he was helpless in the grasp of men who called themselves men of the Tribe.

Finally, they came to a halt before a small stone door. Tu'vog hauled on a creaking lever in the wall and with a relentless grinding and scraping sound, the door retracted upwards, revealing a small, dank, cold, dark chamber beyond. Into this Crom-Ya was thrust.

As he rose to his knees, the stone door slid down with a crash behind him. Now he was in utter darkness apart from a shaft of light from high overhead, narrow, serving more to deepen the shadows than to illumine the cell.

A figure shuffled forwards out of the gloom. A glimmer of light fell on a man's face. Crom-Ya knew those features. He had seen them very recently.

It was Shuggthrod.

# IV

## *Evil Unmasked*

"Chieftain!" Shuggthrod stammered. "They got you, too."

"You betrayed us," said Crom-Ya bleakly. "You traitor!" His hands reached for Shuggthrod's neck.

Shuggthrod sprang backwards, almost colliding with the stone wall. "Now wait!" he said. "You must be confused. You have seen me in two places. Here—and out there."

"What of it?" Crom-Ya said. "I know you are the real traitor."

Shuggthrod stared at him wildly. "Those you met outside," he said, "they are not human. Not people like me. They steal men's shapes."

"You led my men to their death at the hands of the Men of the North," said Crom-Ya relentlessly. "Why? How did they suborn you?"

Shuggthrod gave a cracked laugh. "Don't you see?" he said. "There is evil here. Forget our petty differences. We must join to fight against evil. We are men, you and I. That which lies outside is not."

"I see no man here," said Crom-Ya contemptuously. "Only a pathetic, puling traitor. How did the Northmen persuade you to lead us into an ambush?"

Shuggthrod sighed, and sat down with his back against the wall. "Very well," he said. "If such a minor matter means so much to you, I will tell you. But I tell you this also, that we must unite against the evil that besets us."

"The only evil I see is you," Crom-Ya said, looming over him.

"Very well," Shuggthrod repeated. "I met with the chief of the Northmen, Silver Bear. He told me that if I led you and your picked warriors into a trap, he would make me chief of the Tribe, as long as I bent the knee to him. He is ambitious like you. He too would rule over this land, unite the tribes under him. He said that I would have your furs, your sword, your wives…"

Shuggthrod cringed back as Crom-Ya growled.

"Since I had little but a spear, a few furs, and one slattern to warm my bed, I agreed. The nightmares of guilt have ridden me ever since. And when it came to the ambush, when I saw that you still lived while others had been slain, that you knew me for a traitor, I fled in fear from the field. I did not return to Silver Bear in his cave, demanding what I had been promised…"

"Perhaps it was as well," said Crom-Ya, "since Silver Bear would undoubtedly have had you killed. The Northmen have no time for traitors."

"…instead I fled. I knew not whither," Shuggthrod rambled on, "until I found this place. A place of stone cliffs and caves, but it was made, O my chieftain. Made by men."

"It is what was once called a city," said Crom-Ya. "Before the western island sank, men built many of them in the land that are now sea. But I do not think this one was built by men."

"It was not," said Shuggthrod. "When I came here, seeking a place to hide from your wrath, I encountered those who dwell here. I was met by one in your form. I could not understand it, how you had got ahead of me. Then your face changed—to mine!"

"In their true form they have the body of a man with the head of a serpent," said Crom-Ya, squatting before Shuggthrod's sitting form. "I saw it reflected in the pool in the courtyard. I knew them from my dreams. They are the Serpent-Men. They use sorcery to take on the guise of men. Once they ruled in secret, until that one who is forefather of our race found them out and fought long and hard to wipe them out, long ago, in the time of cities. But some survived, it seems."

"And they mean to begin again," Shuggthrod stammered. "They can take the form of men at will, steal images from our minds and throw them over themselves as a man would throw a fur cloak, but to take a man's form for more than a short space they must work their awful rites, steal his likeness with foulest witchcraft. Their leader will take your form and return to the Tribe, lead it to conquer all the Tribes, lay them all under their dominion as it was in the old time. You and I, my chieftain, we must fight them."

"It seems that my Tribe faces more than one threat. But I will not fight at the side of a traitor," said Crom-Ya, his hands closing around Shuggthrod's neck.

* * *

When the stone door slid open again, Crom-Ya was sitting patiently waiting. In the corner lay a huddled form.

"Then men fight against men," cackled the leader who still wore Shuggthrod's form. "It is well. The better for us, that we can set them against each other and rule them."

"His death was a matter of honour," said Crom-Ya as two others in the guise of his comrades entered the cell and dragged him to his feet. "He was a traitor. I broke his neck as I would that of a swamp rat."

They took him to another chamber. Within it stood strange structures that reminded Crom-Ya of the machinery of the Yithians. His savage mind would have been unable to comprehend them, had he not dreamed of other times, other places. In Pnakotus he had learnt of the whole history of his world, and its future. He had knowledge that was hidden to the rest of his people.

Unresisting, he allowed them to confine him to a metal chair that was part of a larger machine. Another chair sat on the far side. Instrument banks winked with many coloured lights. A metal crown was set firmly on his brows. The leader passed his hands over the winking lights.

On a table nearby lay a familiar object. The leader picked it up and examined it. It was Crom-Ya's sword.

"Where did you come by this?" he asked Crom-Ya, fascinated. "Once, long ago, your kind made such weapons, but it was all forgotten after the cataclysm. You forgot how to forge with metal just as you forgot how to build cities. You fled to dwell in caves like beasts. How was this weapon made?"

"A wizard of the Painted Folk forged it from a fallen star," said Crom-Ya. "I used it to assert dominance over my folk."

"We have heard rumours of the man who ruled his Tribe with a blade of iron," said the leader. "Long have I hoped to meet you. Now I shall take your form and I shall rule, leading your Tribe to conquer. And once again will the Serpent-Men rule over men, as they did in the time before.

"Wait outside the door," he told his companions. "You may drop your man forms and show yourselves in your true semblance. There is no need for such dissembling now. Once the process is complete, I will retain the form of this primitive."

Crom-Ya, with his back to the arch, did not see his captors shed their false faces. Instead he sat patiently waiting for the process to end. From time to time, he tested his bonds.

The machinery reached a juddering crescendo, then went still. Crom-Ya heard strong, confident footsteps as the leader made his way round from his side of the machine. A shadow fell over Crom-Ya. He looked up into his own face.

The leader brandished his sword. "Will I not make a fine warlord? King of you pitiful humans?" he jeered.

With a sudden heave, Crom-Ya wrenched at his bonds. All the time the machinery had been in operation, he had been working at them. Now they were frayed and split. That tug was all it took to break them.

The leader lunged at him. Deftly, Crom-Ya dodged aside, bringing his doubled fists down on his opponent's arm. The serpent man cried out in pain but did not drop the sword. Instead he swung it. Crom-Ya ducked, and the blade struck the machine with a clang. Sparks fountained from within its belly.

Hissing, the two guards charged into the chamber. Crom-Ya's skin crawled. Now he was seeing fully what he had glimpsed in the reflection in the pool. No longer were they manlike; instead they had the necks and heads of huge snakes. They carried metal wands in their hands, tipped with glowing crystal. Seeing two identical men locked in combat, they halted, looking from one to the other.

"Come now," Crom-Ya shouted. "Surely you know who is who! It is he who has the sword!"

A guard fired a ruby ray at the leader and the leader's smoking corpse dropped to the flagstone floor, the sword clattering down beside him. Quick as lightning, Crom-Ya snatched it up and hacked the serpent man's head from his shoulders. The other guard dropped his wand and fled.

Crom-Ya flung the sword like a spear and it struck his opponent in his back. The serpent man fell face down. Crom-Ya strode over, set a buskined foot on his squamous hide, and hauled the sword from his back.

He turned towards the archway, bloody blade in hand. He would not rest until the Serpent-Men and all enemies of his Tribe were slain or driven from the land.

It was to be a long struggle.

# The Cave of Many Voices

Emil Haskett

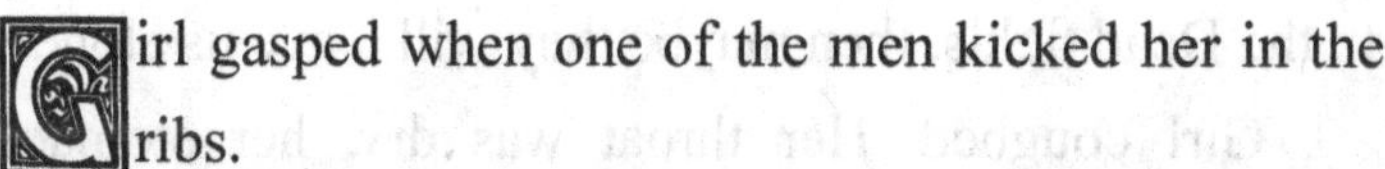irl gasped when one of the men kicked her in the ribs.

"Get up," he spat. "We still have ways to go." She was pulled up by the rope eating into her wrists. The scarred man holding the rope sneered at her. "No sleeping and no screaming."

She could not scream even if she wanted to. Girl's throat was dry from days of walking with hardly any water. Sleep on the other hand was always haunting her. They had taken turns watching over her, and every time her eyes closed, they shook or kicked her.

She could hardly see anything. The air was thick and

damp. The moon could not shine through the fog. Trees rose like sinister giants around them. Her legs stumbled, they were stiff and tired.

She did not know the names of the men. They were hunters and warriors. Men that came and left the village as they wished.

"They are still following us." It was the leader who spoke, the seasoned warrior with grey hair and scars after a bear or wolf on his chest. His eyes strained to see through the thick fog.

"It's the girl who draws them near. We should just leave her here", one of the younger men said, he was still untouched, with no scars or wounds to tell his story.

The leader shook his head. "No, we have to take her to the Dead fields, then maybe they will leave us alone."

Girl coughed. Her throat was dry, her stomach empty. "Could I have some food? I am hungry."

She pointed towards the satchels on their backs filled with dried fruit and cured meat. All of the men turned their eyes toward her. Strong hands pulled the rope and forced her face down in the wet grass.

"If it wasn't for you, girl, we could be home by the fires and feast on this food." She screamed when the rope again burned her wrists and pulled her over the grass. "But here we are marching to the Dead Fields chased by the horned ones."

Everything ached but the grass was cold and soothing on her face. As soon she closed her eyes, sleep came upon her, and with sleep came the dreams. She was floating in darkness. Underwater. There were voices in the deep and dark. Stories that wanted to be told.

Strong hands shook her and forced her back to the foggy night.

"No more dreams, girl."

The world was grey, everything covered in the mist. A shriek was heard, followed by the deep beat of a drum. Something moved in the grey world. Shapes nearing from the trees.

"They are here! The horned ones are here!" It was the young warrior. His hands were shaking as he pulled an arrow and put it to the bowstring.

The leader laid his hand on the bow and lowered it. "We do not hunt or wound the horned ones."

A silhouette appeared in the mist. It was tall and manlike, apart from the great antlers that extended from its head. It shrieked, a loud and piercing cry that might have had words hidden in it. Among the trees and the fog, other shrieks were heard.

"Then what do we do?" The arrow fell to the ground.

"We run." The sudden jerk of the rope yanked Girl's arms forward, she struggled to her feet and ran behind the cursing men.

Drums beat in the dark, shrieks and wailing cries came from the woods but did not seem to be following them. They did not stop until the trees were long gone and they were on open fields where an ambush would be spotted. The men fell to their knees or backs, panting heavily. Girl sat down, her head heavy and falling down to her knees.

"Do not let her sleep. Her dreaming will lure them here again."

The men took watches, poking her with the blunt part of the spear or slapping her as soon as her eyes closed. When the men had rested they continued the journey.

"We will reach the Dead Fields today. We will leave the girl there and return home."

The men sighed approvingly. Girl stumbled to her feet. The grass turned frail and yellow even though it was summer. No animals could be spotted. The ground was filled with dark and murky water holes. The men avoided them, Girl leant down and dipped her fingers in one of them. It was ice cold and so dark that her hand disappeared into it. She licked it from her skin. It was salt.

"That water is poison, Girl. Look at the grass around it."

"I like it." She licked all of it from her fingers. It

tasted like her dreams.

The men watched her with disgust. She whimpered when the rope dragged her to her feet again. Sharp rocks rose from the barren ground. They glimmered grey and greenish. Symbols were carved into them, and also mysterious engravings that looked like bone. There were many of them, coiled up like snakes or snails. Animals that had died long ago.

"There is something wrong with this place." The young warrior looked from side to side, bow ready in his hands.

"It has been under water." Girl had her eyes closed trying to conjure the images from her dreams. Great stone buildings stretching up from the bottom of the sea. "And it will be under water again."

"Do not talk of such things."

Their journey ended before a cave entrance. Dark pools of water glistened in the dead grass. Animal bones and skulls lay mingled around the cave entrance.

A man emerged from the cave. He was old with stripy white hair. His clothes were torn and dirty, no more than pieces of skin and fur. It was as if he was being eaten up from the inside, no more than frail, shrivelled skin on old bones. The old man held his hands towards the sky. "Have you come to ask for wisdom? Do you need to know the future? The secret of the stars. Or where the animals will go next?"

Carefully they approached him. He still stood with arms towards the sky and eyes closed.

"We come to offer this girl."

The old man lowered his arms, eyeing Girl. "She has not even bled yet."

"She will, and then she can give you many children."

"I need food more than women."

"You can eat her if you want."

Girl could feel his gaze, over her thin and fleshless arms and legs.

"Why do you offer her to me? What is wrong with her?"

"She screams in her dreams and speaks strange words." It was the young warrior who spoke. He rolled his eyes, gurgled and screamed in an imitation of Girl. "She lures the horned ones to our village."

The leader pushed the young warrior aside. "She talks of things below the water. Ancient things with voices."

The old man stumbled toward her. Girl recoiled when the old man leaned forward. He smelled worse than the dogs at home.

"Is this true?"

Girl looked down and nodded. Her gaze was upon the dark pools of water surrounding the cave.

The old man gripped her cheeks as he turned her head from side to side. "She can hear the gods? Then you cannot help her. She must stay in the cave with me."

"Many thanks." The men laid the satchels with food on the ground and then spat toward Girl.

They were in a hurry to get home, soon they were no more than small specks on the lifeless plain. The old man gathered together the food, chewing on a dried apple.

"So, can you tell me the future?"

Girl opened her mouth but the old man interrupted her.

"Can you tell me the movements of the animals? Who will be chieftain or when the rains will come?"

"No."

He moved fast for being so old. The slap burned her cheek. "Then what use would I have of you?"

The old man raised his hand again but then lowered it, his eyes across the field, searching for the men who had left her. "They tricked me."

He dragged her into the cave. The rock under her feet was wet and slippery. She leaned against the wall, her fingers again touching fossilised bone. Only a sliver of sunlight shone into the cave room. Smoke rose from a small campfire. The old man sat down by it.

"What's your name?" Girl asked when she sat down.

"The likes of us do not have names. You are Girl

and I am Man."

"Old man", she whispered.

Old man quickly raised his head, eyes toward her trying to figure out what she said.

"Make no mistake, Girl. If you cannot see the future I will eat you when all other food is gone."

Girl's eyes searched the exit, the light of the world outside shone into the entrance.

Old man followed her gaze. "Try to escape." He said, smiling with rotten teeth. "The marshes here are dead from salt water. There are things out there that will twist your mind if you happen to look upon them." He scuffled towards her, she pulled away and pressed her back to the wall. His breath smelled like animals who have been dead in the sun for days. "And when the mist rises *they* appear. The horned ones, the forbidden. They will play their drums, dance and shriek like crazy animals." He leaned back against the rugged wall. "So please, try."

Girl followed every bit of food that Old man took from the satchels and put in his mouth. He chewed and rubbed his stomach. She did not dare to ask for food, and he did not offer. She laid down on the cold stone surface and closed her eyes.

"The dreams were there immediately. She was in water. Floating weightlessly in the dark. She could hear *him*. Feel him. Somewhere in the deep and dark he was dreaming just like her.

It was still night when she awoke. She yawned, the voices were still here as if they were enhanced by the tunnels, coming from the deepest part of them. Old man was snoring. The fire was dying, failing embers was all that was left. She moved quietly, trying to follow the voices. There were many narrow passages, but she could hear the voices more clearly from one of them. It led deeper into the cave.

Red and white lines that almost glowed in the dark were painted on one of the rock walls. Depicting animals. Beings. Stick figures kneeling in front of a giant head with many arms. The paintings continued deeper into the dark. Mingled with the paintings were the white bone-like circles of aeons old animals burned forever into the rock.

"What are you doing?"

Old man was standing behind her.

"Did you make these paintings?"

Old man scoffed and shook his head. "No. They are remains from other poor souls who have inhabited these caves before us. They mean nothing."

"You are wrong. There are stories here. Older than all of us." Girl traced the lines and symbols. "They tell of the great king and the underwater world."

"You can understand it?"

She nodded, pressed her palm against the wall and closed her eyes. Images of a great tribe underwater. Countless servants amassing underwater, the shapes of men and women but moving swiftly like fish or snakes in water. Like her, they were also waiting. She pulled her hand back and opened her eyes. "You cannot hear them, can you?"

Old man did not answer. His gaze wandered from Girl to the paintings and fossils.

"Are there more paintings like these?"

"Yes, but these tunnels go deep underground, some of them are flooded and all of them are dark. And the darkness below has teeth." He closed his eyes, tracing his lip with his tongue. "And the darkness is always hungry."

He dragged her away from the stories on the wall. "Tomorrow you can show me what they say, but now we need to sleep."

She slept cold and dreamless. When she awoke, she heard voices, not from the dark depths below, but from outside the cave. Many men were gathered outside. First she thought that the village men had come to take her back. But these were other men, from another tribe. They were warriors with many spears, bows or clubs hanging from their backs.

Old man was standing before them. Arms held to the sky. One of the warriors threw a dead deer on the ground. It was young and small but would still become many meals. Girl's stomach growled at the sight of the animal

"We need guidance", the warrior said. "The horned ones have been seen close to the tribe. They have taken children away. We found some of them hanging from a tree." The warrior closed his eyes. "They had done things to the bodies. The other children are still missing. Do we have to move?"

Old man started chanting, flailing his arms to the sky. He stood so for quite a while, the warriors shifting their body weight from one foot to another before Old man lowered his arms.

"The gods say no. You can stay. They will not bother you again."

The relief shone on the warrior's faces. "Many thanks," they said, gesturing to the deer on the ground.

Girl emerged from the dark. "That is not what the gods say. They do not speak of such things."

Everyone was silent. All the men turned their eyes towards her. Old man walked over to her. The slap burned her cheek, it was so forceful it felled her to the ground.

"Do not listen to her. She is a girl."

The warriors laughed uneasy, but seemingly content

with the divination they left. Old man scurried off to the deer, searching all over it for a wound and when finding one put his lips to it.

"You did not tell them the truth."

Old man looked up; his smile revealing rows of red teeth. "They don't leave food if I tell them that they will all die horribly."

"The gods do not speak of movement of animals or such petty things."

Old man laughed, holding the dead animal in one of its hind legs. "Then what do they talk about?"

"They do not talk. It is more like… thoughts. Images."

Old man smiled and motioned her to the cave again. "We will eat and then you will teach me."

With a stone knife, Girl cut up the deer. Sorting the carcass into what could be eaten and not. Old man sat with his back against the wall, now and then taking pieces of meat and chewing them.

"Have you always lived in this cave?"

"Long ago I belonged to a tribe. Once I was someone. I had a name."

"What happened?"

"A misunderstanding." Old man caressed a burned and scarred part of his arm. "And I was no longer welcome. Forced to live in this barren land."

When he was full, Old man gave her a bloody piece. "Eat it."

He did not need to ask her again. She ate it quickly. After every bit she looked up to make sure that he did not try to take it from her but he sat against the wall relaxed. She forced through the chewiness of the meat.

"Now that you are strengthened you will teach me how to listen to the gods."

"I cannot teach you. They talk in my dreams."

He did not listen and pulled her into the tunnels, to the painted walls. "What do they say?"

"I told you." She pointed to the great circle with many arms. "We are waiting for the return of the sleeping god."

"I am not interested in that. What do they say about the future? About me?"

Girl blinked. "Nothing. Why would they?"

"You will tell me." His fingers dug into her flesh. The jagged nails drew blood as he dragged her into the darkness.

"Where are you taking me?"

"To the bottom, There are more paintings there, older than these."

Several times he stopped and looked around, before moving deeper into the cave.

"If one gets lost here, one would be lost forever",

he chuckled.

There was no sun, no light. All was dark. Old man's fingers were still tight around her wrist. Then, lights glittered in the distance. It was not the entrance, they were too deep for that. The faint light on the walls and ceiling reminded Girl of a starry night.

The vast room disappeared into the darkness. An underwater lake glistened smooth and dark under the glowing ceiling. Here and there jagged rocks emerged from the water like teeth. The walls were covered in signs, both carved into the rock and painted with red and white paint. The signs were mingled with the petrified white animals. From the cracks slithering plants protruded. They had a heavy and wet smell, like the autumn mushrooms that grew at the roots of old trees. Thick moss covered the walls and floor, the pointy parts of it glowed with a greenish light.

"Is it fire?" She touched it, but it was cold.

"It is a plant. It even grows underwater." He took a handful of the plant and chewed it before spitting it out. His teeth glowed for a short while.

Old man shoved her towards the wall. "You say there are stories in the symbols. Tell them to me. Tell me of my destiny."

Girl traced a fossil with her fingers. She saw what it had seen when it had been alive. Great underwater vistas. A stone village larger than any she had seen before. The dwellings were built with great slabs of rock that formed endless towers and buildings. On the walls and buildings, the glowing moss lighted the dark waters. And in the underwater world, the king lay dreaming.

"The cave, these rocks, have been under water."

Girl closed her eyes, fingertips pressed against the petrified animal. "And they will be underwater again. Everything will be underwater."

The heavy knob of his staff hit her on the shoulder. She screamed and fell to her knees.

"I am not interested in dead animals. I want to know my destiny."

"They do not say anything about you."

The staff hit her shine bone, shooting pain through her body.

"Make them", he screamed and hit her again. "Make me into a great leader, a gatherer of tribes."

She stood up, limping towards the wall and again tracing the twisted signs and fossils.

"They speak of the waves. Great waves that have been, and great waves that will be."

He cut her with the stone knife. Blood pulsated from her arm. "We will stay down here until you tell me what they say about me, or until you teach me how to hear them. And if you do not, I will eat you."

She closed her eyes, hand pressed against the signs on the wall. Her body was floating in darkness under water. She was home. The water was filled with eyes. They blinked and watched her.

"Come back here." Old man shook her, pulling her from the dreamy underwater landscape.

Something broke the surface of the cave lake. A splash. Old man recoiled and surveyed the ripples.

"This is their water", Girl said. "It is both men and the people under the water who have made these signs. "Do you want me to tell you what they say?"

"Yes, yes." Old man brandished the knife. "But I warn you. This is your last chance. If you trick me or talk anymore about waves or sleeping gods I will kill you."

"I am warning you, Old man. These are the forbidden words. The ones that got me banished from my village."

"Say them!" He cut her again, this time on her side. The blade was cold. Blood gushed onto her thighs. "Say them, or the next strike will kill you."

She gasped for air. Blood was rushing through her fingers. Again, something splashed in the lake. Beneath the surface things moved and shimmered. Maybe it was scales. Or eyes.

Girl pressed her bloody hand against the carved signs. Her legs shaking, blood gushing from open wounds with every heartbeat.

"Fhtagn!" Her voice a hoarse shriek, the word coming from beyond herself.

Old man stepped away from her. His eyes widened with fear. "You speak like the horned ones."

Girl turned towards him. There was no stopping the words now. They were everything. They were the truth.

"Ph'nglui mglw'nafh Cthulhu R'lyeh wgah'nagl fhtagn". The words clawed her throat, shook her body.

The paintings stirred and crawled like maggots. Light shone through cracks in the rock wall. Old man rushed towards her, jabbing the knife at her face. It barely missed.

"You are nothing!" Girl screamed and backed away. "You are food. You have no destiny. The signs speak of the great wave and the dreaming god!"

She fell to her knees by the water, the rocks cut into her skin. The salt waves burned her wounds, the lake was connected to the great water beyond the land. The signs and moss glowed around her, the world swirled. Blood gushed over her hands, over wet rock and down into the water.

"Iä", she cried. "Iä, Iä."

The surface boiled. Dark water crashed against the rocks even though there was no wind in the cave room. The old man limped behind her. Knife dripping with her blood. Under the disturbed surface, things were moving quickly up to the surface.

"What have you done?"

"The darkness is always hungry", her voice was deeper, older. "The darkness needs blood."

The water crashed against her feet. Waves that promised to pull her out and under the surface. To hold her. She gasped at the icy touch.

"Make it stop!" Old man had dropped the knife, clumsily backing away from the rising water.

"This is the first wave. The king is stirring in the bottom of the sea." The water was now up to her knees. Something slithered past her feet, as cold as the water. "This wave will only take you. The next wave will bring the awakened king, and then he will take everything."

The water frothed from waves and the movement of myriads of creatures in it. She could feel them around her legs. Snakelike they rushed toward the old man. He screamed and tried to flee. They overtook him. Wrapped spiky arms around him. Pulled him under. When he emerged, blood was shooting from his throat, eyes bulging out of his face. Their eyes met a last time before he was dragged under.

The water rose. She was under it. It was just like her dreams. It was home. Under the water she could hear him much clearer. There would come a time again when the king would rise and the world would revel in chaos in destruction. She smiled, water flowing into her mouth and nostrils, burning her insides. The king's servants were around her, trashing in the water. Wet and cold webbed fingers gripped her ankle and pulled her upwards not into the depths where she wanted to go.

She closed her eyes. All was dark.

Girl shivered. She was lying in the opening of the cave. The mist was like a wall, blotting out the stars, making the world grey and damp. The cave had flooded, dark salt water replaced the rough stone floor where she had slept earlier. The lower tunnels and the symbols were now under the water where they belonged. Longingly she looked at the smooth, black surface.

A wailing stopped her from jumping in, followed by the beat of a drum and a shriek in the night.

She could not see more than a couple of steps further. Drums in the dark. Shapes formed in the mist. Girl shivered, collapsing down on one knee. There were at least seven or eight shapes that appeared out of the mist. They were tall and clad in fur. Their bodies were covered in dark red paint and white scars. The thoughts and voices of the old ones were on their bodies, just as they had been on the cave walls. Skulls hid their faces and antlers stretched out from their heads. A woman strode forward. A great white slash had paled across her chest, the old wound must have been nearly fatal.

"You are the horned ones. The forbidden." Girl fell backwards, trying to stay awake.

The woman knelt. Knives and bone clicking when she moved. The whites of her eyes shone through the eye sockets of the animal skull on her face. Her hands followed Girl's body. Caressing and squeezing. Girl whimpered when the fingers firmly pressed on her cuts and wounds.

"She is bruised, cut and cold, but she will live. She is strong." The woman smiled, teeth shining in the otherwise red-painted face.

One of the antlered ones shrieked out loud in approval. Drums started beating to the eerie tunes of a bone flute.

"We have waited for you. Someone who can hear the old one."

"The old man is dead." Girl coughed. "I killed him."

"Not that bag of bones. He was nothing, a mere bite for the darkness." The woman leaned deeper over Girl. "I am talking of the great dreamer. The eternal king under the waves."

"You can hear him?"

The woman nodded. The bones in her hair rattled. "We have his thoughts and voices carved into our bodies."

She placed her hand on Girl's forehead and then on

her stomach. "Now they will be painted and carved into your skin."

The woman took a knife from her belt. Girl had never seen such a knife, it was slender and sharp. Not made of stone but something else, something old and cold. "One must bleed and scream when one is born."

Girl screamed. The knife wrote stories in her skin. It was not finished until the night had fled and the sky was turning red. One by one the antlered ones touched the bloody signs on her, tasting them from their fingertips.

"We now share what you have seen."

The skull was small, maybe from a young wolf. The woman placed it on Girl's face, tying it to place with dried and twined sinews. Then she pressed her forehead toward Girl's, the bone rattling as it touched.

"You now walk in the night and the mist. You will put fear in the hearts of men. Little sister dreamer, that is your name."

The antlered ones shrieked and danced. She followed them into the mist. Droplets of water formed inside the skull and ran down her face. She looked back once at the dark pool in the cave entrance. The time would come. Soon everything would be under water.

# The False One

Lily Jasmine Bergh

When the squat, bat-headed idol washed up on the shore, Wrænna knew it meant trouble. Not only because the skill it had taken to carve the figure was far beyond the ability of their own craftsmen, but because it was found in the clenched hand of a false one.

A very dead false one.

It was Pip who brought the macabre news. The stripling came tearing into the settlement like a trampling herd of bison, his loincloth askew and dirty feet bloodied from dashing across rocks and ill-willed roots that had sought to inhibit his mad journey from the fishing cove on the other side of the bay to the sloping bank where their clan had settled for the summer. Pip's wild mane, which was ordinarily tied back in the fashion of men who'd passed the rite into adulthood, was unbound and back to looking like a thicket, and as he skidded to a halt before Ragnec, his heaving breath gusting out and preventing him from talking, it waved about his head like dandelion seeds. Ragnec, who had been in the middle of fashioning a promising slab of flint into an axe head, didn't bother to get up. Instead, he threw a disinterested glance over his shoulder before going back to testing the axe's edge with his thumb. "Speak, boy.'

'Dead…' Pip gasped, even as he bent over his knees to cough. 'Pa… fishing… caught….'

In a movement that Wren thought would end in a punch to the boy's guts, Ragnec's fist swung through the air and delivered a series of heavy thumps onto Pip's skeletal back. 'Fetch the boy some water,' he barked to no one in particular, pulling the boy down onto the log where he had been seated. One of the many mucky children that milled about the camp appeared with a water skin, and Pip drank heavily, wheezed some more, and then stared up at Ragnec with big, frightened eyes.

'Pa and I went out this morn,' he said, 'in the canoe. We put out a… a net — If you remember, Ragnec, the method Pa invented for weaving strands together - to see if it would get us more fish—'

Ragnec made an impatient gesture: They were all familiar with Ekil's inventions. Most of them failed. 'Get to the point, boy.'

'We caught fish, all right,' Pip said, his tone suddenly mellow. 'But that's not all we caught. There was…' He swallowed heavily and seemed to struggle against something in his throat. 'There was a… a dead person in it. Caught in the net.' He glanced up at Ragnec, the fear back in his eyes. 'It was one of them, Ragnec. It was all bloated and swollen, but it was one of them.'

The moment the word passed the boy's lips, an eerie stillness settled over the camp. Eyes that had previously been focused on Pip now swung

in fearful anticipation towards Ragnec's tense form. All sounds — from the excited babbling of the children who'd been tossing old bones into a fissure in the cave wall, to the soft humming of Ystra as she scraped flesh and fat from hides destined to become new wraps — disappeared. Even Wren, whose feelings towards the false ones edged towards fear rather than Ragnec's deep-borne hatred, shuddered. She had no warmth over for the creatures, and would happily have seen them all reduced to a Sabre-toothed cat's supper. But unlike most of the other members of the clan, she saw the swarthy humans, humans that were so much like themselves and yet so different, not as a threat that could be eliminated with longer spears and sharper blades, but as something much more sinister.

For what seemed an eternity, Ragnec did not speak. He just stared at Pip, and then westward, in the direction Pip had come. 'What did you do with it?'

Pip wetted his lips. 'I… Pa thought it best to bring it ashore. So, it doesn't foul the water. He… He's waiting for your orders, Ragnec.'

Ragnec stroked his beard, pulling his fingers through the thick, wiry mass of hairs in a gesture Wren had learned meant that he was thinking. Ragnec was not a great thinker. 'Run back to your pa, and bring a pair of men with you,' he said. 'Let's see the damned creature.'

Pip's eyes widened, but he shot to his feet, nonetheless. He pulled his wrap, which had twisted during the run so it covered his thigh rather than his loins, straight, took another gulp of water, and set off back down the path he'd come. A sign from Ragnec set two other young men on Pip's trail. Wren watched the scene play out quietly. Still, Ragnec seemed to feel her disapproval, for he turned and settled a bright eye on her.

'Got something on your mind, Wrænna souldrinker?'

Wren flinched. He spoke her name like a curse. Her fingers tightened around the pestle she'd been using to grind up medicinal plants, and for a moment, she prayed that a swarm of false ones would come running into the settlement and cut Ragnec into pieces. As if sharing her sentiment, a soft wind sighed through the trees. But nothing appeared by the treeline to eat Ragnec, so Wren bit her tongue and stood, meeting Ragnec's stare.

'It is an ill omen, Ragnec,' she said quietly, her tone measured. 'Surely you see that? To bring the body of a false one here… It will anger the great mother.'

For a moment, Ragnec appeared to consider her advice. But then his eyes hardened and he sneered at her. 'I was *chosen* by the great mother to be the leader of this clan. *Me.* Nothing is an ill omen unless I say so. 'He eyed the greenish paste in her mortar with something akin to disgust. 'Go back to crushing your plants, Souldrinker. It is, I believe, what you excel at.'

As he turned his back to her and walked away, Wren felt a quiet sense of despair. In Ragnec's mind, the false ones were simply an enemy clan that could be beaten into submission by physical means. In the same ruthless way that Ragnec had made sure to drive away the clan that had populated this sandy shore before them, he thought the false ones could be driven out of what little viable land remained, too — and no amount of reasoning would convince him otherwise.

By the time Pip and his father returned, the sun had begun to set. Its blood-red descent into the underground bathed the camp and the men transporting the false one in shimmering light. It danced off the men's dusty skin and threw strange shadows that writhed across the sand. Was there not a lifelike quality to those shadows, and a song in the wind that rustled the leaves? Wren thought so: But of the twenty or so clan members, she was the only one who paid it any mind. The others' attention was fixed in morbid fascination on the swollen thing the men carried between them. As the stretched skin on which the body had been carried was laid down before Ragnec's feet, they were all given their first close look at one of the creatures which had been plaguing them for so long.

The false one looked very manlike in its stillness. Its body was decorated with strange markings that looked freshly painted, despite the days the false one must have spent in the water. Its hair, or whatever remained of it, was dark, and the one remaining eye that stared emptily into the sky was the brown of a cave bear's summer fur. Its elongated limbs, and the gills on its neck, reminded of the great lizards that spent sunny days basking on the rocks that flanked the main path to their camp. It was entirely different from the heavy build of Ragnec's clansmen, and yet similar enough that if it hadn't been for its webbed digits, the Deep One could have easily passed for one of them. Its face was frozen in a mask of pain and clutched in its hand, was…

Ragnec grasped the dead man's fingers and peeled

them away from the object, one by one. Even in death, the corpse seemed to resist him. Finally, Ragnec lost his temper, and in one vicious move, he clasped the swollen digits and cracked them, bending them back until they lay flattened against the top side of its arm. The corpse, even though it was impossible, seemed to shudder and emit a quiet scream as whatever it had been gripping tumbled to the ground.

Wren held her breath as Ragnec picked up a roundish figure from the sand to examine it. At first, she thought it might be something carved from bone, but if it was, it was bone from an animal she had never seen before. There was no yellow tint to the material, nor did it sport any cracks or pores. Its smooth surface gleamed dully in the waning light. What sort of spirit the idol was meant to represent, Wren could not tell; While it was carved with such skill as to seem almost lifelike, the bonelike material had been crafted into a squat, ugly creature, with heavy-lidded eyes and a sloppily gaping maw that reminded her more than anything of a bloated toad.

Ragnec weighed the thing in his hand for so long that the clansmen around him started shifting. Then, as if he had suddenly come to a decision, an ugly grin spread across his face, and he looked up at Wren with a cold, cruel smile that chilled her to the bone. His fingers closed about the idol, and he walked, no, sauntered, over to her.

'Wren here has a soft spot for these foul creatures,' he said, loudly enough for the entire camp to hear. 'She speaks, again and again, of shadows and ill omens, and of how our clan would be better served to leave the false ones alone. To LET THEM drive us out of our homes. To LET THEM steal away our children and murder our women in the night. Earlier today, she even opposed bringing this false one into the camp. Tell me, Wren —'he stepped closer to her, too close, forcing her to meet his gaze — 'Did you hope to give this foul creature the blessing of the great mother? Do you think these *creatures* are deserving of a proper burial, as befits our own people? Are you, perhaps…' His voice grew low, dangerously so, '— one of them, yourself ?'

In the corner of her eye, Wren thought something dark slithered across the ground. It felt like something was growing, expanding, waiting; She could not explain it, and she got the terrible feeling that whatever the false one's body had brought with it, it was about to devour them all. 'How can you even ask me that, Ragnec?' She said quietly. 'I am a woman of this clan, and I have never been anything but dutiful. But the great mother—'

He did not allow her to finish. So quick that she did not see it coming, he lifted his hand and struck her across the face. The impact jarred her teeth, and she blinked against the flecks of light that suddenly danced before her eyes. The next moment, she felt something heavy settle about her neck, and she realised with a sinking heart that Ragnec had placed that ugly, beautiful, whispering idol around her neck.

'You love the false ones more than your own people, my dear Wren. So, you might as well carry their false mother about your neck.'

The others in the clan stared with hard eyes at her, and Wren felt the breath go out of her. She did not understand, not one bit.

As the sun's last rays disappeared behind the trees, Ragnec made a show of having the other members of the clan desecrate the body. Wren watched in uneasy silence as they sliced, ripped, and tore at the bloated thing, tossing bits and pieces of bones and spoiled meat to the wolflike creatures that milled about the settlement until there was nothing left but the heart. To the sound of yapping animals, Ragnec lifted the putrid mess of a heart towards the sky, roaring out his victory before surrendering it with an aggressive flourish to the flames.

Wren did not know how much time had passed when it happened. The clan had celebrated the death of the false one until the darkness was so deep that not even the fire did much to penetrate it. Most of the people had simply laid down where they'd been standing: Ragnec sat, half awake and half slumbering, leaning against a boulder. Wren had crawled up on a discarded pelt a good distance away from him and had spent the night listening to whatever it was that moved in the shadows. She could not say what it was, but *something* — something unfamiliar that was not part of the great mother — was watching them.

She was so intent on listening to the wind rustling in the trees, the sudden snap of a branch as some wild animal skirted the perimeter of the settlement, and the heavy breathing of her clansmen, that she did not see it at first. Her eyes stared, unseeing, at the bright heat of the fire, not noticing how one of the blackened bones seemed to suddenly stretch and move. Its narrow shape widened, and from its splintered ends something poured forth, a slithering, unshapely mass that grew and grew until it was the size of a small boulder. The fire hissed as the creature stretched out in it, dousing the flames with its body, and as the last flame sputtered and went out, Wren came back to herself, only to see its dark, toadlike eyes settle on Ragnec's form.

Wren screamed, a shrill, panicked cry that tore across the bank and sent the birds flapping from the trees. In the darkness around her, people moved, but Wren only had eyes for Ragnec. Her scream had brought him awake, and he was staring at her, sleep giving way to anger, and he was getting up, and then he turned his head towards where the fire had been. It was too dark for Wren to see precisely what happened. All she saw was the gleam of Ragnec's eyes, and then a dark mass crashing over him like waves crashing against the shore. The mass, or creature, whatever it was, slithered away from where Ragnec had been only seconds before, and Wren stared in mute horror at the empty patch of sand. There was not a trace of him - Only a puddle of foul-smelling liquid. The thing slithered through the dark, rising and lowering itself, again and again, silencing the terrified shouts of the other clan members.

Wren should have run; She should have sprung to her feet and dashed off like Pip. But her legs refused to obey her, the ugly idol burned against her chest, and then it was too late, the creature was languidly slithering towards her, and she looked up, up as it rose in the darkness, blotting out the stars and the trees and everything else she held dear, and she closed her eyes, praying that it would not hurt.

Something flickered against her cheek. A soft, wet touch, so painful it burned her to the core, and yet the most comforting caress she had ever known. A small, frightened squeak forced its way out of her throat. And then something closed about the idol around her neck.

Wren opened her eyes.

A lithe, fine-boned face with eyes the colour of spring leaves stared back at her. Dark hair tumbled wildly over broad shoulders, framing a swirling pattern of markings Wren knew she had seen before. As her eyes widened in recognition, the lips on the face before her stretched into a feline grin, and the creature's fingers wrapped more tightly around the toad-faced idol resting against her chest.

'Well, well, well,' it said, and she knew that voice, the sinister, wet darkness lurking in the wind all day — the voice that had once belonged to a man her brethren had burned.

# Blessing Time

E.W Farnsworth

Cynwyd was on a once-in-a-lifetime mission—to inter the body of his mother Cynna in her final resting place in the family's dolmen shrine at the place overlooking the Infinite Sea where menhirs rise in rows and Children of Dagon orchestrate the end of the world. The dutiful son was making his way along the Great River that runs through the middle of Doggerland, passing from village to village as the people lined his path to pay honour to the memory of the supremely intelligent and kindly woman whose tireless labours had brought peace to the once warring tribes.

Cynwyd was not alone. His brothers and sisters,

uncles and aunts, cousins and all their husbands, wives and children followed their kinsman and leader through the thickly settled and game-rich valley. Only the grandparents of Cynwyd and of his fair wife Gwenedd remained behind to care for the clan's young children and infants while the majority were away on pilgrimage. The wandering mass of ten-thousand-odd kinfolks put a strain on the general population whose villages they passed through, but no single force was great enough to challenge their passage except for the rebels of a so-called village alliance. Besides, Cynwyd's avowed purpose was not to wage war or wreak havoc but to sanctify the interval called the blessing time, when the peaceful passage of power from one generation to the next is hallowed in a formal rite.

As a precaution against violence, Cynwyd and Gwenedd had prepared an arsenal of clubs, stone hammers, flint knives and bows with plenty of arrows. Each person, male and female, was equipped and drilled with everything needed to defend against an army of equivalent size. This readiness had been counselled by Cynna, and it was one of the reasons peace had come to Doggerland and remained there for a generation.

This night, campfires were kindled in a line of six adjacent village squares, and fresh deer and boar were split and roasted and then shared amongst all. The staple fare of the wanderers was dried meats and fish, seeds, nuts and berries bound with honey, and the newly harvested game they shared while on this march was a tasty luxury. As Cynwyd, Gwenedd and their kinfolks presided over their nocturnal feast, their spies were expected to arrive to advise what they would encounter in the days ahead. All night, a rotating guard of honour, composed of giants, watched over the body of Cynwyd's mother as everyone else either revelled or slept.

From the time when night fell, Cynwyd's wanderers had sung, recited poetry, danced or, wearing frightening masks, acted out myths and ancestral stories by firelight. Among the masked figures was Cthulhu, with his waving tentacles. Alongside the fearsome octopus god appeared menacing demons and powerful spirits representing the sun, the moon and the sea. The tallest and most potent of the actors among them filled these sacred roles as they brandished stout clubs and huge stone hammers. Deep in the nearby forests of stony pine, tall pine and oak, hundreds of red eyes of rabbits and foxes observed the shadows of the festivities.

"Tomorrow you will face the challengers. Naturally, I am afraid for you," said Gwenedd.

"Fear not, good wife. In a vision, I have foreseen what transpires each day of our journey till I meet Cthulhu face-to-face by the Infinite Sea. Only beyond that day can I *not* see the future clearly."

"You take such awful risks, husband."

"Taking great risks is the price of leadership of a family or a people, Gwenedd. I would lose our clan's respect if I did not stand forth to overcome challenges. Look into yourself and ask whether you would remain with a snivelling coward."

"Cynwyd, I shudder to think of it. Like you, I come from a long line of leaders. Courage has been a way of life for us all, but we have never been reckless. We have managed surprises well thus far. Tell me again what you have foreseen from this night forward."

He drew a deep breath wondering what he could divulge. "Tomorrow I face the challenge of mortal combat with the largest giant in Doggerland. Four days hence the whole clan must deal with warriors of the rebellious village alliance. Seven days after our final battle against the alliance, we shall arrive at the menhir garden by the Infinite Sea. There, I must go forth alone to meet Cthulhu."

"So far, you have been lucky. I shall stand by your side when I can. My thoughts will be with you when you must go alone. Tell me what you have foreseen of me—and us."

"We shall be together and happy till I visit Cthulhu. After that meeting, everything is likely to change, but I have no insight as to how things will differ from now. Why are you weeping?"

"The thought of losing you makes me sad. What if Cthulhu decides to take you to his dwelling under the Infinite Sea?"

"Let's enjoy our brief life together while we can. All humans must perish. The question is not whether we shall die but how can we die honourably."

"So, tell me how you plan to slay the giant tomorrow."

Glad to have his wife ask a practical question for which he had an answer. "I shall take the giant down from the bottom and crack his skull open while he struggles on the ground. Woe betides    any who care to support him after he falls."

She smiled at his plan and the certainty with which he had explained it.

The man and wife fell fast asleep until the darkest night before the first purple light when their spies came to tell them the giant challenger had arrived for combat and the village alliance was coming together as foreseen four days hence in a broad meadow full of flowers.

At dawn, Cynwyd bathed nude in the cold river for stimulation. He conducted his morning exercises before he tied back his hair and donned his bearskin. Gwenedd had by then laid his weapons on a deerskin near the centre of the place of combat in the village square.

The giant roared his challenge so there was no question why he had come.

"Cynwyd, hear me! I, Guordic the giant, challenge you to a single-combat battle to the death. I want you to know that when I have slain you, I shall spread your guts in the village gardens to make the plants grow. Speak your last words, if you have any. Be brief as I am anxious for glory, and my friends and companions are hungry." The giant bared his teeth and flexed his muscles, and his retinue growled and clapped in delight.

Cynwyd waited for a moment before he replied. Then in a booming voice, he said, "Guordic, whose name means *fat*, your obesity matches your name. As your group is hungry as well as rowdy, your corpse fat will be most nourishing whether they choose to eat you freshly slain or bled-out and aged. Select your weapons and step forward. Unless you desire long torture before your death, I shall make your last moments memorable for others but short for you."

The giant shrugged and selected two enormous hammers, so large he could barely wield the instruments. Though either weapon would have slain any man it hit, the two hammers were difficult to control, even for a giant. In contrast, Cynwyd selected a small hammer and a flint knife, well suited for agility and stealth. Guordic and his retinue howled with laughter at these meagre choices.

The village elder said, "Let the combat begin!"

Guordic swung his hammers together with a deafening sound. He then whirled the weapons on either side of his body in circular motions as he moved forwards rocking from side to side as he swung the hammers separately. Cynwyd stood perfectly still until the giant had advanced half the distance to his position. Then, as his opponent's left-hand hammer began to rise from its nadir, the hero rushed to that side of his opponent and slid across the grass, quickly breaking both the giant's ankles with his small hammer as he passed under the large whirling left hammer. The excruciating pain of those blows caused the massive man to lose balance and wobble, but he could do nothing about Cynwyd's flint knife cutting through the back of the tendons above both of his heels.

Like an enormous oak felled by a seasoned forester, the giant was toppled by crafty Cynwyd, never to rise again. Cynwyd did not hesitate a moment but used his small hammer to open Guordic's skull between his bulging eyes and plunged his knife into the bloody cavity. The village elder gestured that Cynwyd had won the challenge. He then cried out to the assemblage: "Anyone wishing to challenge Cynwyd may approach the square." But no one stepped forward as a challenger. Guordic's friends and companions claimed the body of their defeated champion and left the vicinity to catcalls and jibes.

Meanwhile, Cynwyd, Gwenedd and their people packed and continued their journey. Everyone talked about the intelligent strategy their hero had used to defeat the giant Guordic. Some likened Cynwyd to his father, Wynwyrd, but the wise knew his mother Cynna had trained him as a warrior. "This demonstration," said the wise, "was a sign that he had been destined to follow in her footsteps."

During the next three nights, Cynwyd's spies brought word of the host formed by the rebel village alliance. Guordic's followers out of spite had joined the rebels, who now numbered several thousand desperate men and women.

The opposing forces eventually became situated on either side of a vast meadow full of green grasses and flowers. The spokesman and spokeswoman for the alliance sought a conference before the battle. Cynwyd and Gwenedd agreed to meet them in neutral space between the assembled forces.

The spokesman for the village alliance, a fearsome veteran covered with scars from former fights, sized up Cynwyd and said, "I, Nydryd the fearless, have heard how you vanquished my friend Guordic the giant. The challenge before you now is far different from that of single combat with a dimwit braggart. Before we begin fighting, I want to give you the option of honourable withdrawal. The only other option under the circumstances is ignominious defeat followed by systematic slaughter, to the last living person."

Cynwyd nodded. He had heard bullies rant and rave on many occasions. Underneath their braggadocio was cowardice. So he answered the fool in the language he understood.

"Nydryd, your skin shows how many times you have fought during your martial life. Once this day has passed, your survivors will decide whether to preserve your pelt for posterity or to consign it with your dead body to the funereal flames. As you are well aware, there is no such thing as honourable retreat.    As for your vain boast to kill everyone in my army to the last survivor, I answer, let woe be the reward of the vanquished on either side."

Gwenedd, who held a bow and arrows in her left hand, stepped forward, pointing her right hand at the female warrior who was standing beside Nydryd. "I shall be coming for you, particularly, young blonde beauty, and I promise that your bodiless head will dance on a sharp stake before this sun sets."

The blonde stood to her full height and shook her

fist at Gwenedd saying, "My name is Ulyr, and I want you to know my children and grandchildren will play with the bones of your hands and feet. All the women who venture here with you shall be eviscerated by me and my sisters."

Cynwyd said, "Enough of taunts and imprecations! Go back to your companions to say farewell, and then prepare to die, for when we come together only one side will be victorious."

For a long while, the two armies shouted at each other and made false starts across the meadow. Finally, they rushed headlong at each other brandishing their weapons. Gwenedd and her female archers mowed down the front ranks of the alliance and kept up their hail of well-aimed arrows even after the combatants had clashed together. Cynwyd used his small hammer and his flint knife to kill the enemy combatants as he sought out Nydryd in the throng. The two faced off only for a moment before Cynwyd flung his knife into Nydryd's throat. The bloviating blowhard grabbed at the knife, but he only made his wound much worse. His arterial blood spouted everywhere, as he fell to his knees and then on his face.

Word spread fast through the rebel alliance that Nydryd their hero had been slain, and many immediately turned and fled from the meadow in terror. Gwenedd kept searching for Ulyr till one of her arrows found her opponent. When the young woman lay dead among her many fallen comrades, Cynwyd's mate pulled the flint knife from dead Nydryd's throat and used it to sever Ulyr's head from her body. She impaled the blonde head upon a sharp stake and raised it like a banner above the field.

Saying, "Thus always to traitors!" Gwenedd marched forward as the women warriors of the alliance broke ranks and stampeded from the field. Stopping to plant the head atop its stake on the battlefield, Gwenedd unleashed her remaining arrows into the backs of her retreating opponents.

Cynwyd ran up beside her with a handful of arrows he had just pulled from the bodies of her victims. Gwenedd signalled her archers to form on her position. When in formation, they moved toward the fleeing army, careful to make every arrow count as they advanced.

Meanwhile, Cynwyd rallied his male fighters and sent them to cover both flanks of the retreating masses. That way, the female archers had a clear distinction between their enemies in the middle and their male comrades closing from either side of them.

On occasion, groups of the alliance would swerve to counterattack their pursuers, but they were for the most part discouraged and battle weary. Unaccustomed to fighting as a coherent army and having lost their leaders anyway early in the battle, they fled confused and disorganised. Any who turned to attempt surrender met the fate of certain death, so they ran helter-skelter until they fell and succumbed to the arrows of Gwenedd and her archers or the clubs, stone hammers and flint knives of Cynwyd and his men.

Among the slain, the giants were notable as they were the most feared members of the rebel alliance. Gwenedd raised the heads of the females among the host on sharp stakes. Soon the meadow was full of grisly reminders of her promises to Ulyr.

In the late afternoon, Cynwyd put a halt to the chase and declared victory. He ordered his survivors to pile up the dead so they could be burned in the meadow by the local villagers before they putrefied. The fires that night were celebratory but not for the broken alliance. Of all Cynwyd's army, only fifteen of his kinsfolk, eight men and seven women had been slain. They were given honours and cremated at once. Their ashes were gathered to be buried with the remains of Cynna at Land's End.

Already memorial poems were recited and heroic songs were sung about individuals' exploits during the day-long battle. Cynwyd discussed the results of the combat with his wife.

"The day was ours, Gwenedd. You fulfilled your promise to that witch Ulyr."

"Ulyr and her fellow-harpies' heads will grace their stakes in the battlefield till the local villagers decide to bury them with their headless corpses. More to the point, your vision of an unquestioned victory was fulfilled."

"We shall grieve for our fallen relatives as we continue toward the Infinite Sea with their remains. Some of the fleeing rebels are likely to try to attack us, but they will not be successful if my vision holds true."

Cynwyd was too excited to sleep that night, so he cast his mind forward to pierce the veil of unknowing about Cthulhu. When his spies came to report in the early hours before dawn, they told of retreating rebels being caught by giant tentacles coming from the Great River.

"See Gwenedd! We are getting indications of Cthulhu's involvement even before we reach the Infinite Sea."

"The question is whether the wrath the god meted out to the rebels will apply to us as well."

Cynwyd tried to discover the answer to Gwenedd's question in his dream state before daylight, but he felt his normal clairvoyance was blocked in some way. In contrast, his visualisation of Cthulhu sharpened day by day. It was as if the monster god was communicating with his consciousness to convey a definite sense of a huge and horrifying, definitely *inhuman* physical appearance.

The pilgrimage continued that morning, and during that and each of the other six final days, the residual rebels did attack them occasionally, but without the force or finesse to harm or deter them. Even under torture to the death, captured rebels would not confess why they continued to fight. On the final day before their arrival at Land's End, four rebel giants attempted to overcome the four giants who guarded the corpse of Cynwyd's mother, but they were easily slain before they could accomplish their objective.

The ten-thousand-odd pilgrims camped at the foot of the sloping area that led to the lookout that was Land's End. Cynwyd saw that menhirs were spaced at intervals up the slope, and the family's dolmen was situated on the ledge at the pinnacle. There the four giants carried the body of his mother, which they helped him inter before retreating. Cynwyd remained standing before the family dolmen alone. He watched the gradual transition from red sunset to mauve dusk to pitch darkness. As Cthulhu had not yet appeared, he wondered whether he had chosen the correct day and hour for his meeting with the octopus god. His feelings of dread and doubt mingled with feelings of despondency and despair.

He need not have worried. Cthulhu's physical presence revealed itself in the darkness, a huge, hulking figure towering over the end-point of land while buoyed by its tentacles in the Infinite Sea. The creature's face seemed to be a veil of small tentacles partially hiding an enormous all-seeing eye and a beak. The abiding presence made no sound, but around it Cynwyd could clearly hear the incessantly pounding waves of the primaeval sea. His mother had told him the sea extended from this promontory forever to the west, and no one had ever sailed across that bounding main with its swelling, surging, billowing and breaking waves.

Cynwyd's communication from Cthulhu came not through his ears but from deep within the depths of his mind or perhaps of his soul. He smelled the salty air redolent of seaweed, iodine and an ocean spicery. He felt the cold spray of the surf as it crashed rhythmically against the rocky shore. Cynwyd froze as Cthulhu caressed his cheeks with its largest tentacle as if the god were trying to wipe the funereal tears perpetually from his eyes.

"Cynwyd, you have brought your mother Cynna to me as she said you would. I can sense her satisfaction at being laid to rest next to her husband Wynwyrd in your family dolmen. For your faithfulness in service to her and to me, I grant you the same protection I extended to her, together with her second sight and luck. If ever you should need me, just invoke my name, and I shall be there to help you. Now, wait right where you stand as I fill your mind with the distant future."

Cynwyd stood there a long time after receiving Cthulhu's promise and sensed the future knowledge infusing his mind. He saw Doggerland sinking deep into the earth and the waters from the Infinite Sea subsequently breaking into the void where the Great River once flowed.

He was then vaguely aware that the old one, who was no longer alone, was retreating with his companions into the Infinite Sea and sinking below the waves.

Exhausted from his encounter, he walked back down the row of menhirs to the place where his wife Gwenedd awaited him. He did not speak to her, and out of respect, she did not interrupt his reverie. Instead, he gently took her hand and led her to their camp where the four giants guarded them through the night.

For the next two weeks, Cynwyd's pilgrims celebrated the coming of Cthulhu to their leader. They understood the significance of this meeting as Cynna had foretold it on numerous occasions throughout her life. They feasted on shellfish of all varieties sprinkled with lemon juice from the fruit of the lemon trees in the vicinity, but they did not partake of octopus or squid in deference to Cthulhu.

Poets could now complete the poems they had started anticipating the moment of Cynna's interment. Cynna was now in her final resting place in the family's dolmen shrine at the place overlooking the Infinite Sea where menhirs rise in rows and Cthulhu orchestrates the end of the world. The dutiful son had made his way along the Great River that runs through the middle of Doggerland, passing from village to village as the people lined his path to pay honour to the memory of the supremely intelligent and kindly woman Cynna, whose tireless labours had brought peace to the once warring tribes.

Now Cynwyd had proven his worth to succeed his mother as the ruler of their clan for the remainder of his life. He had vanquished the giant Guordic in single combat. Then with his wife and family, he had defeated the village alliance. Finally, he had faced Cthulhu alive and received the gift of clairvoyance from the god. It was now time to lead his people back to the place they had come from to reunite with the grandparents, the children and the infants. As he retraced the path, he memorised the features of the landscape so he could tell his successor what must be done when the time came for the next generation to take control. Gwenedd also harboured thoughts of the next transition for he had told her they would live together happily all their time and both die within the space of a single day.

# The Final Betrayal

Simon Bleaken

We pushed through the tall grasses of the plain, our ears alert and hearts racing. We were close enough to taste the taint of blood in the air. As the dense grasses parted before us, we peered out upon a flat expanse of bare rock, rising a few feet above the surrounding vegetation. A flock of birds burst into the pale afternoon sky in a wild flurry of wings and raucous shrieking. We ducked down, momentarily startled, before edging forwards.

Our missing people were there, right where our shaman, Bloodclaw, had said they would be. They were each bound to tall posts, their naked bodies bruised and bloodstained. Their empty eye sockets were frozen towards the sky, faces ravaged by the birds. Their bellies had been sliced open and hollowed out, their genitals removed and their limbs snapped and twisted at unnatural angles.

At first, we could do nothing but stare.

We knew little about the people that had done this. We had heard their voices in the night chanting to whatever unknown gods or spirits they worshipped, and glimpsed their forms silhouetted against the roaring flames of their camp as they danced in wild reverie to the pounding of drums. We had heard the screams too, the last lingering echoes of previous victims crying out into the night.

They were a tribe unknown to us, and we had been keen to avoid them. They outnumbered us and were clearly hostile, and while some among us were anxious to avenge our fallen kin, we knew we were no match for them and their strange sorceries.

We were new to this land, exiled from our old territories and forced to migrate further North by the arrival of another band of newcomers, a degenerate cult unknown to us but easily identified by the antlered headdresses they wore. Now, we are working hard to establish a new settlement. However, it seemed in trying to evade one barbarous group, we had stumbled straight into another equally as dangerous.

The five of us had avoided the cull by pure chance, having been in a hunting party when the strangers attacked. They swept through our settlement, and had our shaman not managed to escape with a handful of survivors, our whole tribe might have been wiped out.

I turned from the desecrated remains and looked at the horrified faces of the members of my group: Stone, Bird, Sky and Reed. They had all been afraid, but resolute in trying to get our people back. But now, faced with this grisly massacre and the awful truth that there was nobody to save, their resolve was breaking apart like lake-ice in the spring thaw.

"We should go," Reed whispered, gripping his flint-tipped spear hard enough to make his knuckles go white. His thin face was etched with alarm. He was the youngest among us, having only just undergone the rite of adulthood. "If they find us, they'll kill us."

Stone flashed him an enraged glance. "You'd leave our people like that?"

His words struck a chord within us all, a stark reminder that these mutilated remains were friends and family. It was our duty to ensure they got a proper burial so they could journey on into the next world.

"No," Reed added sheepishly, "but someone should be protecting the survivors."

"They aren't the ones who need help right now," I said. I understood his concerns but knew our surviving people were in good hands. They were being watched over by the two people I trusted most: Bloodclaw, one of the wisest men I knew, blessed with the wisdom of the ancestors and the guidance of our gods, and Star, my mate, who was proud and fierce, every bit the warrior I was. I knew she would do whatever it took to save our people.

We clambered up onto the low ridge of rock, cautiously checking for any signs of the strangers. There were none, nor did we see any traces of a camp, but the heart of that small plateau was scarred and blackened by countless fires that had burned there. The ashes and charred remnants were still warm from the night before. Around each of the wooden poles holding our slain kinsmen, deep whorls had been carved into the rock floor, each now filled with spirals of congealed blood, as if in offering to something.

We were just cutting the first of the bodies down and debating the best means of returning them for burial, when Reed, whom we had tasked with keeping watch, discovered an opening at the far end of the plateau. We gathered around and peered inside, and I shuddered at the nauseating stench emanating from it; a sickly-sweet smell of rot and decay, of death. The aperture was large enough for two men at a time to fit inside and led, so far as we could see, into a sharply angled passageway that snaked steeply downwards.

"Do they live down there?" Bird shot me a questioning glance. "Like animals?"

"We could seal this up," I mused. "Trap them down there."

"What if they're not in there?" Bird added a note of caution. "We should see where it goes first."

"No!" Reed protested. "They outnumber us. This could be a trap."

"This could be our only chance to stop further attacks," Sky answered.

"Bird is right," I sighed. "We need to be sure they're down there, and that there's no other way out."

"So, we go in then?" Sky grinned eagerly. He was an old warrior and was keen to teach the strangers a lesson, desperate to let his spear pierce their flesh and taste blood. I could see it in his eyes, but I also knew the danger his desire for vengeance posed. It bred recklessness, and we couldn't afford any mistakes.

"We must be quiet," I reminded them.

The air felt noticeably warmer as we stepped into the shadows of that opening. I think on some level we all knew this was wrong. It was hard going too, our spears proved an obstacle in such tight confines, and we had to take care to avoid scraping them on the walls, or getting them caught. It was clear that if we were forced to fight in these passageways we would struggle.

In mere moments the outside world was replaced by thick walls of claustrophobic rock, the heavy beating of hearts, the soft shuffle of feet on stone, and the scraping of spears despite our best efforts.

The air was foul with the stench of decay, and the tunnel pressed in alarmingly as if we were descending into the gullet of some great stone monster. Above us, the ceiling was blackened from the passage of torches, and the walls were lined at intervals with strange shapes that only became apparent as we drew closer to them. At the sight of the rotting bodies lining the walls, Reed screamed and bolted back up the passageway, his spear clattering as he abandoned it. Bird made to go after him, but I put a hand on his shoulder, shaking my head.

"Let him go."

"What people would do *this*?" Stone muttered, examining the corpses.

There were dozens of them. Some were obviously far older than the others, now little more than skeletal remains clad in rotting animal skins. The most recent remains were more shocking, their ravaged faces and eyeless sockets oozing maggots and crawling with insects, their broken limbs twisted at their sides and their hollow chests mirroring the brutal disembowelment of our people. It was clear that we weren't the first to suffer at the hands of this barbaric tribe.

"All the more reason to end these bastards," Sky glowered.

With each step, the air from below grew more humid. The further down we went, the less light reached us from the increasingly distant opening. Soon pervasive twilight became utter blackness, and still, the passageway showed no sign of ending. Finally, just when I was about to suggest abandoning this descent, from some far-off point ahead we caught the faint flicker of firelight. We hurried as silently as we could towards it, and all felt a sense of relief when the tunnel opened out into a subterranean chamber.

The space was large and echoing. At intervals, torches burned, but for the most part, the walls were lit by the pale greenish-yellow glow of faintly luminous lichens that thrived in the humid depths. By their sickly pale light, we saw dozens of other openings in the walls and realised that a twisting warren of tunnels and caverns led off from this one.

Despite the humidity down here, it was now clear the tunnel we had descended was not the only source of ventilation or access, robbing us of any hope of sealing this place up. We should have retreated then, collected our dead and moved on. But curiosity proved too much and we crept further in.

This next chamber was far larger than the last. More bodies lined the walls here, though they were little more than skeletons clad in tatters of rotting cloth. Small niches set higher up within the walls held long rows of skulls. It was impossible to judge how old these might have been, but the sheer number of them was shocking. Some were twisted and split as if they had burst open from inside. The sight of them filled us all with renewed unease, but the real shock came when we turned to examine the walls behind us and realised a dark hulking shape loomed over us.

In the gloom it was difficult to get a sense of the actual outline or proportions of the thing, it seemed to shift and change in the dim light, but overall it was rounded and squat, with a bulbous belly and half-closed heavy-lidded eyes, like some nightmarish conglomeration of bat and toad.

When, after a few tense seconds, the thing hadn't moved, Sky bravely edged closer.

"It's a statue," he whispered.

"Are you sure?" Bird asked.

The glistening surface, beaded with moisture dripping from the cave roof, looked alarmingly like furry flesh. It was only Sky, cautiously prodding the surface with a spear and then a finger, who finally confirmed that the thing was not some sleeping monstrosity. As we drew closer, we saw blood had been smeared across the front of the statue, and congealing viscera was piled in a deep bowl before it, clearing an offering to the thing.

"What is it?" I asked.

Sky spat on the ground before it. "Must be one of their gods."

Something skittered in the darkness overhead. We looked up to see a vague shadow, black even against the gloom, scuttle across the ceiling. It moved fast, and although we couldn't see what it was exactly, the way it moved and clung to the rock ceiling was unlike anything I had seen before. Several of the men cried out at the sight of it.

"Keep it down!" Bird hissed, but even he was shaken.

We held our breath for what felt like an eternity, partly out of fear that the thing might double back for us, but also from a slowly growing dread that we had already made too much noise and had likely alerted whatever else might be down here to our presence.

But when it didn't return, and when there were no new sounds from the darkness, we all let out a collective sigh.

"That thing went into the chamber we came from,"

Sky whispered.

"Then we should find another way out," Bird suggested.

"If we start wandering," Stone hissed, "we'll get lost, or run into something even worse."

Bird eyed the tunnel entrance. "I'd rather take that risk."

"You'll get us killed!" Stone protested.

"Not if we're *quiet*," I said, urging both of them to lower their voices. I had concerns about just how well sound might travel down here. Some part of me wondered whether hidden eyes were already watching us. I pushed my fears aside and examined the three other passages leading off from here. "The air seems fresher here," I gestured at the left passage with my spear.

"This whole place stinks," Stone scowled. "All I smell is mould and shit."

"Stay here then," Sky laughed, "you'll blend right in."

"This way," I took the lead without looking back. I knew Stone would follow the rest of us without question, even if only to avoid being left alone down here.

The tunnel twisted and then descended, plunging us deeper into the stone heart of that place, and I wondered just how far beneath the ground it went. Then we emerged into another chamber and our eyes widened.

It was like stepping into another world. The space before us was vast, opening out beneath a natural vaulted ceiling. In places, fissures within the roof allowed bright shafts of daylight to spear through the darkness. The humidity was stifling and robbed the breath from our lungs, the climate shockingly different from the surface as if some malign sorcery were at work here. Pale mushrooms of colossal size stretched into a forest that towered over us, along with more slender fungal stalks terminating in leprous yellow globes, pale sticky finger-like growths or red spikes studded with spores. Long strands of mossy vegetation hung from the rocks in dense veils and pallid ferns reached out masses of thick fronds. The floor underfoot was cushioned by mulch, moisture dripped from high above, and an earthy scent filled the air.

Rising over everything was an even larger statue of that same bloated bat-toad monstrosity we had seen earlier, sleepy eyes half-open and a long twisting tongue jutting from the corner of its wide mouth. How such a thing had been created, and when, I couldn't begin to guess, but a fresh surge of uneasy dread washed over us. The worst part was the way the light played over the surface, giving an unsettling illusion of movement. The heavy-lidded eyes appeared to flicker for a moment and the wide mouth seemed to twitch.

We pushed our way past the greasy, dripping trunks of the pallid fungal growths, alert for any signs of movement. None of us had forgotten that we were deep in the territory of that other tribe. Nor had we forgotten the strange creature that had slithered over the rocks in the preceding chamber.

All of us felt watched. So far this place had been too empty – too unguarded – for my liking. That sense of being observed grew stronger as we made our way through the dense jungle. We would have turned back, *should* have turned back, had it not been for Stone's continued insistence that he could feel a fresh breeze coming from somewhere up ahead. He was the best tracker in our tribe, and his skills had proved invaluable in the past.

When the base of another statue came into view it was Stone who first noticed the ancient skeletal remains arranged in small alcoves around the edges. I might have ignored them, thinking them at first to be simply more of the victims of this terrible place. But it was Stone's sharp eyes who spotted the patches of brittle umber fur still clinging to the bones, the sharp talons on the hands, and the curious three-toed feet that marked these remains as something other than human.

"What are they?" Stone shot me a worried glance. "Were these men?"

"Does it matter?" Bird hissed before I could reply. "It's just more proof that we don't belong down h–"

That was as far as he got before an arrow embedded itself in his shoulder.

Glancing up, I saw the other tribe standing over us on narrow ledges, more of them emerging from openings in the rock walls all around us, springing the trap I had feared all along.

"Move!" I screamed, urging my people back into the cover of the fungal forest. I paused only to help Bird to his feet. He was struggling to draw the arrow from his flesh. I dragged him into cover, arrows raining down around us.

We retreated blindly through the trunks, tripping and stumbling, pushing aside the pale fronds in a desperate panic. The arrows continued to fly at our backs. We heard them impacting against the canopy overhead, one or two making their way through to pierce the ground behind us.

I sensed a new threat when the arrows suddenly stopped. Glancing around I caught sight of someone moving through the trunks behind us and felt the sting of a dart in the side of my neck. I staggered, my legs turning to jelly, trying to keep my momentum going, trying to keep myself upright. But my vision was blurring and a hot acrid taste filled my mouth.

I tried to call out, the world spinning around me, but saw only the ground rising to meet my face.

* * *

I awoke to the deep pounding of drums, the roaring crackle of flames and the wild shrieks of frenzied celebration. The stench of burning flesh was in the air amid the smoke, and as my throbbing head processed the sounds now assaulting it, my eyes came back into focus.

Bird and I were bound to tall pillars of stone in a chamber we had not seen before. Here, the bare stone floor had been swept clean of any vegetation. To our right was another towering idol of that infernal-bloated god, and at its feet were more of the strange three-toed skeletons in shallow alcoves. Ahead of us lay a short processional avenue of thin standing stones, each stained with some kind of tarry residue. Beyond them, the floor rose upwards in a series of low shallow steps to a central point where a large fire blazed. Some of the dancing bodies silhouetted against that fire were odd, their limbs appeared strangely boneless as they twisted and moved to the pounding drums and the howled, frenzied chanting.

A primal terror seized me.

"You're... awake?" Bird rasped. I strained against my restraints to see his bloodied face peering at me. His nose was broken and one of his eyes was bruised and almost puffed shut. The remains of the arrow still jutted from his shoulder.

"What happened?" I croaked.

"We put up a good fight, but they surrounded us." He nodded to one side. "Stone and Sky weren't so lucky..."

I followed his gaze to two heavy granite slabs that lay nearby. Stone and Sky were upon them, naked. They too had been savagely disembowelled; their rib cages snapped open and the remains of their entrails congealing around them, while their empty eye sockets stared blindly up at the fire and the wild revellers cavorting around it.

I turned my head away.

"They'll come for us soon," Bird whispered.

"Do you want to die here?" I hissed angrily. "These people have taken enough from us."

"What more can we do?" Bird fixed me with a look of terrified defeat. I realised I had never seen him looking so broken before.

I didn't answer. I didn't know what to say, I only knew I wasn't about to let them gut me as an offering to whatever depraved god they worshipped. I pushed my fears back with raw anger. I fought against my bonds, twisting and straining against the ropes that held us, but to no avail. I knew Bird was watching me, I could see the final glimmers of hope fading from his eyes. I knew he would have followed me to the end of the world, only now I was starting to think he actually had.

I thought longingly of my mate, Star. She was sheltering with the rest of our people in the caves we had used during our first winter in this land, waiting for our return. She was expecting our first child, and I knew whatever it cost me, I had to get back.

I felt the bonds around my right arm slacken a little and kept twisting against them, gritting my teeth as they bit into my flesh. I hoped the friction of the rope against the rock would break it.

"Listen!" Bird's eyes went wide in the half-light.

The drums had stopped.

I looked up, holding my breath.

The dancing had stopped too. The revellers were motionless outlines against the flickering flames. Although it was impossible to be sure, I felt that all eyes were now upon us. As we watched, hearts racing and fear coursing through us, I noticed three figures approaching from among the shadows around the fire.

At first, they were little more than growing silhouettes, but gradually I realised two of them were carrying knives and I fought back a burst of fear. Bird was already whimpering, squirming against the rock at his back as though trying to sink into it. I smelled the pungent stench of his urine and determined that whatever came, I would go out with more dignity.

When they drew close enough that I could see their faces the moment of revelation was like a fist driving into my gut. I stared, unable to think, unable to understand. My mouth opened, but no sound came out.

Two of the people standing before me were strangers, part of this new tribe. Their heads were shaved, their scalps covered in ritual scars and their faces decorated with swirls of blue war paint. Sharp fragments of bone were twisted through their ear lobes.

The third figure was Star.

"Don't be afraid," she smiled softly. "You've been spared for a reason."

"*Star*...?" my voice was little more than a shocked whisper.

"I'm doing what Bloodclaw never would," Star glanced at something impaled on a nearby spike of wood that I hadn't noticed before. It took me a moment to recognise the head of our shaman, it was so bloodied and battered, the face almost caved in as though smashed by a heavy stone.

"He was not fit to guide us any further," Star said.

Bird and I exchanged a horrified glance.

"Release them," Star instructed. The two strangers stepped forward and cut our bonds. "They'll listen to me."

Having freed us, the two strangers stepped back,

melting into the shadows like spectres, but I suspected they wouldn't go far. Star, meanwhile, stepped towards us and held up her hands.

"Don't try to run," she implored. "They'll kill you if you do."

"Why are you here?" I asked. She took my hand but staring into her eyes was like looking at a stranger.

"Their god, Tsathoggua, spoke in my dreams," Star whispered. "Even as we explored this new region, he touched my mind. He has been whispering to me for weeks now. He is stronger than our gods, so powerful, so old." She looked over at the severed head of our shaman and laughed. "We put so much faith in Bloodclaw, in all his visions and signs, but he knew nothing of Tsathoggua. He wasn't worthy of such an honour. When I realised that, I knew he had failed us.

"Tsathoggua offered me power and a place among his followers if I gave him offerings. He calls to those who will carry on his veneration, here in this place – a distant outpost of his followers, the Voormis. They no longer dwell here. Their bones are all that remains of their kind. But, those who have taken up the mantle of their religion carry on the rituals and offerings. Here we can hide and prosper, can stay hidden from those that would destroy us."

I stepped back, pulling my hand from hers. "What

have you done?"

"I saved our people."

My lip curled in outrage. "Saved them? You *betrayed* them!"

Her eyes flashed defiantly, and she drew herself up to her full height. "We only sacrificed those I knew would refuse this great gift. Their blood sealed the pact with Tsathoggua's faithful. The rest will be given a new life here. That was the agreement."

"You told them where to find our people?" Bird asked, the old anger edging back into his voice.

She nodded. "I waited until you were out on a hunt. I knew you would come in search of the missing people. I also hoped that once you saw… once you understood… you would see the wisdom of merging our tribes into one."

"You thought we would abandon our gods and betray our ancestors so easily?"

"There is power here. We would be foolish to turn away from it."

I shook my head. "You've destroyed everything we worked for."

"I have given us the only chance to survive!" she said, anger flaring in her eyes now. "We need strong allies in this new land."

"Look around, there's nothing but corruption and

madness."

"The joining is already done," she said simply. "Our people arrived while you slept. They are waiting up at the fire for us."

Even as she spoke, my attention was drawn to the rocks lining the processional way. The sooty, tarry residue that stained them was moving. Individual patches were lifting themselves off of the surface of the stones and crawling, like smaller versions of the thing we had seen skittering across the cave ceiling earlier.

Lifting my gaze to the people assembled around the great fire, I realised that there too shadows were spreading over the walls and ceiling, drawing closer to the crowd in defiance of the firelight that should have banished them. Our people assembled before the flames were all too busy watching us to notice the changes.

"Come with us," Star reached out for my hand again, a smile filling her face. "I still want you."

"There's only death here," I said, the unease in my stomach rising greasily up my throat at the sight of that crawling darkness. "We've all been betrayed..."

Her brow creased and she opened her mouth to speak, but that was when the screams began. The darkness gathering above our people oozed like tar from the rocks above, spattering down and searing the flesh of those beneath it as it fell onto their faces and arms. We saw their frenzied outlines against the flames, writhing, contorting, trying to flee or tear the living darkness from their bodies. Several of them staggered backwards into the fire in their panic. A few stumbled close enough that we saw the blackness constricting around their bodies, cutting into the flesh and even severing limbs as it did so, but there was no blood from those oddly withered wounds.

Star cried out and started running towards them.

I went to grab her arm, but something swept my legs out from under me and I fell heavily against the ground, skinning my elbows and knees as I landed. Around me all the shadows were coming to life, inky darkness skittering and shifting as pools of living blackness swarmed the walls and curled around the remains of the three-toed skeletons in their alcoves. This whole place suddenly swarmed with living shadows.

"We have to get away!" Bird hissed as he helped me to my feet, but my only thoughts were of Star and our people. I turned to see her running between the stones leading to the fire. There was nobody left standing up there, just shapes feebly crawling on the ground before the crackling fire. I saw more of the moving darkness pounce with a cat-like grace from the surface of the processional stones. It landed on Star's back and she fell with a scream that pierced my heart like a blade.

I would have run to her, but Bird dragged me away with a pained grunt.

"She's dead!" he roared.

I shook his arm off and turned back, but there was only shadow between the stones now, a blackness that seemed to shift and twitch of its own malign accord.

Fresh movement from above us caused me to glance up. The other tribe was watching us again, from more of those narrow ledges high above, where they had retreated to witness their latest sacrifice in safety. I spied several of them nocking arrows, and at the sight of that, we turned and ran, weaving as we desperately sought a means of escape from this hellish chamber. There were two openings in the far wall, and we plunged blindly into the first, finding ourselves back in the tangled warren of passageways once more.

With all sense of direction gone, we stumbled, panicked and half-blinded, through that confusing maze of tunnels. It's impossible to know how long our crazed flight lasted. To us, it felt like a lifetime. We saw no other living things, just endless chambers of the dead – sacrifices or bodies of the faithful; it was hard to be sure. Perhaps there was no difference between the two.

Initially, I wondered why the other tribe wasn't giving chase. I hoped that they considered two stragglers not worth the effort of hunting down and were letting us go. But gradually we came to understand that they weren't following because they didn't need to.

Something else was hunting us.

This sudden understanding spurred us on, as did the terrifying realisation that those sounds closing in behind us were not those of humans. They were wet, liquid noises, like something flowing and sloshing – surging through the passageways, and neither of us dared look back. Accompanying that horrible sound was an awful stench, filling the air and growing stronger as it drew closer.

Finally, Bird looked back only to scream and stumble, eyes wide and his face twisted in terror.

At that, I chanced a backwards glance myself.

Filling the tunnel was a thick slimy bulk oozing and clawing its way towards us as if all the other crawling shadows had fused together into a single colossal mass. The faceless sooty-black form bulged and gleamed, bony claws scraping the walls as it forced its tarry mass through the narrow space. Two lipless mouths peeled wetly open in that dripping head revealing rows of bone-yellow barbs lining the inside like forests of needles. The foetid, musty stench that accompanied it was sickening, as was the slimy sucking sound it made as it pushed against the tunnel walls to propel itself faster, sprouting arms and coiling limbs as it pawed at the stone.

I saw a branching tunnel open up to the left. I screamed at Bird to take it, but got no reaction from him. He was lost to his terror, running blindly and mindlessly, and I grabbed his arm and dragged him with me as I bolted down it. The tunnel was shorter than I expected, opening out into an all-too-familiar jungle of towering fungal stalks and profusions of pale ferns.

I glanced around and saw that the narrow side passage had slowed the thing momentarily, but not stopped it. Its glistening form, some kind of living fluid, had simply shifted and flowed into the narrower aperture and was still pursuing. When I turned back, Bird was gone, having fled deeper into the dripping vegetation. The settling of the ferns gave me an indication of his direction, and I followed, hoping that he had some sense of the way back to the surface from here and wasn't just plunging blindly ahead.

The dense undergrowth obscured my vision, and the mulch underfoot sucked at my feet with each step. Within moments I had lost all sense of where the outer walls of the chamber were. I couldn't see or hear Bird, but I didn't dare stop.

That was when I heard a thunderous crash from behind and felt the ground shudder. Masses of spores exploded into the air like a spreading cloud, and I knew the creature had charged into the forest, tearing aside the huge stalks as it went. In that moment of stark realisation, I knew I could no longer waste time looking for Bird. Only my own survival mattered now.

As more stalks fell or were ripped aside, the choking cloud grew denser, filling the air like a thick fog. I clamped a hand across my mouth to avoid inhaling the spores which now coated my body, my other hand stretched before me, fighting through the veils of fronds in my path. The shaking of the ground warned that the creature was close, but I was all but blind in that dense spore-shrouded vegetation.

Then suddenly my outstretched hand encountered the rough rock wall of the cavern. With an anxious burst of renewed energy, I followed it along with both hands now, no longer caring about anything but escape.

There was another tearing crash from behind, and a slender pale yellow stalk toppled right beside me, sending up another plume of spores. I caught a brief glimpse of the creature turning wildly, limbs and twisting appendages bursting out from all over its shifting form – and then it lunged for something.

I found an opening in the rock and scrambled inside another narrow passageway. Even as I ran the scream that echoed behind me revealed Bird's fate, and I knew just what the monstrous creature had snatched up. I glanced back, seeing nothing but a dense swirling cloud of spores. But I knew I was now alone.

After that, my memories are hazy. Fragmentary recollections of endless dark tunnels, of constantly glancing back in fear at the slightest sound. When I finally found another passage back up to the surface, I scrambled up it, half-convinced something would drag me back into those caverns just when the world above came into view.

But nothing did.

I burst out into the night air, gulping it down like I had been holding my breath for an eternity, and stared up at the bright moon in the sky as if it were the most beautiful sight I had ever seen.

It took me a moment to spot the body.

Reed lay before me on the bare rock, his body riddled with arrows and his throat slit. I crouched and closed his staring eyes. He'd warned us from the start that this had been a trap, only he had failed to understand the magnitude of it.

I left him there. There was nothing more I could do for any of them now.

I walked in a daze, aimless and numb, for mile after mile, until a wave of dizziness swept over me and I stumbled, almost fell.

My body was burning up, my mouth tasted of blood and my vision swam. I sat heavily on a fallen tree, shivering; my legs suddenly too weak to go on any further. My arms and neck were itching, and my stomach churned as if something were uncoiling within me.

Worst of all was the headache right behind my eyes.

The approaching dawn painted the horizon in mauve, pink and gold. I stared at the sun slowly lifting into the sky, but any beauty contained within that scene was lost on me.

A new day was here, and yet my world was over. I was far from my home, exiled in a strange and hostile land. My tribe, my family, was dead, slaughtered in a hidden realm where wonder and horror walked side by side.

And, it seems, in escaping I had brought some of that horror with me.

In the growing light of the coming day, I saw the strange growth that had formed on my arm, like a raised red boil that pulsed and twitched as though alive. Already there were angry red lines spreading out of it. A quick check of my body revealed another on my throat, and one on my face below my right eye.

I must have inhaled some of those spores after all.

It was less than an hour later when the top of the lesion on my arm peeled open with a curious tickling sensation, and the tip of a tiny fungal stalk sprouted into the light. I felt no fear or alarm. Perhaps this emotionally numb state was all I had left after everything I had lost in the last few hours. Or, maybe this was just a part of the change that was taking place inside me. As shock shifted to acceptance, I actually found myself laughing an empty, hollow laugh.

Since then, dozens more have sprouted from my body. It feels as if my whole body is itching and crawling.

The headache is getting worse too, as though my skull might crack in two.

I know the other tribe will be hunting me. I suspect they are already fanning out across the grasslands and plains, arrows and spears readied to sink into my flesh before they drag my remains back to their dark god.

But I am not going to run from them.

There's nowhere left to go.

Instead, I will wait here, and see what kills me first.

# Holding Back The Flood

Tim Mendees

Scenting the metallic taint of blood mingled harshly with the iodine of the brackish waters, Caden carefully moved aside the towering reeds with the tip of his spear. Raising his free hand to halt the progression of his weary and hastily assembled war party, he kept low and waded into the river. Bruise-coloured clouds moved sluggishly over the sinking sun casting brooding shadows over the languid waters. Several shapes floated gently on the surface. He squinted to discern the identity of what he was seeing. He quickly wished he hadn't.

What had first appeared to be clumps of flotsam, weeds, or perhaps the resting forms of river otters, revealed themselves to be something far worse. It was the very men and women he had striven to save. Cursing softly, Caden took in the ghastly sight of the bloated cadavers bobbing like driftwood, and pondered his next move. The village the dead belonged to sat on the opposite bank nestled in tangled yew trees and feral bracken. The rough beehive dwellings and scattered tents looked deserted.

As Caden stood in painful contemplation, one of his party, a whelp named Kal, moved up behind him, ignoring his command. "What is it, father?" Kal whispered, waggling a reed to get the head man's attention.

Caden turned, his lips tight and his expression grim. "Slaughter," he said flatly. "We are too late. Death has come to them with savage fury."

All the colour drained from Kal's face, "what of Jerl? . . . Any sign of her?" He had a catch in his voice as he spoke. Concern for the safety of his betrothed had been the catalyst that had sparked his urgent petition for action in the first place. After much bickering between the village elders, Caden had finally decided to lead a small party of his toughest warriors into the neighbouring lands.

"I can't say," Caden held aside the reeds and pointed his spear at the body of a woman. Bloated beyond recognition and minus a head, it was tricky to identify.

"It's hard to tell." Using his spear to drag the body closer, he knelt for a closer look. Its skin had started to slip as the adipose tissue had begun to decompose. "She's been here for days," he rolled the body over and examined her chest, paying attention to the stretch marks below her breasts, "this is a mother, it's not Jerl," he paused before cursing under his breath. "It is the cunning woman. She who held back the waters from their homes. It seems the Antlermen have decided to *remove* all those that stand against them." Caden wiped his hands on the wet grass then stood and peered over towards the village. "This place is doomed."

Kal felt his gorge rising and turned away from the horrific sight. He had known the instant the frightened whisperings of the fisherfolk on the edges of their hunting lands had reached his ears that something was gravely amiss. All the signs had been there ever since that strange island had been sighted off the coast, portents that spoke of dark days and blood in the water. If only Caden had listened sooner. Fighting the urge to confront his father, Kal pushed his way through two ashen-faced warriors and back onto what remained of the dry land. The river was swollen and had already started to burst its banks.

Caden watched his youngest son with concern. Kal was headstrong and prone to action without first giving careful thought. He would have to keep a close eye on him over the next few hours. If his temper got the better of him, it could spell the end for them all. Life hung in a delicate balance, the survival of the villages bordering the forbidden lands depended on their cooperation with those that controlled the tides. If Kal was to do something to upset that balance, their land would be as doomed as its neighbour. Gesturing towards his men, he motioned them down to his position.

One by one, Caden and his men dragged the dead onto dry land and laid them out as Kal watched. With each passing cadaver, his heart pounded in his chest. It was only after examining each one that it would return to beating as normal. In this brief respite, he dared hope that Jerl had somehow escaped. As the last body was hauled ashore, relief washed over him in powerful waves.

"She's not here," Kal said to Caden as the head man looked sorrowfully at the display of carrion. "Jerl may still live."

Caden chose not to engage, instead crouching to inspect the wounds. Each head had been deftly snipped off at the neck with the accuracy of a master butcher, leaving neither rough scraps of flesh nor jagged edges. "What manner of weapon could inflict such damage?" He muttered to himself, neither expecting, nor seeking, an answer. "No flint made these incisions."

"Did you hear me, father?" Kal raised his voice over

the lapping of the water and the screech of the seagulls that wheeled overhead. "I said..."

"I heard what you said, boy."

"Then let's mount a search, we have no time to waste on the dead when some might still live."

Caden shook his head sadly. "I fear I know where she is, and I also fear that any efforts we make to recover her would make things a lot worse."

"What are you saying, father, that we should just give up? Simply abandon Jerl to her fate?"

"What I'm saying, boy," Caden snapped, rounding on his upstart offspring, "is that no good will come from charging off after her without first finding out what we are dealing with. We will scout the area for tracks, then return to camp before deciding on our next move."

"And, while we sit on our hands, Jerl could be slaughtered," Kal paused to choose his next words. He didn't choose wisely. "If we hadn't tarried for so long, we may have saved the Northern tribe, if you had just listened..."

His tirade was abruptly cut off mid flow by Caden striking him across the face with the heel of his right hand. It knocked the startled youngster off balance and sent him spiralling to the floor. "Don't you dare question me, boy," Caden snarled, looming over Kal, cracking his knuckles for effect. "I have the survival of *our* village to consider. Rash action leads to defeat, you know this. Do you want our mothers and daughters left out for the crows?"

Kal opened his mouth to protest but didn't get the chance to force out a single sound.

"No! I will hear no more of your mouth. It is decided," he turned and indicated two of his warriors. "You, take my son, search the banks on this side of the river for tracks. I want to know how many were taken, where, and by whom, understand?"

The two warriors nodded in perfect unison.

"The rest of you, come with me. We will check the village for survivors."

Kal had bristled at the way Caden had said, *my son* but hadn't dared any further altercation. Though he was young and strong, he would have been no match for his father had it come to real blows. To be head man, you had to be the alpha male. From time to time, younger men would challenge for dominance, they never got very far, however, Caden was an absolute beast when his blood was up. Kal watched his father gather his men and commence wading over to the opposite bank. Spitting an oath under his breath, he turned to the two men he'd been teamed with. One of them, a shaggy-looking specimen named Neeva, was grinning like a loon.

"What's so damn funny?" Kal huffed as he joined

the others.

"You," Neeva retorted, a big dopey grin plastered across his face. "You never learn, do you? You should know by now that nothing good comes from meeting your father head-on. You need to be subtle, make him think it's his idea."

"It still wouldn't work, he's happy to sit on his rump while our land goes to ruin."

"Nay, brother," the other man, Afon, stepped towards Kal, his younger sibling, and levelled a crooked finger to the young man's face. "I'll not have that. Our father does his best for us. Where would we be without his leadership? I'll show you where," he swept a hand over the line of headless corpses. "Right there. We'd have been left for the crows long ago if it hadn't been for father's leadership."

Kal bristled, his temper getting the better of him once more. He turned and stood chest to chest with Afon. "So, you think we should do nothing? You're just as much of a coward as he is."

As soon as the words had left Kal's lips, his throat was gripped by a powerful hand. "You think me a coward, do you, brother?" Afon reached for the flint axe at his hip, "let's see if you can back up your words." Shoving Kal back, he unhooked his axe from his belt and moved into a fighting stance.

Not wishing to show any further weakness, Kal took out his axe and squared up to the challenge. Beads of perspiration appeared on his forehead like a blanket of morning dew, he knew he was no match for Afon but his wounded pride wouldn't let him back down. Being made to look like a weakling by his father, the tribe alpha, was one thing, he wasn't ready to let his brother do the same.

As the men circled slowly, Neeva tipped back his head and roared with laughter.

Kal and Afon both stopped and faced the third man, confusion dancing in their eyes.

"What are you laughing about?" Afon growled, turning his violent attention away from Kal and onto Neeva.

Without thinking, Kal did the same.

Neeva roared even louder.

As a unit, Kal and Afon moved towards Neeva, prepared to bash his skull in if he continued his mirth.

Neeva stopped laughing and smirked. "See, all it takes to get you two idiots to stop squabbling is a common enemy... shall we go and find one?" With that, he turned and started to walk along the bank of the river, poking at the reeds with his spear. The two combatants looked at each other again and lowered their weapons. Suddenly feeling foolish, they followed Neeva in silence, scanning the sodden ground for tracks.

This hadn't been the first time that Neeva had been forced to come between the pair. As sons of the head man, they were often butting heads like two testosterone-fuelled stag beetles. The first time, he got physically between them and received a boot to the groin for his trouble. Since that day, he had employed a different tactic that never failed. Insult or ridicule one or both to the point that they forget their argument and redirect their anger toward him. He was a master at defusing explosive situations simply by being insufferable.

His cheek still stinging and his ego hanging in tatters, Kal overtook his companions and made towards the mouth of the river. He hadn't walked for long before he reached it. The worrying thing was, it was further inland than it had ever been before, by roughly half a mile. Kal stopped, biting his lip pensively.

"Neeva, come, take a look at this."

Climbing out of the water, Neeva moved to Kal's position. He didn't need to ask what the problem was, he could see for himself. Spitting a curse under his breath and absent-mindedly fiddling with the charm hung around his neck, he gazed out to sea. The waves rolled in a deliberate fashion towards the headland. With each susurrant impact, the water crept ever so slightly forward, as though devouring the earth, inch by inch... bite by bite.

"How many cunning women still live, do you think?" Neeva's normally jocular expression had been dragged downward by the gravity of the situation.

"I know not, my friend. They have been eliminating them one-by-one. Ours and that old hermit that lives out near the dead lands remain, aside from them... not many, I fear." Kal trailed off, looking across to the land on the other side of the river.

Neeva sighed, his muscular chest sagging. "I wonder why the old hermit has been left untouched? After all, he has the cunning, and is only a stone's throw from the Dead Lands. I would have thought he'd be first to go."

"Hmm," Kal scratched the fluff on his chin thoughtfully. "Perhaps he is working with them, or his cunning simply poses no threat?"

"Could be..."

Neither man had heard Afon approach, he was a little ways off scouring the weeds and shrubs that sat back from the riverbank up a steep incline. To the surprise of Kal and Neeva, he let out a sharp whistle that shook them out of their reverie. The two men turned and gave questioning gestures. Afon pointed his spear through a thicket and motioned them to follow... he had picked up the trail of *something*.

Ascending the acclivitous land to Afon's position, Kal and Neeva crouched low at his side and followed the tip of his spear with his eyes. The bush had been split in two by the passage of some kind of bulk. "What could have caused this?" Kal whispered.

"I know not. Look how the stem has been broken off at the root. This is a hardy shrub, that would have taken much force."

"A body being dragged?"

"Possibly, though it would have had to have been a giant of a man to have caused this."

Neeva looked at the elder of the siblings and raised an eyebrow. "So, what are you saying?"

"I don't know, but I don't like it. There's nothing natural about any of this. We should go and fetch some more men, I have a bad feeling..."

Kal let out a snort of derision, broke ranks, and set off on the newly-formed trail. Neeva looked at Afon, and shrugged before following. Resisting the urge to bash in his brother's skull with a nearby lump of chalk, dislodged from the mud-sodden bank, Afon cursed under his breath, then reluctantly followed.

A path around a metre in width had been gouged through the foliage. The thick tangle of heather, bindweed and ground elder had been almost erased, shorn down to the root by the unknown force, only a few plants stubbornly clung onto life. It continued in a snaking fashion along the ridge for a short distance before plunging sharply down into the salt marshes. The three men scrambled down the bank and looked at the corridor that had been carved through the head-high reeds and stinging nettles. Even Kal was struck by how unnatural it was.

Again, Afon stepped in front of the others and motioned for them to return to the bank. His eyes were wide with nagging dread and his lips clenched into a thin line. He didn't dare speak, though he didn't know why. There was just something hanging in the air that had a stranglehold on his larynx. Kal moved forward until he was almost chest-to-chest with his sibling and opened his mouth to speak but was silenced by a heavy rustle and the sound of dragging waters off to their right.

The three men froze, drawing weapons and looking in the direction of the disturbance A few feet away, the tops of the vegetation started to dance, sending a startled squadron of brightly-coloured damsel flies into the sky. Kal crouched low and readied his spear, the others drew axes as the presence continued to shamble towards them. The sound of the water and drone of insects had been joined by a noise far more unnerving, a kind of wheezing gurgle punctuated by croaking groans. As it drew nearer, the trio of warriors prepared to engage.

Jittery from the rising tension of the ponderous slop and slurp of the footsteps, Kal jumped to meet the threat as it broke cover but was knocked off balance by Afon and dug his spear into nothing but air.

"Hold, you fool," Afon bellowed.

Before them, was a man caked from head to toe in blood and filth. He was clutching a gaping wound in his side. It looked like something had taken a bite out of him. The figure took one more step then fell face-first into the water at their feet.

"Quick, help him," Neeva sheathed his axe and dropped to his knees, turning the man over and raising his head from the water. "Kal, help me, put pressure on his wound."

Kal hesitated.

"Out of the way," Afon shouldered him aside, squatted down and took a look at the man's wound. His eyes met Nevva's questioning gaze. He shook his head sadly.

"I know this man," Kal said after finally regaining his composure. "He's one of the peddlers from the market. Jerl used to get provisions from him."

"What's his name?" Neeva slapped the man's cheeks in an effort to rouse him back to consciousness.

"Um... I'm not sure."

"Think, damn it!"

Kal flinched as though he'd been slapped again. Neeva rarely raised his voice, so when he did, it was startling, to say the least. "I think it's Dairmuid."

"Dairmuid, can you hear me... Dairmuid!" Neeva's raised voice accompanied by a final wet slap roused the fallen man from his slumber. "That's it, you're safe now. What happened here?"

The man, Dairmuid, opened his mouth but the only thing that came forth was a choked gobbet of blood and saliva. Afon used a torn strip of animal hide to wipe his lips then held his waterskin to them. After the trickle of cool river water had cleared his throat, Dairmuid tried again...

"Men with antler headdresses came... It was a slaughter. We had no chance... they came without warning," Dairmuid's rasping whisper gave way to a series of coughs and splutters that sent more blood dribbling down his chin, matting his orange beard.

"What of Jerl, does she live?" Kal loomed over Dairmuid, making him flinch and struggle for breath. "Speak!"

Afon growled low in the back of his throat, rose, and shoved Kal back. When he went to move back closer, Afon levelled a finger caked in the man's blood to Kal's chest and shook his head.

"What happened to the women, Dairmuid? We have found only the corpses of men and the cunning woman," Neeva asked.

"Taken," Dairmuid sighed, fighting to give the words breath.

"Taken? Taken where?"

"I know not. A red-haired woman led them away. They came this way... I was following when..."

Afon turned away from Kal. "This path, what created it?"

Dairmuid's eyes grew wide with fear. "The beast!" He cried before beginning to hyperventilate and spasm uncontrollably as shock took him into its fatal grip. Neeva tried to hold him still and aid his breath but it was to no avail. After a final agonised rattle... Dairmuid stopped breathing. Closing his eyes and laying him down in the mud, Neeva muttered a solemn prayer as Afon checked the man's apparel for anything that may prove useful.

Kal cursed and glared down the path created by Dairmuid's *beast*.

Almost as if in response to the tragic scene taking place below, the heavens opened with a deafening peal of thunder. Lightning flashed and flickered as the rain began to hammer down in rods.

"Come, we should return to the others," Afon asserted, making a start towards the raised bank separating the river from the salt marshes.

"What?" Kal was incredulous. "No, we can't. You heard him, Jerl still lives."

"That's not what he said," Afon shot back. "He said the women had been taken. For all we know, they were taken in chunks of meat. You just heard what you wanted to hear."

"Nonsense!"

"Mind your tongue, little brother, if you carry on the way you are going, you may lose it."

"Shut your mouths, the pair of you!" Neeva pushed past them, his head cocked and his fists clenched. "Listen."

In the distance, they could hear a continuous roar that grew louder by the second. It was distinctly audible over the hiss of the rain. Afon's face drained of colour. He had heard that noise only once before... when he witnessed a huge wave wipe a small coastal village from the land as easy as wiping sweat from his own brow.

"Quick!" He screamed as he took off at pace towards the bank. Scrambling on his hands and feet to stop himself from slipping in the mud, he reached the summit just in time to see a colossal wave crest before crashing over the land on the other side of the river. He let out a wail of anguish, the water was racing towards the village of the Northern Tribe with such force that he knew that his father and his men were in great danger of being washed away.

Neeva joined him and looked on in horror. His mind

was racing, trying to process what he was looking at. The wave had hit the other bank alone. It was like there was some kind of invisible barrier separating the two sides of the river. It was unnatural, that much was for sure.

"Come on, we must help them," Afon said before looking around for his brother. "Where in creation is Kal?"

"Over yonder, look!"

Kal was following the path through the salt marshes.

"Damn him," Afon spat. "You had better go and bring him back. I'll go and help father."

Neeva nodded, secretly thankful to take his eyes off the uncanny deluge and slid back down to the marshes, his feet splashing in the rising water. Despite the wave not hitting his location, the run-off was raising the waterline at an alarming rate. Setting out after Kal, he jogged as fast as the suction of the mud would allow... at least *the beast* had cleared him a path. His mind was racing trying to guess just what this terrible creature could be, a rampaging mammoth or monstrous bear, perhaps?

Not far ahead, Kal was trudging onward with grim determination. He was so focussed on his mission that he failed to hear his friend's approach until he was only a few feet away. It didn't help that the rain was drumming the standing water while the sky grumbled and boomed.

"Kal, stop this madness, we have to go back," Neeva

yelled as he caught up.

"You go back. I'm going to search for Jerl. You heard whatshisname, she was taken this way. If I hurry, I may be able to save her."

"What of your kin? Are you just going to leave them to the mercy of the tide?" Neeva placed a heavy paw on Kal's shoulder, stopping him in his tracks.

"Look, they can look out for themselves, Jerl could be alone. I'm sorry, Neeva, my mind is made up."

"So be it, but, I'm coming with you."

"You? Why?"

"For a start, your brother would have my hide should any harm befall you..."

Kal frowned, "and secondly?"

"Secondly... I fear neither of us has too much choice, look!"

Kal looked back towards the river as the water came spilling over the ridge and down the bank in a raging torrent.

"Run!"

Kal didn't need prompting twice, he was already sprinting along the path with Neeva hot on his heels. Behind them, the water roared as it swept along the marsh ripping up vegetation and sending myriad waterfowl and insects fleeing for their lives. Kal looked back and lost his footing on a clump of reeds, he spun, landing on his back in the water. Neeva stopped, grabbing him under the arms and hauling him upright.

"It's no good. We can't outrun it," Neeva panted.

Kal pointed to his left. "There, the high ground, quick."

Setting off through the reeds, shoving them aside and tramping them down, they fled towards the steep incline leading out of the marshes and up towards an ill-aspected copse. Neeva hit the slope first and scrambled quickly to the top. Kal reached it just in time, clinging onto the root of a twisted yew tree as the water slammed into his side, sweeping his legs from under him. Neeva dropped to his belly and held on to Kal with both hands. After a moment of struggle, the two men reached the safety of the high ground as the water slowed into a rising and falling rhythm.

* * *

With the rain lashing their upturned faces, the two men sucked in oxygen like it was a rare commodity. After a couple of minutes, Kal sat up, took one look at the marshes, and cursed. It was no longer a marsh, it was now part of the sea... they were sitting on the new shore. The tops of reeds were barely visible under the swell, those that did poke their heads out were smothered in foul brown foam from the stirred-up mud and sediment.

Away to the West, only a fraction of the bank that had bordered the river remained, and beyond it nothing but water. This new headland showed no signs of life save for a discombobulated squabble of seagulls that screeched and flapped in confusion.

Salt tears rolled down Kal's cheek but were quickly washed away by the rain. Neeva, overcome with emotion, rounded on his friend, grabbing him by the arm and yanking him to his feet. "Now what? We should have been there."

"And done what? What could we have done to help them? We'd be as dead as them. At least, this way, we can try and avenge their deaths."

Before Neeva could deliver a suitably scathing retort, a furtive noise drew his attention away from his irritating companion. "Hush, I think something is nearby... Over there, through the trees."

Kal turned and headed quietly towards the gloom-shrouded copse. Encircled by twisted yew trees whose branches entwined like fingers in a gesture of worship, the spinney was almost impenetrable. The trees had formed a natural wall bolstered by fronds of ivy, clumps of bracken and tangles of bramble. Parting the curtain of leaves with his spear, Kal peered through the limbs. He could see nothing, the sky had darkened considerably as the storm set in and the dense foliage plugged any gaps between the trees. The only light afforded was by a dim luminescence from patches of leprous fungi that clung to several boles and nestled between serpentine roots.

"I see nothing," he said, turning to Neeva.

The larger man tapped his nose and made sniffing gestures.

Kal inhaled. Even though his sinuses were burning from all the churned-up sea salt, he caught the scent of a powerful odour, an odd mixture of wet animal, fish, and rotting meat. It was accompanied by faint traces of smoke. Evidently, whoever was lurking in the thicket had been enjoying a warming fire before the downpour. Satisfied, he turned and nodded to Neeva. Together, the two men started to scout the perimeter for a place of ingress.

A little way off to the East, Neeva stopped dead in his tracks. "Kal, look..."

Kal joined him and nodded in agreement. They had found the path created by *the beast.* It stretched from the newly-formed shore, up the bank and into the trees. "Look at the size of the gap it's made." he gasped, looking at the freshly-carved tunnel. It was around seven feet in diameter and the ground looked like it had been swept clean.

"Afon was right, there is nothing natural about this."

Kal snorted once again, "nonsense, it must have

been a mammoth."

Neeva approached the entrance and examined the sheared ends of the branches and twigs. There was no sign of breakage. The ends were smooth as though the tunnel had been melted through the use of exceptionally high temperatures. "No way did a mammoth cause this, unless it was on fire."

"Don't be foolish, Neeva. This tunnel was obviously already here. It's probably been here many moons. None of our people have dared set foot in the forbidden lands since the men wearing antlers first arrived on our shores. How else do you think the debris got cleared up? You don't think they did it as they fled with the women of the Northern Tribe, do you?"

Neeva shot him a look that could have brought down a sabre-toothed cat at fifty paces.

"Come on, Jerl and the others need us," Kal started to march down the path with no thought for stealth.

Neeva rolled his eyes and followed. He was reaching the point of exasperation where he was sorely tempted to club his companion with a rotten log. Still, he thought better of it, after all, Kal could turn out to be the only kinsman he had left. This realisation galvanised him into action. He would do his utmost to ensure Kal's survival, even if he was on a suicide mission.

"Kal, keep quiet. We don't know how many we are

dealing with."

Seeing the look in Neeva's eyes, he slowed his pace and kept low. The duo fell into step with each other as they followed the path towards a clearing. Following the procedure they employed while hunting deer together, one man took cover to the left of the tunnel mouth while the other the right. Hiding amongst the wizened trees, they surveyed the scene before them.

In the centre of the clearing, amongst fallen tree-trunks encrusted with moss and more of the glowing fungi, was the smouldering remains of a fire surrounded by several apex tents crafted from branches and animal hides. The encampment looked to have been recently deserted. The only occupants of this evident waypoint were two hunched figures wearing antler head-dresses. They were sitting on one of the trunks taking turns drinking from a water-skin. From the way they swayed, Neeva quickly deduced that what it contained was far harder than water.

Signalling for Kal to take the one on the right, alive if possible, he broke cover and started to creep towards his target. Forgoing its larger, bone-handled cousin, he drew a razor-sharp flint hand axe and clutched it tightly in his right fist. Skirting the debris of countless feasts, they approached swiftly and decisively.

In perfect unison, Neeva gripped one man from

behind, pulling back his forehead and raking the keen edge of his weapon across his neck, while Kal struck the man with the flat of his axe, knocking him to the ground and straddling him. "Where are the women of the Northern Tribe?" he bellowed, raising his axe above his head.

Dazed and confused, his victim merely lashed a toothy grin that sent shivers down Kal's spine. The man below him was barely a man at all, though he must have been once. Gaunt and hunched with scabrous skin and tufts of wiry hair, the long-limbed creature chuckled throatily. Its face was more dog than man with an elongated muzzle and prominent canines. Its breath reeked of rotten meat... he was sitting astride a ghoul. Kal was so reviled that he nearly pounded its skull to paste in an effort to erase the horror from his retinas. Only thoughts of Jerl stayed in his hand.

"You're too late," the ghoul cackled. "They will have reached the Cave of Mingling by now. They are no longer *your* women... now, they belong to Dagon."

"Cave of Mingling? Where is this cave of which you speak? Tell me now, or I'll end you now."

The ghoul broke into peals of mirth.

"Silence!"

Neeva approached Kal. "What manner of man is this? See the antlers, they have been attached to his skull!"

"He's a ghoul. I've heard tell of men like him. Once men like us, they have been transformed through sorcery and now feast on the bones of the dead. I believe the antlers show their allegiance to one of their gods."

"Iä Shub-Niggurath! Iä The Black Goat of the Woods with a Thousand Young!" The ghoul grinned and rolled his eyes in exultant jubilation.

"Silence!" Kal demanded. "Tell me, where is the Cave of Mingling?"

"Never!"

"Then, die!" Kal brought down his axe to the centre of the ghoul's forehead with a sickening crunch that split the creature's skull and spilt its brains into the mud. After wiping his axe on the ghoul's hide-skin garments, he stood and stalked over to the other cadaver.

"This one is different, look, those slits on its neck and webbed fingers... It looks more frog than man."

Kal nodded. "This must be one of those from the sea."

"The antlers on this one aren't fixed."

"They are a different type of man altogether. As different from the ghoul as we are from a badger."

"Then, why does it wear the antlers?"

Kal shrugged. "I know not. A sign of unity, perhaps? Like those of the other tribes who joined up with them.

Maybe the antlers become fixed over time?"

Neeva narrowed his eyes, "how do you know so much about these fiends?"

"Simple, my friend. Where you, Father, and all the others dismissed the tales of the fisherfolk and paddlers as nonsense, I listened."

Once more resisting the powerful urge to punch Kal in his smugly grinning mouth, Neeva sighed. "So, what now?"

"Now, we continue to track them through the trees," Kal pointed to the far side of the clearing where the tunnel began anew.. "This *beast* of theirs is hardly stealthy."

Nodding an assent, Neeva took the lead. Rain was still pouring down from the sky and, by now, had started to turn the clearing into a lake. If it continued, the waters would continue to rise and the sea would claim more land. If nothing was done soon to hold back the flood, their homeland would be drowned forever. But what could possibly be done? This conundrum occupied his thoughts as they picked their way along the tunnel of trees and out onto the rolling hillocks of the dead lands.

"The trail goes that way," Kal pointed due south, "towards the Great Bank."

Neeva nodded as they trudged onward with the rain lashing their faces and the wind doing its best to sweep them off their feet. Coming out onto a hillock that overlooked The Hidden Valley, a place sacred to the Antlermen and strictly forbidden to people such as himself. He held a hand to Kal's chest. "Hold... Look, the Old Shaman's dwelling. I can see light, he must be home and have a fire lit."

Kal nodded. "Hmm, let's go and see if that false mystic can tell us what we are dealing with. He must have seen their coming and going."

"Agreed. Plus, it won't hurt to warm ourselves by his fire for a while."

Making a beeline for the rough beehive dwelling, Kal and Neeva followed the gentle slope down towards the valley that led directly towards the foreboding rows of standing stones and burial mounds known as the Dead Lands. This was uncharted territory for both men. Trespass was punishable by death. Whatever lurked out in that sinister wilderness, the forces that stood in opposition to them didn't want anyone to find out. These monuments and resting places had been there long before the first settlers. Nobody knew where they had come from nor who had put them there. The entire stretch of land was an anomaly.

"Old Man!" Neeva called out upon reaching the entrance to the ramshackle stone structure. "We seek your wisdom. I am Neeva, and this..."

"I know who you are, Kal, son of Caden, and Neeva,

father unknown," the voice from within sniggered to himself. Clearly enjoying a joke only he was privy to. "Come inside, if you're coming, don't just stand there blocking the view, the lightning is stunning."

Bemused, Neeva gestured for Kal to go first. Reluctantly, he did. Stepping into the conical structure fashioned from irregularly shaped stones and mud taken from the marsh, he was greeted by a welcome burst of heat that radiated from the small fire pit in the centre of the structure. Around it, the old hermit had fashioned bedding from a vast collection of animal skins and feathers. It was far cosier than the tents and shacks his people lived in. Still, having to move their village periodically due to the rising waters hadn't left them much time to build more permanent dwellings.

"Why have you come here?" The old man asked, though his expression betrayed the fact that he knew only too well.

"We seek my betrothed, Jerl, and the other women of the Northern Tribe," Kal explained. "They have been taken to a place called the Cave of Mingling, do you know of such a place?"

"Oh, yes, I know it, and I say this... Turn back, forget Jerl, and head for the high ground. Only death awaits you there."

Kal did a surprisingly admirable job of keeping his

temper in check. "I cannot simply flee and leave Jerl to her fate."

"You should," the old man chuckled. "She's no longer your betrothed... she is now a bride of Dagon."

As Kal moved to deliver a blow to the man's face, Neeva intercepted him and placed himself between the two men. "Explain yourself, hermit. What is the Cave of Mingling, and what do you mean, *bride of Dagon?*"

The wizened old mystic stroked his tangled beard and took a gulp of water before beginning. "They have been taken to a place where they will become breeding stock for those that come from the sea. They call this *mingling,* it's a great honour, apparently. This is the purpose of The Cave of Mingling. I'm afraid, Kal, son of Caden, newly appointed head man of a doomed tribe, that your betrothed has been taken by *another*. The children of Dagon continue to grow in number. Soon, their gods will sink this land. Their mission complete, they will move on, continuing the cycle until the stars are right."

"What happens when the stars are right?" Neeva asked.

"Cthulhu will rise from his house in R'lyeh, where he is imprisoned, dead but dreaming."

Neeva shuddered, he had heard that name before and seen the cave paintings of a creature that looked like the product of a hellish union betwixt man and squid. "You say Cthulhu is dead, yet, I have heard men say they have encountered this creature, how is that so?"

"Did you not hear what I said, Cthulhu is dead... but dreaming. He can manifest through dreams. Those stones down there, the menhirs and altars, create a place of visions... a way for the Children of Dagon to communicate with their lord and master. His rising will not be for many, many moons... In the meantime, The Children of Dagon will swell their numbers in preparation, getting ready for a time when the world is drowned."

"What of these *ghouls* and the tribesmen who have joined them, the so-called Antlermen?"

"A marriage of convenience, like Kal's union with Jerl. Simply uniting two tribes with a similar goal. Though I doubt a union betwixt ghoul and Deep One would prove fruitful, they have other uses. What do you think happens to the breeders once they have done their duty? There's plenty of dead flesh to go around. It's an uneasy truce, and one that will end when the time comes..."

"How do you know all this?" Kal snarled, his eyes flashing with impotent rage. "Come to think of it, how do you still live, this close to their sacred land, how have you not been slaughtered like the cunning women of the wandering tribes?"

"I know this because..." The strange old man took out a rolled-up vellum scroll, Neeva snatched it from his hand.

"What is this? Is this animal hide... I've never seen it so thin before. How was this done?"

"Never mind that," Kal snapped. "What has a rolled-up animal skin got to do with this?"

At that moment, much to the amusement of the hermit, Neeva unfurled the scroll and looked in confusion at the strange scratches and dots on its surface. They were vaguely reminiscent of the clay tablets that cunning women carved runes upon but at the same time utterly alien. He could tell they were weaving a narrative but, to its meaning, he was completely in the dark.

"It is the language of Hyperborea. A place that, like this, was reclaimed by the Old Ones, and now lies under sheets of ice. It tells me all I need to survive."

"How?" Neeva peered over the top of the vellum. "How can you read these scratches?"

"I went to the place of dreaming, gazed through the gem of the wizard Eibon. Now... I see all."

"And, this is why you go unharmed?"

"The stories within are powerful, my shaggy-maned friend, within are words of power. Words that protect me from harm."

"Such as?" Kal stepped forward, adopting a feigned interest in the man's babble. He slyly gave Neeva a wink as he did so.

"Words such as... Cthäät!"

"Cthäät?" Kal raised an eyebrow. "This word protects you?"

The old hermit nodded.

"Thank you, cunning one. Now, if you could give us directions to the Cave of Mingling, we will be on our way."

"What? No! It is madness to go there. The red-haired woman and her beast will destroy you! No human male is permitted to enter the cave."

"But, surely, the reason you gave me the word of power is so that I can enter unmolested. Is there something else I must do? A disguise, perhaps."

"Yes," the hermit nodded, drawing back a sheepskin and taking out two sets of antlers. "Wear these and speak the word, you will be safe... at least, for a time."

"So, you would have me dress in the headdress of an Antlerman, sneak into the cave and speak the word if danger arses."

The hermit nodded.

Neeva had to smile, Kal was finally learning. He had convinced the old fool that it was his own idea.

"Thank you, oh cunning one. Now, if you would be

so kind as to show me the way."

Rising, the hermit gestured to the door. "Wait one moment, I will don a cloak and guide you to the cave. It is easy when one knows the way. Otherwise, you could easily become lost."

Neeva and Kal left the building and stood out in the rain while the hermit gathered up what he needed for the journey. While they waited, they both practised speaking the strange word, rolling it around their mouths and spitting it from their lips. Soon, the hermit joined them and guided them down the valley, across a flooded plain and towards a rocky outcrop at the sea's edge.

The rain hadn't let up since they had discovered the dying peddler in the marsh and showed no sign of surcease. The sky continued to glower as lightning flashed and flickered as it forked out to sea. Their limbs weary and their feet struggling to keep traction in the omnipresent mud, they followed the hermit on towards the cave.

* * *

"There, that is the place," the hermit raised a wizened and bent finger towards a cave mouth shrouded by evil-looking vines and towering cypresses. After a moment's thought, he turned to Kal. "You should go alone, you will have a better chance of remaining undetected."

Kal nodded.

"Wait, not a chance. I'm going with you," Neeva asserted.

The hermit snorted. "Then you will both die. Look at you, you're far too ungainly for stealth."

"But, what of the beast?"

"Come, Neeva, it is just a mammoth. We have dealt with things far more formidable," he pointed to the talisman around Neeva's neck. It was fashioned from the fang of a sabre-toothed cat. "In any case, I have the word of power to protect me from its tusks.

Neeva turned to the hermit. "Is he right? Will the word protect him?"

The hermit smiled. "He has nothing to fear from any mammoth. Come, let us not tarry here. If you are going, go. But, I warn you, if you both go... you will both die."

"He's right," Kal placed a hand on Neeva's arm. "I have to do this alone" Guiding him away from the prying ears of the old man, he lowered his voice conspiratorially. "In any case, I need you to ensure our escape path is clear. We may have to make a break for it. I don't fancy the old crow's chances in a fight."

Neeva reluctantly agreed. "Here," he took off his talisman and slipped it over Kal's head, "Let it bring you good fortune."

"Thank you... Keep your eyes sharp, my friend,"

Kal nodded as he set his shoulders square and strode purposefully towards the cave. The entrance was set above a cluster of tide pools that burst into scuttling life as his footsteps disturbed them. Crabs and brightly-coloured shrimp darted under rocks and behind clumps of diseased-looking seaweed. Unhooking his axe from the thong around his midriff, he pulled aside the vines and stepped inside.

The first thing that struck Kal was the glow. Despite his expectations, it was far from lightless due to a dim lambency provided by clumps of the same glowing fungi from the clearing. It appeared to have been purposefully grown at regular intervals. The second thing that snatched his attention was the overpowering smell. Somewhere between stale blood and seawater, along with fishy overtones, the pungent aroma made his eyes water.

Pressing onward down the meandering tunnel, Kal marvelled at the smoothness of the walls. The limestone showed no signs of tool marks yet couldn't possibly have been formed by nature. A constant trickle of water ran down the centre of the passage in a v-shaped gutter. He was going further and further down into the heart of The Great Bank with every step. And with each yard covered, the atmosphere grew ever more stifling. The tell-tale sickly-sweet stench of death was starting to overpower the iodine from the water. He hadn't smelt anything so foul since he had stumbled across a week-old boar carcass out in the woods.

After what felt like an eternity, the passage widened and came out into a square antechamber. The water from the gutter flowed into a deep pool in the centre that was encircled with two-foot-high pillars of glowing fungi. The strange luminescence danced on the surface of the water. The walls of the chamber were adorned with unsettling murals of strange horrors that made his skin crawl just to look at them. Insectoid horrors, tentacular monstrosities, and things that simply defied description leered down at him with mocking indifference.

To the far side of the central pool, another aperture leered out of the darkness like the maw of some chthonic abomination. Dragging his eyes away from the disquieting décor, Kal made his way cautiously towards the opening. Reaching the mouth of it, he stepped inside and instantly came face to face with a startled horror that was just as surprised as Kal was. This was one of those from the sea, bulky, strong of arm and fleshy of lip. Kal instinctively lashed out with his ake and cleaved a gap in its skull. As it fell, it let out a gurgling stream of invective that was instantly answered by croaks and murmurings from further inside.

Kal backed out of the tunnel as three more of the creatures appeared, brandishing weapons that shone and glinted in the blue-ish light. He had seen lumps of silver ore before, but never seen them fashioned into blades. The flint-axe in his trembling hand was about as advanced as his people got. Backing away from the threat, he skipped around the chamber, putting the pool between himself and his attackers.

As they continued to advance, he stood firm and grinned. "Let's see how you monsters like this... Cthäät!"

The Deep Ones stopped and looked at each other, surprised to hear a human speak the language of Tsathoggua.

When the word seemed to have no discernible effect, Kal cleared his throat and tried again. "Cthäät!"

This time, the Deep Ones started to laugh and back away.

Unsure as to why they were laughing, yet pleased that it was working. Kal yelled it a final time. "Cthäät!"

Now, the Deep Ones raised their webbed hands and joined the chant. The cave started to shake and rumble as the waters in the pool started to roll and bubble. Kal started to edge backwards towards the sloping passage to the outside. Something was rising from the depths of the pool. Something huge and gelatinous. Kal cried in horror as it broke the surface. This, then, was the beast, and it was no mammoth. It was a bulbous mass of iridescent protoplasm covered in hundreds of baleful eyes.

*Tekeli-li!* The monstrous creature piped in apparent fury at being summoned by one such as he. It slopped and slurped with multiple mouths as it hauled itself from its aquatic nest and onto the cold hard stone.

His axe falling from his grasp, Kal turned tail and ran for his life.

With his lungs burning and his heart hammering, he charged up the sloping passageway never once looking behind him. He dared not even a single glance for fear of losing his mind altogether. Soon a fulgurant light at the mouth of the cave ahead, announced his escape from that nightmare. For a second... he dared a hope that he would survive.

* * *

Getting fidgety from the interminable wait, Neeva turned to the old hermit who was watching the cave mouth with anticipation. His lined face betrayed the hint of a smile. *He must be sure of our success.* Neeva thought to himself as he wandered over to engage him in conversation.

"How deep is the cavern?" He asked, breaking the heavy silence that had lingered between them since Kal's departure.

"I couldn't say. I have never been inside. I have never dared get this close to The Cave of Mingling before."

"Then, why come now? Come to think of it, you put up little resistance."

The hermit sighed. "I was once as you are, a warrior, headstrong like your friend. I couldn't trust him not to make things worse for us all."

Neeva frowned. "What do you mean, *make things worse*?"

Just then, the air was filled with terrifying screams. Neeva broke away from the hermit towards the cave mouth just in time to see Kal crash through the vines and fall to his knees in the rock pool. Neeva drew his axe and went to give aid but was halted in his tracks by the sight of a slippery appendage shooting from the cave. It snaked through the air, coiled itself around Kal's head, and tore it off as easily as a child pulling the head off a daisy.

Neeva screamed and charged the hermit, his axe raised above his head. "Betrayer! You will die for this!"

Displaying nimbleness uncommon in one of his age, the hermit dodged aside while drawing a gleaming blade from under his bearskin cloak. He brought it up in a parry that splintered the bone handle of Neeva's axe. Knocked off balance, Neeva's gangly legs betrayed him and he was sent sprawling to the floor with a strike from the hilt of the hermit's blade.

"Wh... what manner of weapon is that?" Neeva

gasped, struggling for breath.

"It was forged from star metal by the Serpent Men from the fjords of the North Way. It is called a sword. I warn you, I am proficient in its use and I will separate your head from your shoulders as easily as the shoggoth did to Kal."

Neeva's heart burned with rage and sorrow. He wanted to show his strength, and pledge revenge for his fallen kinsman, yet, all he could muster was a feeble, "why?"

The hermit lowered his blade and shook his head sadly. "I'm sorry, I truly am. I didn't want it to come to this, but I saw no other way to stop Kal."

"Stop him rescuing Jerl, why?"

"For the good of those on the higher lands to the west. If he had deprived the Deep Ones of their breeding stock, they would continue to raise the water until nothing remained. This land is doomed. I have seen it in visions. In moons to come, it will stand as an expanse of water between the higher grounds to the west and east. Nothing can stop this process. It is already in motion. The Storegga Slide is underway and, soon, all will be flooded. This way, many souls will be spared. They will move on to new lands to await the rise of R'lyeh."

"If Kal had succeeded, more would die?"

"More than you could possibly fathom. In time,

the fate of this land will be discussed and sung about by wise men and ballad singers alike. They will call it Doggerland and it will sit aside Atlantis, Hyperborea and Leng as lost lands. Warnings to all of the dangers of the Great Old Ones. Only if men survive can our story be told. And, only then, can we fight back."

The Hermit sheathed his blade and offered his hand to the fallen warrior. Neeva took it and struggled to his feet. "So, what now?"

"I'm heading north, towards what will be known as Northumberland... I suggest you do the same. It's either that, or death." That said, the strange old hermit bundled himself up in his cloak and set out along the coast.

Neeva watched his progress for a while, considering sneaking up behind him and getting revenge for Kal. In the end, he decided against it. Instead, he would go back to the hermit's hut and rest before following in his footsteps.

For the moment, however, he simply stood in the rain and watched the sea inch ever closer.

# Alternate Histories

# Cosmic Macabre

### Carlton Herzog

*Already I have been a boy and a girl*
*And a bush and a bird, and a silent fish in the sea.*
— Empedocles, Purifications.

The enigma of the octopus is the enigma of the cosmos itself. Just as there is never one tentacle, there is always more than one reality. As for us, we exist in a trench as dark as the ink the octopus secretes. We mistake unpredictable causes and effects for disorder, when in fact, they are the logical outcome of an order we cannot see. One that is too complex, distributed, and advanced for our monkey brain mathematics.

Perhaps, if like the octopus, we had evolved a brain in each appendage—digits included--we would be less disoriented by our happenstance existence.

But I have gotten ahead of myself with my exegesis on tentacles and the dark murmurs of the void. In the pages that follow, I will have ample opportunity to make my case for beatification as the Patron Saint of Pessimism. Going so far perhaps as to argue non-existence is preferable to life and offering the sobering reminder that even when the glass seems half full, the liquid inside is poison. But again I have digressed.

Know first that my wife Annie and I are trapped in a forsaken topography for which no idiom exists. Here anatomical frameworks are devoured, enlarged, rearranged, redacted, and shrunk. Many life forms are little more than portmanteaus, creatures stitched together with genetic scissors and glue by a sadistically imaginative invisible hand.

For all its weirdness, we believe that the ground on which we stand, and will shortly die, is the rattling ghost of Doggerland before it became submerged. Since we cannot read the timestamp of this haunted terrain, we cannot know if this be Doggerland past, present, or future. If this be the past, it is our fervent hope that some wayward bone digger will find my journal of nightmares. It will be up to the finder to decide whether my story was all in my head or it really happened. Certainly, our grotesquely deformed bodies and the Orb I will clutch, if found, will lend some credence to the tale.

Our timeslip began with an unusual broadcast from BBC 4. "We interrupt this program for a special news bulletin. We have just received a report that thousands of burnt and mutilated carcasses of giant octopi are washing ashore along the North Sea coastline. They appear to be colossal versions of the North Atlantic, or spoonarm octopus. The spoonarm is a small, short-armed octopus between 6 and 10 cm in length, with an average adult weight of around 45g. It has an eerily malleable body, sucker-studded arms, skin that can transform into a convincing facsimile of seaweed-or sand-in a flash, and an independent brain in each tentacle. Ordinarily, its mantle is globular, and covered in warts, especially around the eyes. The enlarged versions measure a solid fifty metres. Their tentacles seem adapted for land locomotion. Further, the globular heads are covered in eyes rather than warts.

The viewers should know that in addition to these Kraken, various chimaeras have been found. I'm told that there are instances where several grey seals have been fused into a single organism, along with sea bird wings, lobster claws, fins and beaks.

The event piqued my interest and that of my wife

Annie. We both worked at the London Natural History Museum as Junior Curators of the Paleolithic Collections. While we loved our work, we had an abiding nostalgia for fieldwork. We would often visit the village of Covehithe and stroll along the beach looking for artefacts. It is a place of Deep Time. Once I found a flat white object, a fusion of stone and bones, that turned out to be a mammoth's tooth. A few months' later, Annie found the jaw of a wolf with milky blue teeth and a harpoon carved from the antler of a deer. After that, I found a human skull packed tight with soil and full of worms.

When we arrived at Covehithe, members of the London Marine Biology Association, a contingent from Oxford, and a Krakenist cult were analysing the carcasses. As one might expect, there were also any number of curious citizens out for a look and a trophy. Annie and I separated ourselves from the scientists and curiosity seekers. We proceeded to explore the lonelier stretches of the beach. Since we were old hands at this game, we came prepared for any foreseeable contingency including an extended stay. I always brought my journal to record what and where we found our washed up Doggerland treasures. But even with our expertise, we could not have pictured what lay in store for us in the days ahead.

Our journey in the dark backward began with a

serendipitous discovery. We were wading in shallow water. My foot struck a hard object. I reached through the kelp that encased it and felt its contours. After some deliberation, I decided to give it a good yank. It was surprisingly light, as if it were made of gossamer. At first, I thought I had extracted the British equivalent of the Tollund Man, a perfectly persevered two thousand four-hundred-year-old body of a man found in a Danish peat bog. But it was not like any man I had ever seen.

The thing was covered in a luminescent green fungus, presumably the agent of its crisp preservation. It looked as if a man and a woman had been fused into a single six-legged body. The two heads melted into one another producing a grimace of sheer agony and terror. One set of arms functioned as the creature's front legs, the other as prehensile claws with elongated fingers ending in talons. The four former human legs imparted rear locomotion and the ability to assume a stable upright posture. The Double Thing had spines protruding from its back and flanks. Tentacles with sucker mouths coiled around the body. When I rolled it over, I found that its belly contained an enormous mouth with jagged teeth.

But there was more, for the creature clutched a glowing orb that seemed immune to the ravages of time and circumstance. Against my better judgement, I pulled it free from the chimaera's clutches. My Latin was too rusty to do the writing justice. But Annie knew many an ancient tongue and after a few hums and uh huh's rendered understandable what was to me pure Latinate gibberish.

You are trapped in an illusory labyrinth which is entirely the construction of your language. It is so thoroughly saturated and animated with notions of time that you assume time is linear and continuous. But that is wrong. Time doesn't just have breaks and gaps. It has many avatars, kinds and modes. It is discontinuous and polyform. This Orb of Safu is an Aleph. It allows the person who holds it to exist in many chronometric frames of reference at once.

As I examined it, turning it over and over, it glowed and vibrated. Slowly, our world changed as if it had been sprinkled with pixie dust. Where there had been a sea, now there was sand and marshland. I was thunderstruck as was Annie.

Annie said, "My God, the sea is gone, gone. If the North Sea has been replaced by land, we must have gone back in time to Doggerland."

I grasped for a rational explanation for what we were seeing.

"Perhaps, the Orb's vibrations are of such a potency to dissolve linear time and other boundaries of the atomic universe and thereby render them fluid. That would explain our current predicament but not the infestation of cryptozooans along the coast."

"Then why not use the Orb to get us home. I would do it myself but I'm not wearing my ruby slippers and we didn't come in a DeLorean."

'Let me picture our point of origin while holding the Orb," I said.

But nothing happened. We gave each other dumbfounded looks. Annie, not being one to mince words, exclaimed, "We're in the soup. Shit, this might not even be earth."

I tried to calm her down with some reassuring words. But I was in a panic.

"We need to stay calm. I think our best course would be to explore the place. Maybe we'll find a clue as to where and when we are. Come on love. It'll be like old times in Olduvai Gorge."

"I hated that shithole. Hot, dirty and nasty."

"I can't argue    with you there Honeybun    ."

I took her hand, and we began our walk-about into the land unknown.

The sheer density of life was overwhelming. All around us things jumped, hopped, flew, glided, floated, slithered, and burrowed. The air was thick with the pulsating sound of birds: chattering, lamenting, babbling, twickering, rattling, bugling, and crying. Much to our amazement, we saw a flock of flying squid pursuing a flight of fish-tailed albatross above us. They snared one here and there with their tentacles and dragged them down to brackish ponds of orange water. The sight of a tentacled coiled around a desperate albatross rising from the water to get away only to be pulled down again both fascinated and repelled me.

Annie picked up a broken branch and said, "I will bash their fucking heads in if they make a play for me. Flying fucking squid. Bloody bonkers that. And yet here we are."

After that, we encountered one biological heresy after another. There were land corals. Not of calcified micro-organisms, but of heaped human bodies projecting without order. They existed as fleshy haphazard tangles of mortified souls grasping at whatever passed by for sustenance. Prehensile hands clutched careless rodents, while semi-melted faces moaned and cried in disjointed syllables that may or may not have been a language.

Some treetops dripped a sticky blue ichor that gathered itself into herds of headless blobs propelled by pseudopods. They shimmered with a vile light and stank obscenely. Above them, drifting sentient clouds filled with a thousand eyes, churned, and changed shape, reflecting perhaps the workings of their gaseous minds. We stood aghast as when one floated downward, engulfed a wild boar, and then rose again leaving behind a smoking skeleton.

Every now and then, we would stop so I could pen these words. One occasion, a large bullfrog hopped in front of us. It stopped for a moment and looked us over with its enormous bulging black eyes. Then it spoke.

"Twas brillig and the slithy toves

Did gyre and gimble in the wabe

All mimsy were the borogoves

And the mome raths outgrabe."

Annie exclaimed, "A frog reciting Lewis Carroll's *Jabberwocky*. Is there no end to this madness?"

The frog replied, "Don't you two gob smackers get it? Doggerland is *Alice in Wonderland* on crack. Here everything is permitted, from snark hunting to whiffling through the tulgey wood and burbling as you go."

"How can you, a frog talk?" Annie asked.

"In this place, where there is no ontological purity, how can I not?  Your limited mind has an appetite for forms and structure. But here forms dissolve and reshape themselves. That much should have been clear when your "North Sea" was replaced by this land mass."  Reality is a plural thing. There is no single version of it. Rather, there are hundreds, thousands of versions to be found in the dark backward. And they all refute your belief in a monistic reality.

Now, I have hopping and fly eating to do

So, it is with an amphibious heart I bid you adieu."

The frog leaped high into the air, so high it was caught in the tentacles of a low flying squid. The squid used its free tentacles to rip off the frog's legs and deposit them in its ferocious maw. After that, I could, with the aid of my binoculars, see the squid swallow the remainder whole. It was yet another example of pathological life that should not exist in any rational scheme of things. A religious person might regard what we had seen as evidence of what we sloppily call the supernatural. But it is simply another kind of nature that lies beyond human comprehension. Impersonal, blind, and indifferent to human expectations.

Annie had reached her breaking point. She reached in her pack and took out her vape tubes.

"Before I take another step in this cosmically weird place, I need to get mellow. Otherwise, my head is going to explode. Want a taste lover?"

I desperately wanted to get high. But I didn't want to compromise my reaction time, given the profusion of monsters that inhabited this strange land. And I wanted to stay clear-headed so I could find us a way home.

"I'll pass for now. But if you need it, then go ahead. We both don't need to be freaked."

As Annie sucked in the hash oil fumes, she became

calm and then chatty and ebullient. I envied her state of mind but knew that I would be doing the thinking for the both of us.

We continued our impromptu expedition into the pandemonium that was Bizarro Doggerland. There were explosions of colour--from wildflowers and sounds from the throb and stridulations of insects—all around us. We walked through areas bursting with life where grasses and reeds grew, and swirls of moss spread out in great lakes of luminous green as bright as neon lights. There were silver plumed grasses, savannah thistle, knapweed, wild fennel, stork bill goosefoot and wormwood. Giant eight-legged white flowers with woody stems and glabrous leaves walked over glittering expanses of mud and sand made electric by jumping sand fleas, crabs, shrimp.

Annie said, "It's so beautiful here, the creepiness notwithstanding."

"It is indeed," a thunderous voice said.

We turned and saw an enormous earth worm protruding from the soil. It swayed hypnotically back and forth. It opened its mouth and said, "Such a beauty was Delilah. Tis a pity she was a whore. But is it not true that every beauty, however excellent    , always has some corruption in its proportion? Amazing is it not how complete is the delusion that beauty is goodness.

Often beauty and folly are companions. How could it be otherwise for the most beautiful things in the world are the most useless. Beauty is a frail ornament, a passing flower, a momentary brightness belonging only to the skin. For like everything else, it cannot escape death. Don't take my word for it. Go visit the sepulchre up ahead and see for yourselves."

It dove back into the ground. Once more, we had been visited by a strangely grotesque and curiously philosophical creature.

"If we ever get back, we can write a book: *Johnny and Annie in Doggerland*. In addition to the weirdos, we have seen here, we should include the Bandersnatch, the borogrove and the hookah smoking caterpillar," Annie added sarcastically.

"I prefer the Jabberwocky, the JubJub bird and the March Hare. But since we are guests in whatever this place is we can't be picky. The next time a creature chats us up, we need to question it. Find out how we can get the hell out of here," I exclaimed.

We pressed on and came to a dishevelled palaeolithic graveyard. We found skeletons of men fatally damaged from heavy blows to their skulls. One had a stone tipped spear lodged in the barricade of his ribs close to the heart it pierced. There were bodies of women and children, their heads covered by leather caps decorated with deer teeth and snail shells and bodies placed on the outstretched wings of swans. The human remains gave way to others more disturbing. We found the remains of giants that stood four metres tall at the shoulder. They had spirally twisted tusks projecting from their upper jaws and claws for hands.

From our vantage point, we could see a group of hunters with hair growing all over their bodies. They carried spears with bone barbed points used for fishing. With my mini-binoculars, I could see the sharpness of the backward slanting teeth and admired the elegance and fluidity of the blade's line. We stayed low to avoid detection since we didn't know if they were cannibals.

As we laid low, Annie said, "I'm knackered and I'm gagging. We need to find a place to rest and pop the canteens."

Once the hunters had moved out of sight, we found a small hummock and took a break. We watched a great herd of mammoths moving diagonally along our line of travel. That sighting seemed to be further confirmation that we had time slipped back to Doggerland. But time had become more problematic than that.

"Johnny, we have been walking for some time, but the sun hasn't moved a bit in the sky. And the clock on my phone shows nothing but zeros," Annie noted.

"Maybe the writing on the Orb is right about the

plasticity of time. It could be that it moves differently here wherever here is. Let's keep moving."

We had gone another hour or so when we came to a bog. Like all bogs, it was a riddle since it was neither water nor land but both. It was a place of spongy structures, sudden mists, miasmas, and self-igniting balls of flying fire. Stew of digestion and embrocation, it could, depending on its chemical composition, strip a body of all its calcium while preserving the skin fingernails and hair. Or it could destroy all trace of flesh and leave behind an intact skeleton. As we surveyed the domed red and green cushions of moss and pools of black water, we spotted burial mounds. A moment later we saw the bog walkers; hooded figures moving on enormous stilts. They were harvesting peat, presumably for fuel and iron to make weapons and tools.

"We need to stay off their palaeolithic radar. It's time to head back. We'll retrace our steps back to our starting point and keep going west into Britannia."

That was easier said than done for a new pageant of nightmares awaited us. We had walked no more than a mile when we saw a cluster of long-legged figures in the distance. I assumed it was another cadre of bog walkers, but as we circumnavigated the group, I saw that it was a horde of ambulatory octopi. It had cornered a herd of rhinoceros. One by one the squealing beasts were snared, torn apart, and devoured in chunks and bits.

Before we could do anything, the ground around us erupted with octopi in all directions. Several stood no more than ten metres away. And as they swept their Argos eyed heads over the land looking for prey, I assumed our time had run out. Any minute we would be grabbed and then pulled apart. An eminently logical conclusion, to be sure.

But this was a place of madness, not logic. For the sky above us fulminated, then exploded in a great ball of light. An enormous something, indiscernible through the glare, cast a great shadow over the cephalopodic feast. The octopi forgot about their meal and turned their attention skyward, flailing their free tentacles and screeching like wounded birds.

Blue fire bolts shot from above incinerating the monsters. Some burned then burst into a thousand pieces. Others were seared, others split in two. Within minutes, the entire herd had been reduced to ash and cinders.

Annie and I stood there unharmed but dumbfounded. Our confusion grew when a hologram materialised before us. It was a decidedly beautiful woman in ancient Egyptian attire.

"I am Cleopatra, formerly Queen of the Nile, now captain of the warship Nyctalops. You must leave this unholy place. For the ground on which you stand is not ground, but the hide of Otha Mal, the Father of All Beasts, Bringer of the Evil Dawn. The fiends you have encountered are his bodily parasites and offspring."

She was a study in beauty, even as a wavering hologram: a sensitive mouth, firm chin, liquid eyes, broad forehead, and prominent nose. She was also a medusoid with a cluster of snakes entwined within her black hair and fangs protruding from her upper lip.

I am the living embodiment of the goddess Isis and Protector of Worlds. But what manner of men are you? You look out of time. How came you to this gloomy place?"

I told her that we called this place Doggerland, and that it existed in our past. I told her how the Orb of Safu took us from the present to the past.

"The Aleph! It is spoken of in whispers because it is a primordial change engine. Whatever it touches cannot remain the same," she warned.

"Can we use it to get back to our time?" I asked.

"I cannot say. It is a fickle thing. You regard this as Doggerland past. But it is also a Doggerland future beyond that of your natural time. By a million or so years."

"Can you bring us forward to our present?" I pleaded.

"Sadly, I cannot. Your intimate contact with the

Orb makes you a carrier for its randomness. If we took you aboard, the contagion would wreak havoc on our instruments. In trying to help you, we could very well fly into a sun or a black hole or be lost forever in the seething vortex of time," Cleopatra explained.

"What do you recommend?" I asked.

"At the very least, remove yourself from the land mass you call Doggerland. For we are going to reduce its surface to a burnt cinder. Admittedly, we cannot kill Otha Mal, but we can drive Him deep into the earth, and cover Him with salt water. The saltwater's ions will inhibit his movements for a few millennia. When he resurfaces, we will repeat the process. I suggest you return to your point of origin and hope that the Orb *sua sponte* resets itself and takes you home."

The hologram disappeared. We gathered ourselves and did as Cleopatra suggested. We came to the margin of a small, blackish-green lake. On the far side, I could see a cluster of giant purple flowers swaying and writhing like serpents. They had vines instead of tentacles and with my binoculars, I could see they had used them as constricting coils to snare a palaeolithic man and woman.

"Let's go. We need to help them," I exclaimed.

We ran toward the helpless couple. My plan was to cut them free with my clasp knife. As I hacked and sawed at the tentacles, the man and woman—Neanderthals—

went pale and limp. The tentacles had sprouted smaller tentacles with sucker mouths that were draining the two of their lifeblood. As fast as I cut one tentacle in half, another sprang up in its place.

Annie had taken it upon herself to smash the segmented flower stalks with a sharp rock. The things hissed like serpents from their confederacy of sucker mouths. But despite our best efforts to that point the things refused to relinquish their prey.

In desperation, Annie took her lighter and burned the stalks. They dropped the two troglodytes and went after her. The sucker mouths embedded themselves in her. I cut away the squirming coils, but the suckers were in deep. I dragged Annie away and burned them with her lighter. They did not ignite but squirted off, sprouted legs, and ran away.

Annie's metamorphosis began shortly after that. Subtle at first, it began with facial acne and the loss of hair. After that, she sprouted spines along her arms and her fingers elongated. Outwardly she seemed in high spirits, but I could feel the potency of her fears as she became something morbid and hideous. Eventually the cruel reality of her transformation overwhelmed her, and she dropped to her knees crying,

"Jesus Christ. We are trapped in this netherworld where the sun doesn't move, and the wildlife is one horror after another. On top of that, I am becoming one of the monsters. You need to kill me before…"

I tried to calm and reassure her.

"We'll rest a bit then keep walking. Sooner or later, something must give. Whatever is happening to you is the result of some toxin. The proteins in it are rewriting your DNA. That can be fixed with gene therapy once we get you home. So, you need to suck it up and hang in there."

She gave me a wistful look and shook her head.

"My body's been hijacked by some malign force that will reshape me long before we find a way out of here. You're the one that needs to suck it up and either kill me or leave me behind before I hurt you. My mind is becoming unhinged and I'm not sure I can control the impulses I feel."

I hoisted her to her feet.

"I'm not leaving you behind. We keep going until we can't go anymore. And whatever happens, will be to the both of us."

She managed a faint smile and took my hand. We began walking. Whatever change was taking place had slowed. That gave us both hope we might yet get her some help.

That tiny slice of hope faded. A horde of black beetles the size of house cats went scurrying by us. They paid us no mind. But Annie grabbed one by its legs and used it to smash several before the pack skittered off into the distance. Initially, I thought she did it out of fear until I saw her claws peel away the carapace of one. She tossed it aside and then plunged her face into the giant beetle's guts. She devoured its innards, stopping every now and then to suck up its black blood. I didn't try to stop her. Whether that was from curiosity, resignation, or fear, I cannot say. It may have been the unendurable stench of the creature's internal organs that kept me at bay because I could not stop retching.

Once she had her fill, she lay down, closed her eyes, and drifted off into a contented sleep. I didn't try to wake her. I did consider her spontaneous insect feast to be a watershed moment, one that made me seriously consider leaving her behind. After all, I might become an item on her menu down the road. And her ferocity and lethal adaptations would probably be more than I could handle with a clasp knife.

Annie didn't sleep long. When she woke, the whites of her eyes were gone. Her entire visual apparatus consisted of two unblinking black eyes. Her chin had become prognathous, her teeth enlarged to the size of a horse's.

I asked her how she felt. She replied in deep guttural tones that indicated her vocal cords were less than human.

"I feel like a new woman. Refreshed, renewed and ready for action."

I couldn't look at her. She was covered in bright green and purple patches. Where there had been hair, there were now pulsing violet tumours. She had grown taller by half a foot. In that moment, the only thing to do was press forward and hope for the best. Although Annie was madly grotesque, she had an unexpected positive attitude, and for now, that would suffice.

We had not gone far when we encountered another conversation between the ancient and recent past. Massive skeletal remains littered our current line of travel. At first, I thought they might be dinosaur bones. But as we walked beneath a stupendously high and long rib cage, I grasped the tremendous size of the now fossilised creature. When alive, it must have stood one hundred metres tall and some three hundred long. The other remains were equally monumental.

Our awe at the monster graveyard gave way to fear, for no sooner had we left it than we encountered another tribe of hirsute hunter-gatherer. Fearless Annie, fully imbued with eldritch power, wanted to engage, and presumably eat them. I convinced her a retreat was in order. We circled around them and kept moving west.

Later, we stopped in a small outcropping of rocks. As I lay back, Annie cuddled up close to me. I wanted to run for my life, she was so damned repugnant. But I put my arms around her. In the next moment, a tentacle burst through her shirt and embedded its sucker mouth in my neck. Before it could drain me, I grabbed it and yanked it out before it could do any more damage. But the damage had been done. Its venom coursed through my veins; I could feel the subtle changes in my body. Soon, I would like Annie.

At that point, I was resigned to our fate. Sometime later, the same hunter gatherers we had seen came by. With barks and grunts, they demanded our clothes and gear. Given our current condition, I saw no point in arguing. But when I tried to hand them the Orb, they ran off leaving me with it, my pen and journal. Even their crude prehistoric minds knew the Orb for the ominous and prepossessing power it was.

We lay next to each other as the change took hold. That's when the horror of the moment truly struck me. Over time, Annie and I would become the bisexual creature we had found in the cove. We had, it seemed, been caught in a strange loop. That reminded me of the lines from T.S. Eliot's Four Quartets:

*We shall not cease from exploration*
*And the end of all our exploring*
*Will be to arrive where we started*

*And know the place for the first time.*
*Through the unknown, remembered gate*
*When the last of earth left to discover*
*Is that which was the beginning?*
*At the source of the longest river*
*The voice of the hidden waterfall*
*And the children in the apple-tree*
*Not known, because not looked for*
*But heard, half-heard, in the stillness*
*Between two waves of the sea.*

Now, I watch in amazement as I undergo my Kafkaesque metamorphosis: a tentacle here, a crab claw there, spines, barbs, and all manner of things sprouting from my body. My entries are nearly complete. Good thing since we are fusing together becoming the one who is the many: a boy and a girl and a bush and a bird, and a silent fish in the sea.

# Flesh of my Flesh

Jasmine Jarvis

## *Part I.*

It is said that in the beginning, a God created the universe.

The stars, the planets, he breathed celestial life into the black void. But the universe in all its vast ethereal beauty was not enough, and the God became lonely. And so, he took the brightest of stars and crushed it in his hands, turning it into dust. Holding his hands to his mouth, he exhaled, gently breathing life into the particles, releasing it from his grasp the dust swirled and thrummed, sparked, and began to take shape. Bodies formed in different shapes and sizes. Creatures born of visions on his day of rest.

These new creatures, grateful for what this God had done, immediately bowed to him and swore to be his faithful servants.

At first, the God feared these new beings that he had created. He contemplated extinguishing them for he was worried that he had made a grave mistake in desperation for company. None of them looked like him. But as time went on, he grew to love these creatures, and as he expanded the universe, he appointed them roles and duties. Some he favoured more than others, and these he gave them the title of Angel. As the universe grew bigger, his attention was spread thin and he had not noticed one of his planets, the one he had named Gaia, had begun to change. One of his angels had taken a fascination with Gaia. She was beautiful to behold, and the angel fell in love with her. God had forbidden the angels to touch any of the planets. The angel descended upon Gaia, and with its touch on her surface, it had woken Gaia up and life began to emerge from her.

The angel marvelled at what they had done. Mountains rose, seas formed around lands, and life forms emerged. The angel had done to Gaia, what its God had done to it. Awakened by stardust and eternity. It trembled with excitement at this new achievement. And while God was busy elsewhere in the universe, the angel remained with Gaia, marvelling at her ability to sustain life. Creatures moved from water to land. Large, cold-blooded monsters of simple intelligence battled it out for their survival while the angel watched on. Rotations around the Sun, all life ebbed and flowed on Gaia. The large cold-blooded creatures were soon through their era, and following their demise, they were replaced by new creatures, with their blood now warm and able to adjust to Gaia's cooler climates.

As time went on, the angel began to think more about what the God could do. After the first contact with Gaia, the angel stepped back and only watched over as life developed. It did not interfere. Until now. Could it take a star, and just as God had made the angels from the dust of a crushed star, could the angel create something new? The more it dwelled on the possibility, the more it desired to seek the power of God and create its own beings as a gift to his love. God would never know. What the angel would create, it would be able to survive hidden away on Gaia.

The angel looked at the stars surrounding Gaia, but none were beautiful enough for what the angel wanted. Instead, it reached into its own chest, taking a handful of its celestial flesh, and guided by the visions it had held of a new life form, created something that the angel called human. As God had breathed life into the angel, so too, the angel breathed life into these humans before placing them on Gaia's soft earth where she loved and nurtured them, making sure they were provided for and offering them protection in a lavish garden.

These beings were pure perfection.

Just as the angel upon its own creation had bowed to its God and promised to serve it, so too did the humans to the angel. When they asked the angel what they were to address it as, the angel thought for a moment; its God had never given it a name. Eventually, it replied with "Tsathoggua."

When the God returned, he was informed that one of his angels had gone against instruction and had altered God's most beloved planet, Gaia. God summoned this angel to come to him and he questioned it over what had taken place in his absence. The angel explained what he had done, and how as God loved his angels, the angel too, loved what it had created. With each detail the angel gave, God felt jealousy taking seed within him. For only the God could create stars and planets to fill the space. Only he could create the celestial beings, his angels. This angel had broken the rule and had created life from its own being. He realised that the angel now posed a serious threat to his position. The angel had crossed over to becoming a god.

God thundered in rage and jealousy, moving to punish both the angel and Gaia. He bound them together, casting the angel into Gaia's molten core where it would burn for all eternity, and as for Gaia, the knowledge that she was now the prison for the angel she loved, and that she was the cause for its eternal suffering would be her punishment. He then turned his attention to the angel's creations – the humans. He would destroy them, as they, of the angels' being, could find and potentially release it. As he set about eradicating them, some had fled under the ground, with Gaia giving them shelter while she wept for the ones she could not save. From her core, the angel screamed with every human the God killed.

The angel, Tsathoggua, vowed that upon its release, it would wipe out its creator and the other angels.

The final violation came with the God grabbing at the soil and crushing it into crude forms, breathing life and creating humans that would now have to evolve "from the nothing of which they were created from" referring to Gaia now being lesser than in the wrathful God's eyes.

With the threat of a stronger God now removed, he resumed his hold over the universe. Creating and shaping the space. He revelled in the newfound power he had over the humans and of Gaia. He enjoyed the fear he instilled in them; it was exciting.

## *Part II.*

Over time, the environment on Gaia continued to change and the life within evolved. From searing hot and dry climates to freezing ice and snow covering continents, the new humans managed to survive. Populations expanded, and the busy God decided it was time to delegate roles to the angels to supervise the humans. These angels now became the idols of worship in return for them ensuring provisions of food, shelter, safety, and better weather conditions. The humans moved around, taking with them their beliefs, and carrying amulets and totems of their deities.

When the great ice age had passed, the snow and ice melted away to reveal a lush and fertile land that would become known as Doggerland. As herds of animals traversed the landscape, the humans followed. They realised that Doggerland was a viable environment, and the reluctance to continue with a nomadic life had shifted as tribes now established camps, erected their basic shelters, and learned to live off the land. The coastal regions were established by tribes as prime locations for the harvesting of seafood which became the main staple in their diet. Rituals were carried out to appease the deities of the sea, the land, and the sky. The angels obliged - when they felt like it. When the God was not watching, they liked to see how far they could push the humans and Gaia to the brink of collapse.

With established camps, there were still nomads who would make their way through Doggerland. With them, they would bring stories from where they had traversed. Stories of battles and the settling of new regions. And of a cult, known as the Tsathoggua, that was moving down from the North and making their way to Doggerland. In their wake, dead bodies of young women, the daughters of Chiefs, bound in rope and clothed in something, not of leather or fur, but the colour of blood. When asked about what those in the cult looked like, the visitors would respond in lowered tones so as not to scare the women and children, speaking of beings that emerged from the marshlands, and shapeshifted between human and elk. In human form, the antlers would remain. They were taller than normal and incredibly strong, and they were looking for something or *someone*. They moved from camp to camp along the coastlines, watching the tribes before striking. In the morning the chief's daughter or daughters would be missing, only to be found later, their bodies washed up on the shore.

# Part III.

The Chieftain's wife laboured into the long night. Her breathing was ragged, cut by sobs and screams of pain and fear. By her side was her husband, no one else was allowed in the hut. Outside the sea was dark and turbulent. Flashes of lightning cut across the sky, the air, electric. A bad omen, the Chieftain realised that they were in trouble. No good could come of this, the Gods were angry but surely it had nothing to do with the child that was being born. A little cry carried over the hissing winds, and he met his wife's fearful expression, and at that moment their hearts sank.

A daughter.

When a daughter is born of the Chieftain and his wife, the monsters from the marshlands, known as Tsathogguans, appear when she is of age, and on that night, she will be taken and killed in a ritual. The very creatures his wife had run away from as a child would now find them to steal their child in the belief she would be the one to summon their God. Outside the sea roared and gnashed at the shore.

He looked at his wife who was clinging tightly to their newborn. She seemed to know what he was thinking, and the look on her face told him that she was not going to give her child over.

"No! We are not sending her away! She is *our* child!"

Her voice swelled with fear and rage at the very thought that her daughter would be taken from her, even though she knew that to keep her would put her and their tribe at risk.

"It is for her safety. You *know* who you are, where you come from, and what she will become for *them*. We have the guilt of the innocent deaths of all those daughters of the other chieftains in our souls because you ran away, and I protected you…"

"Our best option is for one of the women to take her inland, away from the marshlands, and there she will raise our daughter until she is an adult and can return to us and our home. I will have my best and strongest men escort to make sure our daughter remains safe in passage. We can't risk her staying here. They will know of her and when her time is up, there will be nothing we can do to stop them. You know that just as well as I do!"

"There has to be another way?" Tears were welling in her eyes as she looked at him pleadingly.

"We will raise her as if she is our son. Dress her like a son, teach and train her like a son. Surely that will keep those monsters from finding her. We will give her your name. No one will know other than us. Don't take my baby from me. I won't allow it."

The Chieftain could see that there would be no

arguing. His wife was exhausted, and he knew that the Gods were angry and there was nothing to be done more that night. With their baby cradled in her mother's embrace, at that moment, he vowed that he would do everything in his power to protect their daughter. They would raise her as his son. He prayed to his own gods that they would keep his family safe from the Tsathugguans. In the morning he would announce to his tribe the birth of his new son.

From that night on, the child was raised as a son. As she grew and began to question her surroundings, her parents told her of the fate of daughters born to the Chiefs along the waters who would be stolen in the dark of the night by monsters with antlers protruding from their skulls and for the daughters to be found dead on the sands the next day, and that for her safety she had to pretend to be their son. She was treated like the boys in the tribe, and the women and girls waited on her hand and foot. Her parents, not having any more children after their daughter was born, worked to keep their secret.

Her mother was always close by to correct her if she forgot her place.

The years went by and as she grew, she found her mind and soul shifting more to the sea. It was like she was one with the water, or more with the something "other" within its depths. It was a calling, a low voice that would whisper in her ear making her turn to face the waters, heeding the call but not understanding why. Her father noticed her behaviour, and he knew who it was she could hear. His wife, when she was at that age, could also hear the voice, which was why she never ventured close to water. For the Tsathogguans, there was one supreme god who would rule over all in the universe, and to release it from its prison, they needed the flesh of its flesh.

The older the Chieftain's daughter got, the stronger this instinct within her became. This could only mean one thing. That she was the key that they would be seeking.

He had stopped her from heading out in the canoes to fish with the other men, for when she stepped onto the shore, the water would froth and churn at her feet.

# Part IV.

The water speaks to me. I hear **him** all the time and at first, it was soft, a whisper, but now that I am approaching womanhood, his voice is louder. It is deep, and its timbre makes me feel like I am losing the earth beneath my feet. I can see the vision of myself sinking into the sea, surrounded by blood as I fall to where he is waiting.

My chest hurts all the time because mother must bind my chest every morning as everyone believes me to be the Chieftain's son. My whole life has been stories about monsters who are waiting for me to reveal myself. They will steal me away and I will be killed in their ritual.

Instead, I am kept with the men. The women treat me like I am a young man. They wait on me, tend to me, and just what would they say, what would they do if they knew I too was a female? The daughters of Chieftains go missing when they come of age, and so a young man I must be. But what will happen when I pass this danger if I ever pass it? Am I to remain in this form?

Stealing a moment in the hut, she stretched and tugged at the tight leather binding her chest flat. Her shoulders ached and her breathing was becoming pinched. Her mother insisted on the binding so their people would not realise she was indeed a girl. If word got out, it would only be a matter of time before the Tsathogguans would find them. Her body had been conditioned, shaped by her upbringing as a Chieftain's son. She was lean and muscular from spending days out chasing and hunting prey. Her clothing was layered to help disguise the undeniable soft feminine curve of her hips. She sighed and looked out and up at the sky. Sun would be setting soon, and when it was night, she was able to remove the binding and breathe.

Out by the ashes of last night's campfire, children played while the women tended to the preparation of that night's meal. Around them, the fishing nets were strewn, picked clean of the harvest earlier that day.

The sea.

Summoned by an unseen force, she left the hut and walked to the shore. It was here that her father now found her standing knee-deep in the shallows, in her hands a gelatinous creature that pulsated as the water churned around her knees. Her father could not hear what the creature was saying to her, but he was full of fear as he dragged her back to the gritty sand of the shore. He grabbed the creature from her hands and tossed it back to the water before spinning her to face him, his hands now pressing down hard on her shoulders causing her to wince and try to yank herself away. He would not let go.

In a low and angry tone, he warned her that she was to never go in the water again. He released her only when she promised to abide by his order.

He then led her back to the camp where a group of young men were about to set out for a hunt. Taking up her bow and arrows, he thrust them at her and instructed her to go with them. Reluctantly, she followed the young men out to the open field, making their way to the woodlands.

They moved quickly and quietly through the wooded area towards where they had been told earlier by a passing visitor that a flock of elk had been sighted in the woodlands. The Chieftain's daughter kept her eye on the shadows that flicked and scattered about, just out of her reach but following her along her path. The young men in front stopped, dropping into a crouch, signalling the prey was ahead. She instinctively followed, dropping low and peering ahead at the elk that had congregated in the small clearing of the woods. The tree branches intertwined above, creating a ceiling where thin shafts of sunlight speared through into the clearing, the canopy cast shadows over the animals as if a cloak of protection, making it difficult for the hunters to single out their prey.

They saw the silhouette of the largest of the herd. The stag lifted its head up, and the others around it shifted as it moved. The light bounced off pelt and antler.

It was the tribe's custom that the stag was reserved for the Chieftain's son to take down. The other men shifted carefully aside to allow her to move forward, closer to the clearing taking up her position, silently drawing an arrow and setting it in the string of the bow. The thumb of her left hand traced over the hunter's blessing etched into the curved wood of the bow, the thumb of her right hand pressed down on the etching on the arrow, asking the gods for a straight and true strike.

With her gaze locked on the dark shape of the stag, she steadied her breathing, drawing the arrow back before the sudden release and the sharp thrum of the taught horsehair bow as the arrow shot through the clearing and into her target. A mighty scream erupted from the stag which sent the herd bolting further into the dark of the woods. The stag rose, doubling in height, its shape shifting from that of a stag into a human-like form with antlers protruding from its head. A creature tall and muscular, it lurched to its feet, swaying from side to side before steadying itself. The monster screamed again, glowing amber eyes filled with pain and rage, as it yanked the arrow from its torso. Clutching the arrow in its large hand, the creature stared in the direction of where she and the young men were crouched, frozen to the ground in fear and horror. Through the brush it locked eyes with *her*, and as it stepped into a shaft of light, she could see it appeared to be the form of a tall naked man with antlers protruding from his head. His amber-coloured eyes went from rage to surprise, then recognition, before his face broke into a sinister smile exposing teeth that had been filed into sharp points. The arrow fell from his hands as he now broke into a sprint in her direction, a guttural growl erupting from his chest, arms outstretched, fingers curled in anticipation of securing the very thing he and his people had been so desperately searching for.

From behind, arrows and spears flew overhead in the direction of the creature, missing him as he cleared the distance between him and his prey.

His sight was set on the Chieftain's daughter.

The young men screamed, and one grabbed at her arm, hoisting her to her feet and dragging her until her legs began to carry her properly, moving her out of the woods. Reaching the field, she glanced over her shoulder. There on the edge of the woodlands he stood, the monster from the stories her mother had told her, and on either side of him, stood the others, all naked and all with antlers protruding from their heads. Her pace slowed as the young men raced towards the camp where the Chieftain, his wife, and the others gathered. The hypnotic voice carried across from the sea, where it reached her now, halting her in her tracks. It was telling her that it was time. She could see the crimson swirling about her, and her heart quickened in terror. She turned towards camp, to her mother standing there helpless, watching in horror.

She could hear her father rallying the men.

The Chieftain's daughter looked back to where the creatures were still standing. The cult of the Tsathoggura. The one she had shot with the arrow, now stood slightly in front of others. Amber eyes watched her intently. She was unable to move. Her body locked up. Her heart and mind would not let her take another step towards the camp no matter how much she willed it, there was something deep within her that held her firmly to the ground. She heard the shout of her father as he sprinted for her, behind him, he was flanked by the men, armed with spears and clubs. The Tsathogguans charged forward. Gravity released her and she began to run for her father.

The Tsathogguan's leader bounded across the ground towards her. He grabbed her from behind, lifting her up from off the ground and hoisting her over his shoulder in one swift and powerful move, before pivoting and sprinting back to the woods. She held her hands out to her father and let out a scream as the darkness of the forest swallowed her. The other creatures turned and followed their leader back into the woods, leaving the Chieftain and his men behind.

That night as the Chieftain's wife cried out for her daughter, the Chieftain was confronted by their people. Fear, despair, and anger ran through them as they demanded answers from their leader.

Why had he lied to them about his daughter?

It was to protect her, to protect them.

From what? What were those *things*?

He sank onto the ground, hands clasped in his lap, his head bowed, he drew in a deep and measured breath before telling them his wife's story.

"An angel had fallen in love with the Earth and its love for her led it to create the first humans from its very being. The God who had created it was jealous of the powers it possessed, and of the creations that came from it, and its love of the earth. An angel's purpose is not to create new life, but to serve the God, and so the God had imprisoned the angel to burn within the earth and wiped out its children.

"The very few that had survived had done so because they were sheltered underground by the earth but, over time, they had turned their back on their creator so they could survive in the new world with the new primitive humans under the rule of the new god. The earth, unable to bear the thought of torturing the angel she loved, and angered by the rejection of its own creations, revealed the truth about Tsathoggua, the false god and his angels, and the creation of the universe to the shapeshifters from the marshes, in the hope that these creatures who had long been maligned by humans and the rule of our gods, would find the angels descendants for retribution. They began the search for the surviving children, whose bloodline stemmed directly from Tsathoggua. These marsh creatures now want to wipe out humans and align themselves with the one powerful God rather than worship the many.

"They found my wife when she was but a small child, and when she came of age, she learned from whom she came from and that she would be sacrificed, and so she fled. I found her and I promised I would protect her. Despite this, the Tsathogguans had heard whispers she had grown and married a Chieftain, and as she was now too old for the ritual, they set about moving through the lands, stealing the young daughters of the Chieftains, hoping to find another with the bloodline of the angel."

"When the flesh is returned to Tsathoggua, the earth will shake, the seas will rise, and all those who denied the angel will suffer its wrath. Our gods will not be able to protect us."

When he finished, the people turned their backs on him, for they realised now that they have been cursed, betrayed by the leader they trusted; their peace now shattered. They demanded that he and his wife leave the camp to never return. He pleaded for them to follow him, that they needed to go to higher ground now, but they would not listen to him anymore. Together, the Chieftain and his wife fled into the night for they both knew what was about to come.

## *Part V.*

The group of Tsathogguans made their way through the woods heading towards water. The leader still held the Chieftain's daughter over his shoulder, his claws digging into her thighs, every time she tried to wrest herself free. The sound of the water lapping on the shore grew louder over the steps of the creatures, and the salt air mingled with the pine and earth. Soon trees gave way to sand, and there, waiting for them were more of their kind. They had come from her camp after searching for her parents only to discover that they had fled.

The leader set her down, and they surrounded her. Tall, imposing figures stared down at her, glowing eyes and antlers clicking as they moved in closer to her. One of them grabbed her and held her still, while another began to tear away her clothing. She protested, kicking, and punching out at their clawed hands, pulling hard to be free of their grasp but it was no use. She tried to ball up, to hide but was forced to remain upright and exposed until another approached her, in their hands, a material the colour of blood, and softer and lighter than the pelts and leather she was accustomed to wearing.

This is what that red in her vision was. It was quickly wrapped around her while low voices began to chant in a language unfamiliar to her. They cleared away, leaving her standing on the sand, clothed in the crimson material. Behind them, she saw small boats moored on the sand, water lapping at them. The leader was now in front of her, in his hands a headdress made of antlers. Placing the crown upon her head, the chanting began, and she was now ushered towards one of the small boats. Silently sobbing, she knew what was to come. The vision was unfolding in real time now and the sea kept calling for her. They bound her wrists and ankles, dipping her feet into the water before placing her into one of the boats which was then pushed out into the water. The leader and one other climbed into the boat with her, and taking up the oars they began to paddle out to sea. The others now in their boats, followed behind, their chants echoing out and over the dark and murky waters.

## *Part VI.*

By dawn, there was a change in the air. The camp, after the chaos of the night before which saw the Chieftain and his wife exiled, was now silent. The seabirds that woke early to catch the morning fish were nowhere to be seen. No one had risen to light the campfire for the morning. Fishing nets remained spread out over logs. The ground was waterlogged, and a stench was filling the air of the camp. In the huts, the people remained in eternal sleep. Their bodies sodden with marsh water, the murky green liquid trickling out of the corners of their greyed-out eyes and from their gaping mouths. Scratched into their skin were the markings of the Tsathoggua. Punishment for hiding the flesh of their God.

## *Part VII.*

The Chieftain's daughter was plunged headfirst into the cold water. The blood from incisions the Tsathogguan leader had made in her arms before she was thrown overboard now spilt into the water and it swirled and mingled with the crimson fabric that gently cocooned her body as an underwater current pulled her down to the sea floor where her body came gently to rest. Her blood and the crimson fabric swirled above her as the ground rumbled and split open. A prickling sensation starting in her scalp made its way through her body, her eyes fluttered once, twice, before slowly closing. Her final vision was of a bright and burning light obscuring the figure of what appeared to be a man. He embraced her, engulfing her in bright light till neither form could be seen. With its flesh returned, the prophecy was now fulfilled, the angel Tsathoggua, the all-powerful God would be free to claim its revenge.

## *Part VIII.*

Other camps along the coastline woke to the eerie silence. The men gathered their nets for fishing, making their way to where they had moored their boats, they stopped at the sight that awaited them. Before them the tide had receded for miles, exposing a blackened reef and sea life choking and dying on the exposed seabed. The fishermen's boats were stuck in sediment. The water out yonder was dark and still. More people gathered along the shoreline, looking at the sight of the sea peeled away from shore. With the release of Tsathoggua, came a roar rushing across from the sea to shore, knocking the people off their feet. The ground shook violently, and the sea began to churn. The sky went black as night; the sun was blocked out by a high wall of water that was now bearing down upon the shore.

Before the coastal people of Doggerland had time to react, it was too late. They were sucked out into the sea. Bodies were pulled under the waves and bashed and broken against the reef and rocks. The water pushed further into land, swallowing everything in its path. No sooner had the violence occurred, it was quiet again. The water settled over its new space, Doggerland was now mostly submerged below the sea's murky depths. A civilisation sealed within a watery grave.

# *Part IX.*

The body of the Chieftain's daughter slowly rose to the surface where the Tsathogguans remained waiting. They pulled her waterlogged body up and into the boat that she had been cast from and began the procession back to what little remained of Doggerland.

Reaching land, the leader climbed out of the boat and standing in the shallow waters, he lifted her body, still in the crimson garments she was dressed in for the ritual, up, and carried her towards the cave. Storm clouds swirled overhead and further out to sea an iridescent glow thrummed just below the churning surface. He had to move quickly as the false gods were now aware that the true and powerful God, the angel Tsathoggua, was about to make its return.

The body and its bearer disappeared into the inky depths of the cave, where he would lay her body upon the stone altar that her ancestors had built in the early days of their worship.

Gently setting her down on the altar's slab, he now carefully slid his hands out from beneath her. The garments they had dressed her in for the ritual, now stained the palms of his hands and wrists. The crimson garments were breaking down with her flesh. He glanced over his shoulder to see if he had been followed before removing the crimson shroud. He gazed upon her, she truly was beautiful, and she was indeed a true descendant of a celestial being. She looked like she was in peaceful slumber. He watched as her pale skin changed colour; violent blooms of purple and dark green spread out under the skin, before turning to foam.

Dissolving.

He remained by her side until all that was left were her bones, stained red by the dye from her garments. She was born from legend, and she had now returned to that legend. The gates of the prison had been unlocked and a God was restored to his rightful place. Her sacrifice absolved the angel's children of their sins. For that, they would be forever in her debt.

Outside the cave, the faithful called. With her form completely dissolved, the one who had carried her into the cave now stood back as Tsathoggua, the true God, born again from the flesh of its descendant, rose from the altar. From its back, tentacles unfurled and writhed. Its skin was as black as the night and shimmered with the stars from the night sky, just as it had been when its own God had first breathed it into being from stardust. It turned to face its follower, revealing its six eyes, all glowing white hot, studying the form in front of it. It was not like the ones it had created, but their worship proved them to be worthy and so Tsathoggua's head began to pulsate until large, shiny black antlers protruded from its scalp. Not only could Tsathoggua create life, but it realised that it could now also change its own form. Not even its creator could do that!

Together the God and its follower stepped out of the cave and into the light to cheers erupting from the devout heralding the reinstatement of the true God.

A new era in faith was about to take over.

# The Common Time Mysteries

John D. Chadwick

The drums of the primordial past now beat out a resounding thud; one, two, three, four; one, two, three, four; one, two, three, four; one, two, three, four.

Far across the earth, beyond the land, beyond the sea, once upon a puck'd cuckoo's beak, tales of magic were once weaved, by a hermit named Leughor, in a shack up upon the shore, made of beach wood and pebble stones, and with a goatskin for a door. It had been said that wise Leughor, was blessed by ancient, eldritch gods; A sign he had upon his head which held his bardic gifts aloft; a rune carved scar above his eyes, as if fine fire used as ink had smote his skin and baked it in, a firm branding like tarnished tin that drew the starry wisdom in. Referenced links to ancient picts were seen by other cunning men who read such things and spoke of him with the honour of priestly kings.

Leughor gazed over the ocean, to the land of once and gone far, to gather thread yarns of folklore, for golden tales of truth he saw. He'd sew the words with seaweed and drift from the sandy beaches where, there he'd decorate each on the sand with fair green leaves and flora. Wild pictures drawn upon the sand displayed the stories told, from before the flood drowned all the land that lay between the North to Gaul and this green island.

Though Leughor lived alone on that ancient shore, loneliness he never felt, folk would always draw to hear his tales of Doggerland, now sunk beneath the North, wild, deep, grim, greenish seas that wept aloud in grief and moaned gargantuan, blustering gales bringing tales to the shore. He told tales of old crones, fierce fay and hanged moles, dwarven folk and elven gold, creatures of all folds; monsters from the damned, dark wolds; of starmen and skyfolk, of toadstools and evil banes, of cauldrons filled aplenty, spears, swords and the slain of tribes with ancient names;  of giants hands, cursed talismans, of eldritch and weird sounds, of angles carved on standing stones and twilit roads and murky dams; where Balg stole his secret kin cooking them on fatty spits; where goblin kings played sinister tricks with brittle sticks on sticklebacks; where sunken ships and sleeping stones swore to protect barrow Lich, weighted, pressed below a blackened ditch, under the quag in dark, brackish depths.

So on to tell a tale once told by Leughor there on the shore, of things he'd seen before the flood that fed the future of all men, cast now into our most mythic known, cherished, fabled lore.

Hear the drums of the ancient past beating out a dread steady thump; one, two, three, four; one, two, three, four; one, two, three, four; one, two, three, four.

Far across the earth, beyond the land, beyond the sea, once upon a puck'd cuckoo's beak, lay land now hidden from sight by senseless sea. It was there folk from the bright stars fell down to earth and claimed the land, with all the fair, wild living things crawling, flying and swimming there, that lay betwixt the eastern dales and Southern fens and above the ground, below the sky, the Northern cliffs and western hillocks bound. Their claim was stated from then but some of those wild, living things did object to this claim, though others knelt and prayed to them and spoke their ancient names rejoicing them as kings and Gods and welcomed in their reign. The others plotted the end of them and became known as men.

These godly, denizens of stars, looked down upon

these brutal men. The men disliked their goodly ways, conical forms, their starfish heads, their stick-like arms and root-like legs. The star folk brought with them the fire, that caused much terror in the night. The men much coveted this with eyes burning red from jealous sight. The warmth and heat could aid their plight and end their bleak disturbing nights. Wars did avail to no man's aid, they fell before the star folk's whim, and thus some men became entranced and declared them as godly kings. Others fled to the far-off hills, they hid away in burrowed dens, saw their kin as no more than sheep, kept and owned and so imprisoned.

The starfolk saw that their own end, was drawing nigh in Doggerland. The food they ate became too scarce but seeing that they had risen those who worshipped them as godkings, they were glad that they had now sown such civilising seeds on men. So, unto the stars they returned, and men became as once before, but now they had the laws of gods to aid them in their paltry lives.

Men that had fled to the hills, now returned to their lowly farms, expecting their kin to welcome them with overflowing hearts. Of course, those risen by the gods saw those who'd left embarrassing. They still wore furs and their shoeless feet were torn and bloodied and sickening. They cast them all down and turned them out, whipped their backs and tore their skin. Refused to give them shelter, food, water or any aid therein. The outcasts now lived as low wolves. They banded together in tribes. The cunning ones became shaman and led them in the tangled wilds.

The land was green then and fertile and a harvest was always fine. The men fed well upon the wilds and for aeons looked up at time, monitored stars and saw sublime aligning patterns in these signs. This led them to cunningly see that time could be measured promptly; the future based upon the past, foretold the golden age would pass. As all things move quite circularly rotating around a cosmic pin, so below all follows that law, the key to everything. What has been will renew so as it is with joy and sorrow, thus what was once will return for ages pass as day to the morrow. This foretold a shadowy truth that if the elder starry gods, who came there once and claimed the land before them leaving once again, would return to enslave all men when certain stars aligned again.

So, they looked for lands to call home. In the far west, above the cliffs in the blue sky that no man climbed, they spied a golden land and smiled. From asunder these white chalk cliffs they spied the glory land above. There antlered beasts on the sky-high rocks wandered high on cloven foot. Now the clever, cunning, shaman amongst the wild, roving brave men, saw this prey there and could predict if beasts thrived above the cliffs, then they must eat on greenery. The land would surely support men too, so high in the hallowed sky, a better home should surely lie there to take as a sacred prize, beyond the cares of starry ones. So, this is how they were inspired, and left for the sworn plains of gold before the coming storm and flood wept sinking Doggerland, foretold.

Now, as all stories that are told always have some added turmoil, to shatter and flatten egos of their heroines and heroes, this true ancient tale must also follow the same rules set in stone. Perhaps these ancient shaman and old cunning men failed to see the signs lit up amongst the heavens. Whatever the reason the starfolk once more fell upon the ground. Humankind, little more than beasts, were considered property owned by these greater folk from the stars who claimed this Doggerland their own.

People, warlike as ever times, saw the ancient starry threat now very real upon the lands that sustained their own survival. The starfolk saw these fertile grounds to feed them too, not just the reeds, the green grass, the trees but also the creatures and all the seeds too. A war with gods would not be wise, but wisdom wasn't so common then amongst the tribes of humankind. With sharpened axes, spears and knives they struck the invading gods down. In turn they were smited too and blood ran thick wine on ancient grounds. Flesh was cut, burnt, flailed, skinned and then eaten by both armies alike. Despite the strength of ancient men, these elder gods would take their souls, adding them to their collection. Blood upon more blood now ran red upon the gore soaked, sorrowed land. The marks of Cane marked all men, and they were forevermore cursed.

Hear drums again from man's dawning, resounding in your very soul; one, two, three, four; one, two, three, four; one, two, three, four; one, two, three, four.

So let me tell another story, now that we have the founding's. This one was told by Leughor too, to the wandering tribes of bull. Our hero is a fervent man, made of stone like bone and gristle. His name was Fildred from the moon tribe that worshipped the goddess, Dana. Guilty of the utmost sin and doubly cursed was his black soul. He murdered his father over gold, mined in the deep, dark caverns before the cold sea flooded all. Cast out by the tribe of the moon, thrown out their gates, left to flounder, Fildred wandered far and wide by land and so was with the shaman when they first spied lofty cliffs above, and decided to climb with them.

With taut ropes spun from feathered loins, cut from birds that wallowed and flocked by the sunken base of the cliffs, they bravely climbed the haggard rocks. One by one they fled the green plains of Dogger, dizzy far below and crawled upon the spiked thickets they found grown upon land now known. Thus, Fildred took his first steps to fulfil his redeeming destiny.

If one who knows of otherwise and is a wiser man than I, let them speak now or hold their tongue. For I was told this tale myself from a wandering man of age, who I met amongst the bracken sleeping there in the pouring rain. He claimed he was there with Leughor and that he heard this very tale of the gristled, miserable, wretched soul, of whom this story reveals, became a golden shining light and shed its blackened cape of sin. This tale of redemption was told to me, now I recount it too.

Hexed Fildred Moon of the sullen chin, knew that he was cursed with sin. The group of shamans knew this not, for a stranger he was to them. They trusted him to go with them, these wise men of holy renown, upon the sharp cliffs and clamber to risk his life and limb and bone. The traversing was dangerous, they all knew that fate would see them in the silted bowels of doom, unless they raised themselves aloft well upon the cold sharpened rocks. All climbed well but still they were worn, their very skin torn from their flesh, leaving the bleached colour of bone upon the staggered, surface stone. This is how those steep cliffs still bear that shade of frozen winter clouds; dyed with bone of brave men that danced on crags to the land in the sky.

Struggling up over the cliff edge, once above they healed themselves. They used poultices of bark from sapling trees to cure their torn flesh. Free from the despair of Doggerland they looked down from high above and saw the Star Folk descending once more upon the lands down low. Fildred swore to avenge his slain kin, whom he saw below devoured by jaws that mauled their screaming faces, sucking their features from their heads, swallowing them in hefty gulps and spewing up their foetid dregs. He swore to cut off the tendrils from these starry, ghastly god folk to use them too, to tether, bind their own kin and bleed a revenge like suckling pigs in squalid fens.

The cool, marshland that glowed in summer gold spanned out, fertile and nourishing below the cliffs that led to this new, lofty dark unknown. Up there in the sky the wild, plant life had grown beyond all control. The animals were monstrous, living entangled in briars and branches hanging with corpses of those who dared climb the mountainous crags to reach what would become Albion. No men were hung amongst the dead, as the people of whom I tell you, were the first to make the climb. The pure horror that they found there was certain to cause them shivers. I would quake myself if I was with them, for animal's heads were torn from their bodies and hung, steadfast from clambering plants, perched within the crevices and hooked spikes grown from the grisly stems of these living, breathing, tangled tombs.

Quick of wit these wise shaman were and knew that only burning fire, could pave their way through this vile place and lead them to places better. A ritual was decided so to choose one who was their best. A holy circle, in chalk dust, spun upon the new ground was cast. In turn each would swig a poisonous dram of the serpent venom that were brought in sacred pouches, up the rugged cliff side with them. Then one by one they stood within the disk cast upon tangled limbs. In turn each would raise hands sunward and call upon the spirit dead to request them to be chosen. Awaiting a sign of telling from out the sacred blue above, each man would take his turn therein and pray that he was arisen.

When it came to Fildreds turn as all before him had badly failed, a light beamed from the sky torn clouds and struck him once on the forehead. It burned the sign of elder gods upon his flesh and smouldered it into his very soul, plunging him near to the dead's fiery pit. On seeing this the shaman feared that fair Fildred, of the sunken brow, was bound to die and so they wrapped him tight in the skins of a cow and hung him high above the new ground in branches to decompose, coiled within like a nest, to be born anew like buds of briar rose.

The shaman danced their sacred dance, shaved their

heads and then barked and howled, others rolled in spit, dung and dirt as others stalked and scowled with mirth, to rhythms beaten on rocks and logs. They changed their shape and spun amongst the thorny thicket and hanged dead, they sang and spoke of ancient gods, all through the time of setting sun until the moon let down her locks with which they climbed to higher states and rode upon the beasts that came from silken moonbeams to heaven. Here they bartered for Fildred's soul and requested he be pardoned.

Yog-sothoth spoke them down and wished their pledge to only him alone, but shaman, being men renowned, excused themselves and asked of him what he wanted mostly from them. He told them that his grandfather was the only way to give the life, dead within the twigs and pollen. Yog was the grandson of the blind, fool who creates deep, down in dream, and Yog is the gateway placed before the realm of that abyss. Yog requested that shaman would forevermore cast his runes and speak his name, so that their dreams and mare's would always feed his bliss. That done then Yog of the Sothoth would allow them guarded entrance, to the hollow, blackened hole before which he stood, then by chance to see the blinded one with their own eyes and ask of him what they decreed and thus they then took council, talked and happily they all agreed.

The deed being done, Fildred's eyes opened slowly from the deathly pits, with disbelief saw the cocoon, which they had made from vine and twig and hair and hide and bone and stick. He slowly regained his old wits. Redemption had come at last, and he felt his inner soul relit. The hunger he felt was beyond that he had barely ever known. He ate through that crusted cup, climbed out and lay himself on the ground. His hunger gone, his thirst quenched, Fildred stood like a giant, hardened stone and anyone who saw him then, they said, 'This man has surely grown.' They said of him, he was anew, a golden fruit from on the vine, they said his blood was precious red and that he and the land were one. They chose to drink of his god blood, eat of his sacred flesh and then, they would be born anew like him and serve him well until the end. When they had ate and drank their fill, his body returned to the ground, they wallowed low and shook with grief, and prayed a deep sojourning sound.

Fildred, like harvested wheat returned, he grew back like luscious bracken. From the earth he came once more, curled and then unfurled again. 'Beyond the thicket, beyond the death of this dark, bleak, sad abyss, that stands before us, this tangled mess of twig, thorn and spiked defence, there is a sacred plain for us that's quenched by rivers, lake and brack. One tree stands there, tall, to give us shade, this place is called Sen Mag.' Spoke Fildred of the life renewed, 'This is our golden, promised land, but to carve our path though this hell, there is something indeed we lack. We need a spark of holy fire, a coal with which to breathe a flame to burn this place of trapped, death down unto that sacred, golden plain.'

So, mighty Fildred climbed back down the rocks with one almighty step, no need for rope had he this time, for he was now wild-honey fed. His cloven hooves were hard and flat, the land split before his tread and deep rivers formed where his feet did fall, and the Star folk wailed 'Fildred!'

A mighty battle that flattened hills as that never seen before, on Doggerland's mythic, ancient plains, smote, clashed, crushed and clattered all. Fildred fought with the will of gods whose ancient names filled weak men with dread, he stomped them all, the Starry ones, and took them for his daily bread. He fought them from this sacred isle and drove them to the daunted sea, and from their bones he whittled flame and returned it to the newly free. With twenty-four men and twenty-four women, Fildred did return. From then on, he was known as a god king, the mighty Parthenon.

The fire set, the tangled web, that horrendous, dark, destroying mesh, burnt to cinder and decay and the path that senselessly bled now led, unto golden, gracious Sen Mag and that sacred, single, tall tree, that gave the people of Parthenon shade and then nourishing seed. The seeds were sown, the harvest grew, the people fed and rightly bred and soon one plain was no more; where there was but one, four were instead.

Once more hear drums beat out their throng and feel it in your heart of hearts; one, two, three, four; one, two, three, four; one, two, three, four; one, two, three, four.

Here now is a tale for all men, told and sung to the tribes of Mull, who came forth from the Northern lands, that lay beyond the raven lands and thus travelled South for rituals, held at the rise of the fifth moon.

Sprightly, out from the loins of Parthenon, sprang the son of Fildred. His Mothers line was the bird song, sang on the lone tree of Sen Mag. Full grown came he, cloven hooved, an attribute of the old mighty, so as to be recognised by all who would see his face and think of him then a stranger there, but know his soul was above holy. He shone like gold upon a flame and yet no shadow did he cast; a furious ball of flame spun from the light of the Sen Mag tree. He spun and blazed the starry night and fools cowered in fear and dread.

'I am Akbaw, sweet Fildrids son. Here to lighten the dull pathway, buried deep in the dark abyss, that spirits of man sail at night in vivid dreams but guarded deep within their still minds by keepers of the twelve gates, dark, demon damned, sent there to test those with the will to proceed beyond their vigil but refuse the unenlightened. Sail with me on a silver barque, together we shall venture forth, on the nightly passage of the soul, so that great Sol will arise anew at every dawn and so survive, unfettered and burn well.'

Two warriors of great renown were chosen then to sail with him. First came Henay the sole scribe's son, gifted with a silver tongue that like a sword could slay the beast that guarded every single gate. He knew the names of everything that the dark gods had ever dreamed, and with this spoken fire he could bind every beast with strong tendrils. The second was a man of bronze cast from the very blessed clay of the great plains that lay so fertile all around the Sen Mag tree. His name was Ibix, a man of few words but when he spoke, he spoke. He spoke like granite and uttered forth solid wisdom that be sworn. Henay stood at the silver barques bow and Ibix at Akbars rear, one to cut through the silk veil of mists and one to protect their backs, for on the nightly voyage dwelt creatures who would do them ill will, but versed in wisdom were all three, so undaunted sailed on for dawn.

They sailed unto the darkest depths unto the dreaded underworld; a place of resounding echoes and velvety shadows flitting across the rock-strewn cavernous spaces of dimension edges, where senses cheat and the strongest, most cunning minds can be deceived by ephemeral illusion passing as sheer reality. All this time K'baa the serpent stalked their majestic, sacred, silver barque to lure these travellers from their course and lead them far off into unknown twilit, sunken, rolling realms, beyond the dreamt ken of the wisest and learned men from the wild woods, seas and mountains.

Unto the perilous spaces with cosmic wind at their rudder, urging onward this righteous ruse, these brave souls sailed forth on vapours, for their just cause and course was true. When old K'baa raised his scaly head from the tumbling waves far below or let them spy his hump of coils slide through the sea before their bow, Henay would gesture sacred scripts, slipping words from his silver tongue to ward away the serpent's breath. Yet fearsome K'baa was never far, the beast shadowed their quake tremor and soon the first gate came to eye and thus marked their first hellish hour.

At the portal stood Shaurash-Ho, the guardian of what lay beyond barring entry all who dared to cross the dimension threshold. 'Who dares cross this ghastly gate?', the father of the ghouls declared, in a voice like crumbling wombs and poisoned roars, echoing in tombs strewn with dust and mould and lurid thoughts and deathly, stinking putrid remains, struck with manic thunder as a great rocket from the tombs.

Yet Henay, held the silver key and uttered forth the secret name of Shaurash-Ho known by so few, 'The Prowler of the tombs; Nagob'.

The guardian bid them to pass, the serpent slipped alongside too, concealed in the foetid grotesque, waves that wallowed, wept and bled below.

This second realm was one of ice and here a fearsome, freezing wind blew the silvery barque on through a lonely, frozen landscape. There even shantaks, cold immune, feared to journey in that lost place. All this time K'baa the serpent stalked their majestic, sacred, silver barque to lure these travellers from their course and lead them far off into unknown twilit, sunken, rolling realms, beyond the reaches of the known wisdom that men dreamed from the forests and pale beaches. Twice fearsome K'baa was never far, the beast shadowed their quake tremor and soon the second gate loomed forth to mark their second hellish hour.

At the portal lay Ithaqua, guardian of what lay beyond barring entry all who dared to cross the dimension threshold. 'Who dares cross this ghastly gate?', with glowing red eyes he declared, in a voice like ice and hail stones and hurricane roars, echoing through frost bitten cavernous hollows, resounding awe in frigid bellows tumultuous icebound cracking snaps and avalanchian rushing's.

Yet Henay held the silver key and uttered forth the secret name of Ithaqua known by so few, 'The Windwalker; the Wendigo'.

The guardian bid them to pass, the serpent slipped alongside too, concealed in the foetid grotesque, waves that wallowed, wept and bled below.

This third realm was basalt rock and here a slippery, black slime oozed upon the cyclopean forms that jutted upward to the dome that hung aloft so high above, on slimy formless protrusions. Into the perilous, murky realm of luminous, globulous, cavernous, dank Voormithadreth had these brave adventurers come. The cold water here was vile, still, stagnant and foul, fragrant like rot; grim beyond all possible words that any good bard could muster. They held their shortened breath in gulps, toxic these vapours were to breathe, though very faint in head they were, in stalwart hearts their courage flamed determined for this hour to tame, as mighty leviathans they braved the foetid sea that writhed around, their sacred, vessels sturdy sides.

The windless sea on which they steered, bubbled with scum, oily black like slick, sooty ooze emitted from out of surface spores that transformed with speed, from form to misshapes like starlings flocking in the dawn and school of herring in the depths. This formless spawn followed the boat, intrigued by its novelty, sentient in curiosity, forming feelers from the black mass it reached out to smell, taste and touch the sailors to determine more and discover if they were food. Yet, K'baa was never far behind, that serpent with its tendrilled beak, came lurking from down underneath, scattering the formless spawn slime, for K'baa hungered madly too for the party's so succulent flesh. His powerful quake, from leaping forth from the surface sanguine slime, pushed the ship of heroes on forth; an essential fluxing of still, sluggish sea (that held them drifting, disorientated and so lost upon the filth and turgid, sop), setting them free, forcing them on towards the next gargantuan gate. Thrice fearsome K'baa was never too far, the beast shadowed their quake tremor and soon the third gate loomed forth, thus, to mark their third hellish hour.

Before the gate a temple stood squat and plain (as those depicted in vaults of the kingdom of Zin), its front open so that within could spy for trespassers upon a sole onyx stone pedestal. That within was a bulbous gloat, a hoglike toad that lazed its vast, sluggish, bloated, mutating mass, dribbling fat, gut-stink down its chin awaiting tortured offerings to quench its gluttonous cravings. Tsathoggua was this guardian's name, long worshipped in lost lands was he. He almost stirred to question them, as their journey so led them there, but such a sleepy oaf as he could barely move so to sustain passing gas from his blubber brain. Before the god opened one eye, Henay spoke true with silver tongue, 'The Sleeper of N'kai', uttered he. The portal's gates creaked, opened wide, shedding vast rust and dust and sludge, feculence, ordure, silt and sleaze down upon our lone quester's heads.

The guardian bid them to pass, the serpent slipped alongside too, concealed in the foetid grotesque, waves that wallowed, wept and bled below.

Onward to the fourth realm they soared, thrashed around by clamorous storms. The silvery barque was cast astray; a toy upon this sea, tossed, turned, flooded, rolled, thrown, stormed, roared by such a rambunctious weather. The gales chanted uproarious words like icy spears set to sink the sacred vessel asunder.

'Ph'nglui mglw'nafh Cthulhu R'lyeh wgah'nagl fhtagn', the cultists from out crop rocks wailed.

'Ph'nglui mglw'nafh Cthulhu R'lyeh wgah'nagl fhtagn', those maddened souls cursed their sail.

'Ph'nglui mglw'nafh Cthulhu R'lyeh wgah'nagl fhtagn', the sea itself frothed in washed foam.

'Ph'nglui mglw'nafh Cthulhu R'lyeh wgah'nagl fhtagn', the stars above bellowed and groaned.

Our heroes clung to their boat fast, tied themselves to the steady mast, refused to hear the madding screams, invading their futile, pure dreams. Then before them rose monoliths. strangely shaped, carved and wyrd beyond all they'd ever seen before then, cyclopean, stone edifices not even carved by mortal men. From depths with a cacophonous roaring sound as sea was expunged from slopes curved, stepped steep in rolls with sharpened edges, perilous heights and angles insensible to a rational, considered, shapely, right, correct construction, R'lyeh itself rose from the mists.

Quarce fearsome K'baa was never too far, the beast shadowed their quake tremor and soon the fourth gate loomed forth, thus, to mark their fourth hellish hour.

Up from the depths the guardian rose like a dreadnought, its wings wide, its four eyes staring with anger, seething with fury, wrath and hate. The tentacular protrusions lashed wildly from its prodigious, monstrous, towering, immense chin. The great, monumental Cthulu, the curse of the dim, ocean depths stood before the chaotic, stone gate; colossus, majestic, awry. The champions sensed his, dementing, astonishing, fearsome, alien mind within their own threatened thoughts, overwhelming their very souls.

His thoughts loudly, rattled in their skulls, 'Who wakes my slumber before the stars are correctly aligned?'

Yet Henay held the silver key and uttered forth the secret name of Cthulu known by so few, 'The Kraken;

Tuloo the Leviathan'.

The guardian bid them to pass, the serpent slipped alongside too, concealed in the foetid grotesque, waves that wallowed, wept and bled below.

Thus, the chaotic gates of R'lyeh spasmed fourth an unnamed coloured hue, which covered all in fluorescence, that shone brighter than one thousand rich, resplendent, radiant stars. When this starry light faded out the last realm had changed once again. The next realm had now transposed the former, maddening torrent and the fierce tempest had dissolved.

The water before them spread out, no more a sea but now a lake. No saltier to the tip of tongue did this water taste, but rain fresh. The barque sailed upon a dream, the night sky glowed white up above, the stars were now like pebbles cast upon a crisp blanket of snow. The fifth hour came as Carcosa, they skimmed across sweet lake Hali. The faint breeze blew a light sprinkle, that sparkled in the mirrored haze from which a city, silhouetted, emerged from within the mirage. On they sailed, in trance, in wonder, guided by their golden slumber, on a set course destined by fate onward to sweet Carcosa's gate.

This joyous land was golden hewed a rich joyous sight to behold, warmed deeply by a black hole sun that flourished in serenity. Magnanimous vegetation lined the resplendent, rosy shore, redolence perfume brimming forth danced on thermals permeating all, whilst flocking, feathered, waterfowl gracing the shallows whooped and called. But such a dream was dangerous; the beauty was mind infecting. Soon our heroes longed for the shore, a wife, a home, a belly full of wine and meat, life fulfilment, a cornucopia of pleasures to replenish their heavy hearts. They turned their barque to the land, blinded by all the beauty there. But as they sailed that blissful goal seemed a forever distant end, never nearer did the three sail and yet the gate they'd sadly spurned faded far beyond to their rear; so distracted had they become.

Crazed by their journey in this realm, our knights bickered amongst themselves. Jealousy overcame their thoughts, selfishness ruled their benumbed minds, their desires grew as did their greed and gluttony replaced their needs as what was once deemed fulfilling now became sick wealth obsession. Henay, fired with a heart of hate, struck out at Ibix who in turn grasped at Akbaws great, sinewed throat, as Ackbaw kicked at Henays heels. The silver barque rocked and rolled unbalanced by their furied brawl, until their rivalry became murderous, evil villainy.

Seizing his opportune moment, K'baa the dread serpent swam with speed, he leapt at the sacred barque and overturned it with his humps. That sweet silver vessel capsized, threw our heroes in the deep lake. They floundered in the golden waves desperate to regain their breath. The serpent turned around once more, readied itself for its attack, then with haste he soon launched again to swallow the sailors at last.

One hump, two hump, three humps then four whipped up the waves into a thrall. Akbaw now sunk, his head well rocked, doused in the cold, fresh water, shook regained his sense no longer stunned by all the beauty in that realm, raced to the boat and turned it straight, then climbed aboard, no recompense, did he give to the vile serpent, all thoughts turned to his drowning men, to save their souls and then return to their divine sweet, sacred, quest. With Henay and Ibix in tow, he grabbed their hands, pulled them aboard. K'baa leapt up, bit, but only air did his slavering jagged, jaws bite, in rage he sunk back to the depths and planned his next vicious attack. With reddened, maddened, rolling eyes he watched them set sail once again with contempt and utter despise for all the world's mere, mortal men.

So on towards the gate they sailed with this realm having lost its sheen, where once was joy they now saw pain, cracked madness and deep suffering. Fivefold fearsome, dreaded K'baa stalking them close, was never too far. The beast shadowed their quake tremor wishing the sailors to devour and soon the sixth gate then loomed forth, thus, to mark their sixth hellish hour.

Terrible Hastur, the guardian, octopoid and so repulsive, slid from the spiralling towers, slithered from long, lost Carcosa, to challenge them at the next gate at the old, fabled cities threshold. Dripping, slime and drooling black ink great Hastur rose on mantis legs, his golden habit billowing in the sudden wind behind him. 'Who dares enter this domain?', he spluttered from his dripping maw.

Yet Henay, held the silver key and uttered forth the secret name of Hastur known by very few, 'The Maddening King in Yellow.'

The guardian bid them to pass, the serpent slipped alongside too, concealed in the foetid grotesque, waves that wallowed, wept and bled below.

Deep along a flooded river amassed by flora and fauna from a long bygone millennium, they sauntered on their mighty boat through mists arising from the drink in lifts and curls and furls and drifts. Soon, they realised that not all around them seemed so normal now. Their silver barque and themselves were the only solid mass forms. All of the present primordial life that grew and prospered around seemed transient and transparent and made of vaporous mist, twists and curls of simple, silken cloud. This bewildered their precious souls for here were beasts of great burden consisting of such rare, vacuous matter drifting in the warm air. There too were savage, scaled monsters with cutting claws and razor fangs violent in their hunt frenzy devouring everything that ran. Yet all these things were barely present like many ghosts from another time. drifting by on feathery breeze from the first ground to virgin skies.

Recurrent through the deep, dark depths and air below the cavern's roof, creatures consisting wisping steams propelled their mad, primordial forms. Lizard brained and slow, giant framed, these living things both flew and swam, darting down from the shadow sky or charging up from the abyss, exploring the strange intruders onboard their prized, silver barque. Their vapid eyes and misty guts, hungered to taste these mortal treats. Their formless tongues tested to taste, their crushless mouthfuls of morsels that vacated their eager jaws. Yet still the wary pioneers leapt and ducked, dodging their sinister foes, cautiously, covering their heads, shielding from empty aforesaid threats subsisting of nought but cobwebs. On and on they still battled the nulls inanely in exhausting brawls, 'til fatigued our heroes dropped bone-weary on their vessels floor. Ibix in this sapped, sorry state spied the next gate with weary eyes, decrying that its coming was nigh mustering strength for his crippled cries. They raised themselves despite attacks that simply passed through their frames and in weakened rapture revered their impending, forthcoming prize. Yet fearsome K'baa was never far, the beast shadowed their quake tremor and soon the sixth gate loomed afore and thus marked their sixth hellish hour.

On standing stones before the gate, immense spheres, with bulbous eyes, and spindly formed amorphous limbs, and death trap mouths on primitive protruding heads from vague, wide necks, teetered on natural, stone plinths. Striving to coexist, they bickered like twins with a favourite toy that neither wanted the other to have, to hold and thus enjoy. Bewildered by the coming crew, sailing towards them on the sea, these squabbling slugs were distracted from their pathetic jealousy. They began to quarrel anew over which had seen the barque the first and to then continue to squabble over if the men could be descended from the two, as they were the root origin from the darkest primordial soup from which primal life had begun. These two guardians were Nug and Yeb, the spawn of great Shub-Niggurath and omnipotent Yog-Sothoth; their union melded in grandiose, cosmogonic, immense fusion, that spun galactic aureole beyond the space and time fabric into dimensions still unknown. Spawned on the then doomed nebula, that imploded with the ghastly, natality on Zlykarior.

Taking the complete advantage of the squabbling, jealous, oaf twins, our heroes course sailed straight on past. Wielding all his secret knowledge, Henay again put skills to task. Through use of silver key and tongue he uttered forth the secret name of Nug and Yeb so barely known, 'Cxaxukluth', for once they were one. The guardians bid them to pass, the serpent slipped alongside too, concealed in the foetid grotesque, waves that wallowed, wept and bled below.

Becoming a tight, bubbling brook the soft water flowed before them. It winded through a darkened wood, where no birds sang, and sound was hushed. Overcome by daunted feelings of being watched from the thickets, the traveller's eyes searched the scrub for any hidden denizens. Occasionally a twig snapped from the deathly, dark, devil trees that rose from impoverished soil standing whist like tombstones tipped, ruined, wrecked and long forgotten. The dusky sky growled low above with thunderous drums before rain, desperate spears of fractured light splintered the heavens, bursting flames from shattered trunks struck far below casting splinters like spat arrows. A haunted landscape, sickened bark, with poisoned growths and rotten roots, toxic plants, infected spores and sinewed, sticky, spiked hawthorns spreading with cancerous flowers that filled the air with foetid stink, welcomed our brave warriors in to its vile, repugnant embrace.

The sailors found the going hard. Their boat kept catching on the banks of the overgrown stream, all riddled with reeds and rugged rocks and roots. They used their legs on the banks, pushing their freight along its route, like bargemen in a long dark, sunlight starved, brooding, tomb canal yearning for the glim, lit oval at the end of the deep tunnel. As they pushed, their thoughts centred on this conundrum they persevered, but every now and then they'd start by something at the edge of sight, caught in the corner of the eye. It seemed the trees were uprooting, sliding up out across the ground and finding new places to rest, so silently in this sad grove and slowly as if they hunted. Every time our heroes stared, these ugly trees halted firmly, like struck arachnids playing dead, so their presence would be ignored. But Ibix stole an upward glance, reacting to a quick snapping sound and there he spied that the high boughs were not quite as they first appeared. These were not trees but grotesque things, sinewy, ropey, tentacled beasts whose bodies only looked like trunks and their legs only appeared like roots. His accomplices caught on fast, the horror chilled their tortured hearts. The dark young of Shub-Niggurath were all around them drooping down searching soil for sour succulence to suck it from the dying ground.

Forked lightning bolts from heavy skies kept barraging the seventh realm. It severed the dark young in two and shook the ground, smashing it down in tumultuous, spiny sparks, but still the sailors pushed onward, forcing their barque on and on, until at last the banks gave way unto a stinking, septic pool. Down they rushed on torrential flooms, rapid whips and frightening foam with bated breath and taut tight lips they clung for life on fingertips turning white, tight with tortured grips, muscles spasming from setting stiff reflexes steering their spun ship. The fearsome serpent, dreaded K'baa, stalked them still, was never too far. The beast shadowed their quake tremor soon the queer seventh gate glowered, to mark their seventh hellish hour.

There before the thick, twisted gate a ghastly, swirling mass of fog extruding octopoidal limbs and slime drooling orifices, stood on thousands of goatish feet ejecting monstrous small creatures from within its black, misty slick in endless spasming seizures. When these creatures tried to escape, the thing swallowed them all up whole, re-ingesting its own spewed fauna, tooth, hair and claw and skin and bone. Shub Niggurath, this guardian, bellowed, 'Who is trespassing here?' with a putrid, odorous stench of rotting fish heads and stale beer. Yet Henay held the silver key and uttered forth the secret name of Shub-Niggurath, rarely known, he whispered it in silver tongue, 'The Black Goat of the Withered Woods with a Hundred Thousand Dark Young.' The guardian bid them to pass, the serpent slipped alongside too, concealed in the foetid grotesque, waves that wallowed, wept and bled below.

Into a cosmic realm they sailed, a gelatinous, globular, viscous, vascuous, verdurous, vibrance bubbling both effervescently emerald and pliantly pulpous. This realm and guardian were one, a live, conscious, territory. The gate as much its very mind as a portal to the next realm beyond this puzzling paradox. This endless entity even now knew their quest and welcomed them all into its infinite innards spiralling, ephemeral sprawl. Yog-Sothoth was the well-known name that made its foes quake, struck with fear, but the sailors' priests worshipped him and prayed and sang odes to him and thus the mighty Yog-Sothoth allowed them to pass graciously. Yet for K'baa, the sacred serpent, this welcoming was not so kind. Protective of the hero's souls Yog-Sothoth spurned the tendrilled foe and cast its scaly, wyrmly form from his warm emerald embrace, spitting him into the cosmic, aether beyond all dimensions. Here he fell further below than ever before; frozen in the very core of heavy matter, so densely solid and crushing and impenetrable to all. There he remained in lone exile for aeons in solitary stone, long awaiting, yearning release. The hero Innsgolt of Endeast, on a trial of penitence, to garner grace from Shaurash-Ho, would save K'baa from his lonely fate in other stories often told around fires to ward off the cold.

Passing through the great jewelled portal that marked the eighth hellish hour's end, Yog ushered blessings and bade them courage on their terrible path, for worse may yet befall the crew upon their humble, hero quest. They thanked and praised majestic Yog, promising him sacrifices of many virgins, goats and lambs and to herald his mighty name for all eternity, a pact surviving to this very day. So, on they sailed to the ninth realm and all the mysteries they'd find, amongst the strangely mercurial nature of Nyarlathotep's mind.

In this terrible, torn up realm was a universal graveyard of rusted frames of iron. Here decrepit, roaring machines mined the once illustrious soil, roaring with abhorrent clanking, industrious grinding, sparking jets of flame into a flaring orange sky with cruel, crimson clouds raining blood on perishing ponds where life had once thrived; now long gone. Perpetually metallic manic thumps, beating like vast drums of war, sonically battered the fragile air as whining flute like surging, stiff, whistling, whoops in a demons orchestral dirge, droned long screamed notes of tortured pain, in brutal, distorted, shrieking, piercing wails; the flautist insane and repeatedly suffering. All the land quivered with humming, vibrating the debris littered, strewn amongst dilapidated buildings, architecturally strange to our heroes' burning eyes, the concrete bricks were new to them. Sulphuric vapours scolded, scorched their nostrils with dizzying effect. The heat from the tortured cracked ground, wavered visions across the land, reflecting the defiled, frying sand that covered everything in gusts. Paradise was lost and unfound, progress had obliterated every juncture of common sense and culture disintegrated.

The silver barque hastened on, riding a vast crest of fiery, toxic slurry, chemical waste and ruined, melted, plastic shapes. Flames rose scorching around its sides threatening the fearless crew's lives. The edges of the freight began to melt and slowly liquify. To save the ship from vanishing into the molten, smoking quag, they then poured what little fluid that they carried on their journey, from flagons, onto the decking. As it bubbled, steam rose scolding them, blistering their skin; pustules wept from burning open sore welts that ran down their ulcerated, seared, reddened, broiled, sizzling wet flesh. Their skin began to peel away, their charred hair smoked like candle wicks, better fortune perhaps they'd fare penniless on the River Styx.

Through steaming eyes, glutted with blood, Akbaw saw (past the burning light), the portal ruin to the next realm. He battled his dissolving senses to maintain that no illusions marred his eroded judgement. His hazy vision deluded a friendly face awaiting there by the gate of dire corrosion and with a beaming simple smile pertaining joy at their approach, calling them with a friendly hail. In truth there stood Nyarlathotep, the guardian of this grave realm. The smile was no more than a sneer on his matt, glib, obsidian face, that stole all light within a gold, azul and pharaonic headdress adorning his elongated cranium shaped as an ant's thorax. His calls were not one so cheery, in fact, the opposite was true, this master of the chicane arts and trickery, objected to their trespassing upon his realm and bid them slow torturous deaths. He gifted rebirth so to die and live again a second time to stretch their burning agony for his own grim, cherished smiles. Yet, Henay held the silver key, quietly croaked the secret name of Nyarlathotep barely known, 'The Black Man of the witches cult.' The guardian bid them to pass, the spoiled barque barely virtued, a molten slab on the grotesque waves that wallowed, wept and burnt below.

The freezing space before them froze the splitting barque and so sealed its form into a drifting blob of misshapen silvery slip. This saved the craft from running free in metallic dribbling, drab drips, liquified like warm mercury. The crew clung on most bitterly, mourning their once glorious boat; a relic of more fortuitous travelling unto the weird lands that they had found less challenging. Still skinless and so badly scorched they lived within a squirrel breath of passing out and slipping off into their sad untimely deaths.

Into the darkest, blackest void they drifted on in bleakest night. No stars shone bright to guide their plight, no sound, no air, abject of forms, just cold vacuum consuming all, sucking them forth so terrified. Brave Ibrix held as best he could with stubby fingers on his scabbed melted hands. Stripped of flesh and grip, his thumbs had since melted away. So desperate as not to slip he bit down hard with gritted teeth determined to prevail his life despite his ghastly, flayed, mangled form. Henay barely bettered his friend, with one leg left below his waist, the other burnt into a scab had blistered and crumbled under him. Despite riddled with tremendous pain, he called, prayed out Yogsothoth's name to save them in this brutal place, but no air came forth from his lungs to aid him in this silver way. Akbaw too was a crisp, roasted scab. His face had long since melted into the barque, creating a tangled form of man and ship uniting them in one and, yet, he thought thoughts for the both of them. Whereas his friends still held on tight to the deformed ship for dear life, Akbaw couldn't lose his bloodied grip even if he had felt like it. His conscious thoughts steered the vessel deep into that sheer endless night. His one eye facing to their helm became their navigation guide. The final trick, the curse and whim, that Nyarlathotep had given was the first amalgamation of organ and machination. A terrifying, grotesquely blasphemous abomination.

Still with gut determination, the magnum innominandum, that held them in this blackened prism, inside its evil volition, decided their inquisition in his realm was imposition and fired by his own ambition named them now his own possessions. Preventing their long procession, without the intimidation, but only cold isolation, he suspected the frustration kin felt at this resolution. So, with self-glorification and overjoyed jubilation, he forgot his cogitation, caught up in exuberation.

As Ibix croaked a weighted question, 'Where are we, what's our location?'

Henay, without clear intention, replied, 'Darkness' with sedition.

The silver key lacked pretension; accepted the annunciation. 'Darkness' was the true expression, the guardians factualisation. Now bound the guardian's vexation, renounced their dreadful detention and the inane repetition of this realm's bleak, black condition. With abrupt defenestration the guardian's ejaculation fired the crew in a direction straight through the gate's perforation. But forced by the tempestuation, of the sudden evacuation, Ibix lost his attenuation, fell into dark perpetuation and infinite deprivation. The others gained liberation; the deadlock was beaten at last.

Speeding through the eleventh hour as a comet, burning with fire, their torrential tears for ibix evaporated into mist surrounding them in this dull realm in vapid, sheer, bright, white, glum veils. Through vapours, clouding their locale, in thick wafts of vapid fluid, gaseous drapes of silken threads, obscuring everything in sight. They roared across this abysmal place of dire and dismal, drizzle, as condensation formed upon their sad remains and ran along the length of all they still had left making everything slide on wet silver, dissolved into the hulk of their once glorious, sweet boat.

N'yog Sothep ruled this dreary realm, as omnipresent in contour as his dread brother before. This brutal fact shuddered their hearts. From the frying pan of blackened doom into the fire of endless gloom, had our heroes been fleetly thrown, into these limp insipid plumes. Stale N'yog Sothep observed in them a plaything to bully and tease. His power to manipulate the fabric of all space and time, was rapidly put to great use. Every instant that the brave crew seemed to approach his tiresome gate, he set them back a far greater distance than they were set before bewildering their vacant course. His twisted game was ceaseless, he of course never tired of it, as his flat disposition was as relentless as his bland jest.

Even though doomed Henay had fell, slipping from the warped, cursed hulk and vanished into the dead mists, he only landed back on board the damaged boat's contorted deck, once more to slip to his sick fate.

However, from the height (or depth) that sorried Henay always fell (or rose), he spied the dull portal gate to the twelfth, hellish kingdom. He uttered the guardians title, a paradox which was baffling, 'The Nameless Mist' was the name like shamelessness but still shamed or nothingness where something still left over there could still remain. Despite the conundrum that this odd mystery self-concocted, N'yog Sothep was bitterly bound. The gate was opened, and he bid his playthings to promptly proceed. But falling far, Henay now missed the malformed deck and plunged into endless, colourless, misty voids. His screaming reverberating long after his body vanished.

So, Akbaw sailed onward alone, discontent dwelled in his bosom. The sad loss of his friends and crew, persecuted his rocked stone heart. Yet through the gate, the battered boat drifted on from beyond the haze, onto Azathoth's freakish realm to complete this quest before day arrived without the sacred sun, casting out all the promised land into damned, devilish doubting, anarchy and churlish chaos.

Outside the ordered universe, in darkened, unlit

chambers shaped inconceivably, weird and strange (beyond the space and time threshold), Azathoth, the most ancient one, gnawed, drooled and dribbled in endless thoughts. Echoes in a hole in his head where his gormless brain should have been, rhythmically reiterated with whining, accursed fluting that spun from out his maddened mind and resounded all around him. This sad, tragic, amorphous blight of nethermost confusion blubbed, bubbling and speaking heresies, blasphemous oaths and most cruel abundant curses, in patois that nothing else could understand. From within the centre of all universal infinity, this giant, tortured behemoth rocked and shook with insanity. Its dreadful mutterings were formed into galaxies and stark stars, pink nebula and deep, black holes and life on and off turning orbs, enraptured in the orchestral symphony of all known matter. Azathoth was the source of all; creation was accidental.

Akbaw saw the grim, bitter truth, and in turn went wholly insane. The quite maddening, pressures from before (that had already turned his sanity into sludge), now paled in the comparisons. He drifted past this monstrous sight, like a speck in Azathoth's eye. The ancient god seemed unaware and if he was, he just didn't care, continuing to gibber on creating interstellar mass; all consumed in mystic, cryptic, eldritch, arcane absurdity.

A single noun caught Akbaws feet; it glowed with such intensity, that flames took across the barque, becoming a mass explosion; a blazing, burning fireball. This soared across the milky way and into the world's sacred sky, a sun to brighten all the land, to warm the seas, the shores and plants. So, on it ran for a whole day, sinking down below this small world, taking its passage through the realms again until the break of dawn, to retake its infinite path until great Akbaw finally burns out in stone cold, senseless space.

So, hear again those ancient drums and know them now for what they are; Azathoth's almighty, torn thoughts creating everything's patterns regardless of the lives of man. Just relax and free your old woes for nothing matters, after all. As Leughor knew, oh, all too well, from the other tales that he told to warm the hearts of all mankind. Go carve his sign on rocks and stones that overlook the sand. See the mythic place arise, it's ancient unsunken, Doggerland.

# About the Authors

Over the last twenty years **Gavin Chappell** has been published by Leidstjarna Magazine, Penguin Books, Countyvise, Horrified Press, Nightmare Illustrated, Death Throes Webzine, Spook Show, and the podcast Dark Dreams, among others. He has worked variously as a business analyst, a lecturer, a private tutor, a local historian, a tour guide, an independent film maker, and editor of Schlock! Webzine, Rogue Planet Press, and Lovecraftiana: the Magazine of Eldritch Horror. His influences include Tolkien, Robert E Howard, Michael Moorcock, HP Lovecraft, Lin Carter, and Terrance Dicks. He lives in northern England.

**Carlton Herzog** publishes supernatural horror, science fiction and crime stories. His work is noteworthy for its portrayals of characters who are outsiders to ordinary life, depictions of otherworldly dimensions, and dark visions of human life. Filled as it is with strange terrors and brutal absurdities, his writing bends reality until it cracks. He is a USAF veteran with B.A. magna cum laude and J.D. from Rutgers. He served as Articles Editor of the Rutgers Law Review.

**Jasmine Jarvis** is a published author of speculative short fiction stories. She is currently studying a Bachelor of Arts, majoring in writing. Jasmine resides with her family in Townsville, North Queensland, Australia.

**Vincent H. O'Neil** is the Malice Award-winning author of the Exile mystery series from St. Martin's Press and the military science fiction Sim War series (written as Henry V. O'Neil) from HarperCollins. He's also written two horror novels called Interlands and Denizens, as well as the futuristic fiction novel A Pause in the Perpetual Rotation and its companion work, the non-fiction self-improvement manual The Unused Path.

His short work has appeared in Mystery Tribune, Bourbon Penn, Escape Pod, Mystery Weekly, Hypnos, Scene4, and Lovecraftiana magazines.

Learn more at: www.vincenthoneil.com

**E. W. Farnsworth**, an Arizona writer, is widely published online and in print. While he is a constant student of the original Old English poetry, including the masterwork Beowulf, Farnsworth imitates the language, tropes, customs and forms of the entire Norse and Icelandic saga tradition in his collection Hrethelsaga. The author's use of weapons and locations accord with the latest archaeological findings, which indicate the ubiquity of Viking settlements from today's Norway and Sweden throughout England to the New World. Unlike his predecessors, this author is proud to let the "pagan" Viking tradition stand on its own merits rather than merely allowing it to form a thin veneer for underlying, fundamentally Christian moralizing. For example, Farnsworth's new Doggerland stories are based on recent archaeological discoveries in Brittany, France, as well as the evolving Cthulhu mythos. The author discourages attempts to "interpret" his tales metaphorically. They were written as bedside stories to be read aloud to children or other adults.

**Simon Bleaken** lives in Wiltshire, England. His work has appeared in magazines, ezines and podcasts including Lovecraft's Disciples; Dark Dossier, Tales of the Talisman; Lovecraftiana; The Horror Zine; Schlock! Webzine; Night Land (Japan), and on The NoSleep Podcast. He has also appeared in the anthologies: Eldritch Horrors: Dark Tales (2008); Space Horrors: Full-throttle Space Tales #4 (2010); Eldritch Embraces: Putting the Love Back in Lovecraft (2016); Kepler's Cowboys (2017) Best Gay Romance 2015 (2015) and Twilight Madhouse vol. 2 (2017). His first collection of short stories: A Touch of Silence & Other Tales was released in 2017, followed by The Basement of Dreams & Other Tales in 2019 and Within the Flames & Other Stories in 2019.

By day he works for the NHS but divides his free time (when he should be writing) between reading, combating a severe case of Skyrim addiction and even the odd spot of ghost hunting. He is also a full-time slave to two cats.

**Tim Mendees** is a rather odd chap. He's a horror writer from Macclesfield in the North-West of England that specialises in cosmic horror and weird fiction. A lifelong fan of classic weird tales, Tim set out to bring the pulp horror of yesteryear into the 21 st Century and give it a distinctly British flavour. His work has been described as the lovechild of H.P. Lovecraft and P.G. Wodehouse and is often peppered with a wry sense of humour that acts as a counterpoint to the unnerving, and often disturbing, narratives.

Tim is the author of over one hundred published short stories and novelettes, seven novellas, and two short story collections. He has also curated and edited several cosmic horror-themed anthologies. When he is not arguing with the spellchecker, Tim is a goth DJ with a weekly radio show on The Feelgood Station, and the co-presenter of the Innsmouth Book Club Podcast & Strange Shadows: The Clark Ashton Smith Podcast. He currently lives in Brighton & Hove with his pet crab, Gerald, and an ever-increasing army of stuffed octopods. timmendeeswriter.wordpress.com

**Eric Labrie Giles** is a former Canadian musician and music composer who diverted into writing some years ago. He specializes mainly in dark stories, science-fiction, dystopian, weird, cosmic and horror stuffs. Algernon

Blackwood, Ray Bradbury, H.P. Lovecraft, and Dan Simmons stand among his favorite authors, alongside with Ambrose Bierce, Robert W. Chambers, and so many other. Between 2018 and 2022, Eric has seen over forty of his works published, either as part of themed anthologies, selected group projects, or as stand-alone.

**Lily Jasmine Bergh** is a weird fiction writer and fantasy novelist who has a particular love for the 18th century, men in tweed caps, and steampunk machinery. She currently lives in Western Scandinavia and splits her time between running a vintage-themed marketing agency and dreaming of becoming the next Robin Hobb. Her superpowers include lympic-level procrastination skills and an unparalleled ability to kill plants.

Jasmine shares her home with her partner (a bearded computer programmer who may or may not also be a very hot gym junkie) and a geriatric poodle who can't tell the difference between the postman and a burglar.

**S.O. Green** (they/them) is a genre-fluid writer and editor living in the Kingdom of Fife with husband, John. Author of the post-apocalyptic novelette, Sin Chaser, published by Eerie River Publishing, as well as over 80 works with imprints including Dragon Soul Press, Black Ink Fiction and Nordic Press. Writer, vegan, martial artist, gamer, occasionally a terrible person (but only to fictional people).

**Emil Haskett** is a Swedish author. He writes mainly in Swedish but has recently started writing in English. He has published the urban fantasy novel "Where thou shall not tread", available in Swedish and English, and has also published several short stories in different anthologies. He prefers to blend fantasy, science fiction and horror.

He lives near old Swedish woods full of shadows, secrets and stories, that is where he gets most of his inspiration, by digging deep from Swedish folklore, unearthing creatures that should have been left undisturbed and putting them in a modern setting in his stories

A writer who specializes in the Horror, Science Fiction, fantasy and crime genre. **Chris McAuley** has been the lead writer in novels, comics, audio dramas and games. He is the co-creator of the popular StokerVerse, along with Bram Stoker's great-grandnephew Dacre Stoker. He has also created a science fiction and fantasy franchise with Babylon 5's Claudia Christian called Dark Legacies. Chris has worked with some of the top names in Star Wars, Star Trek and Doctor Who.

**John D Chadwick** is a writer, illustrator, animation

filmmaker, spoken word performer and co-host of The Innsmouth Book Club podcast. A former university senior lecturer and writer/illustrator in residence at the Yorkshire Sculpture Park, his work has been exhibited, published and performed through several media since his film Spiritual Love was nominated for Levi's Young Narrative Filmmaker of the Year at the 1996 British Short Film Festival. His portfolio can be viewed at https://www.behance.net/jdchadwick and https://www.facebook.com/jdchadwickart

**Claudia Christian** is an actress, performer, writer and musical artist. She is best known for her role in Babylon 5 as Susan Ivanova and for her many voices over roles in the Call of Duty series and World of Warcraft. Along with Chris McAuley they have crafted 'Claudia Christian's Universes'. These are a series of narratives from various genres such as Fantasy, Science Fiction and Horror.

**Lee C. Conley** is a musician and writer in Lincolnshire, UK. He lives with his wife and daughters in the historic cathedral city of Lincoln. Alongside a lifetime of playing guitar and immersing himself in the study of music and history, Lee is also a practitioner and instructor of historic martial arts and swordsmanship. Lee is one of the founders of Bard of the Isles literary magazine and is now also studying a degree in creative writing while working on his debut fantasy series The Dead Sagas, which includes the novels A Ritual of Bone and A Ritual of Flesh, as well as also other works of speculative fiction and horror.

Find out more at www.leeconleyauthor.com

# More From Mythos

## Antisocial Housing - Tim Mendees

978-9198750959

## Visions & Abominations -Tim Mendees

978-9198750843

Find us at:

http://www.nordicpresspublishing.com